December Girl

For English teachers everywhere, who light the spark of a dream.

Prologue

Ireland, 3,200 B.C.

The sea was grey and the skyline missing. A whiteness had descended along the east coast. The leathered boat dipped up and down, the small waves lapping and dashing as they rowed. The rough granite sat squat in the boat, steadying the small currach, as the men, with their auburn hair matted and long, made their way slowly through the sea.

They sailed from the sea to the Boyne, floating over dark water, fronds waving from below. It grew still as they rowed upstream, past the rushes and the marsh. On land, rough ropes pulled the square stones from the boat on to the oiled logs lined up on the shore.

They rested that night, sleeping beside the stones, their fire smouldering in the spring dew. The weak sun warmed their arms that morning and as it rose in the sky, beads of sweat dripped from their brows, down their necks and flowed freely under their arms to their torsos.

They sat when the stones reached their resting place, ready to be carved and formed into their passage tomb. Some lay their bodies against the stone, feeling the warmth, the scratched surface and the spirit of the stone. They smelled the granite, breathing in its air and thought of the great tomb the stones would build. The warmth was a gift. The stones were a sacrifice. A delivery from the Gods to the sun.

And this was the beginning of Dowth.

Part One

Chapter One

MOLLY

London, August 1896

Putting my hand on the door of the shop. Stepping in. Queuing behind that old woman with the mauve hat who wouldn't stop nattering about her sore hip to the grocer behind the counter.

Him laying out my bits on the brown wrapping paper. Small loaf of bread. Half a dozen sausages. A lump of corned beef. A slab of dripping.

Handing the coins over. Putting my hand on the door. Pulling it open. And turning to face the pram.

Empty.

Oliver.

Gone.

I looked around, thinking maybe he'd fallen out or someone was behind me holding him. Maybe he'd been crying. There was a man walking a big dog on the other side of the road. And a horse pulling a flatbed cart rolled by. But there was no one else on the street. Just me, my empty pram and the package of groceries in my hand.

I threw the groceries down and ran all the way to the end of the street. It criss-crossed a busy road and there were more people walking, footsteps filling the path. I put my hand out at a woman coming along with her own pram.

'My baby!' I say. And she stops, almost looking scared of me. 'My baby's gone! Did you see him? Did you see anyone? With a baby?!'

She shook her head.

'He's been taken,' I say. 'Out of the pram.'

I pointed back up the street to where my pram sat, on its own, outside the shop.

I looked around, circling, taking in all the people on the street. Looking for someone holding a baby.

I ran past the woman and ran to the end of that street, stopping people and asking them the same question. I stepped into the middle of the road, almost under the hooves of a horse and I asked the people on that side of the road too. But no one had seen him. And they all looked at me like I was a mad woman.

I was in a vicious panic now. I could hear my heartbeat in my ears. This couldn't be happening, I thought. This isn't real. No one actually came and took my Oliver. There's been a mistake, a misunderstanding.

I looked into the shops, opened the doors and asked if anyone had been in with a small baby? The shopkeepers came out, rubbing their aprons, and stood at the doors looking up and down the street. A little crowd had formed around me now, people stopping, wondering what all the commotion was about.

A policeman was summoned. A young bobby, with his tall hat on his head. I told him what happened, all my details, what Oliver was wearing, where I lived. No, he couldn't talk, he's only a baby, I said. No, he couldn't have gotten out and wandered off. He wasn't creeping. He was only a baby.

All the time I was waiting for someone to walk up, holding him, saying they'd just taken him off for a minute, that he was a bonny baby and they were sorry for the trouble they'd caused. But no one came, except the nosy parkers and the curious, all gathered round me and suddenly I was screeching in the street.

I let the panic take over. There were screams now. I could hear them coming from my throat. I was wailing. They were trying to get me into a shop to give me a cup of tea, to calm me down. But I didn't want tea. I didn't want off that street where maybe Oliver was, somewhere.

I told the policeman that he had to go searching, that whoever took him couldn't be that far away. He said they would start enquiries but that he needed all the details first and that I needed to calm down.

I took deep breaths in. There were hands patting me on the back. The woman with the pram was still there, a concerned look on her face, patting her own baby's head.

My body was shaking. There were tremors in my hand when I put it to my mouth. I touched my head, searching for comfort, wondering what I could do. What did a mother do when her baby was stolen?

Someone produced a brown bag and I was hunkering on the ground watching it blow in and out with my breaths. It didn't calm me down, instead, I felt sick.

'We're wasting time,' I say. 'We need to find him. He could be in any of these streets.' I wave my hand.

I looked at the policeman and I saw the blank look on his face. He didn't look as if he had any intention of taking to the streets in search of Oliver. He looked like he didn't know what to do.

'If you come with me, I'll take you down to the station,' he says.

'I don't want to leave here,' I say. 'He could still be here, around, with someone.'

'We'll make an official report and get the word out,' he says. The people around him nodded.

'We'll keep an eye here, love, see if he comes back. Don't you worry,' said a shopkeeper in a brown flat cap.

I felt as though they wanted me out of there. That seeing me go off with the policeman was the best thing for it. That they would shake their heads and say, 'isn't it awful, that poor girl' and then go back to their shops and their lives and their customers and all the while, my whole world had been tipped on its head. The bottom taken out of it. My Oliver, gone.

I got the pram and followed the policeman as he walked ahead, striding with purpose. All the while I searched the arms of the people around. Was anyone holding him? Could he have fallen out?

I had an awful sense of foreboding. I knew by my stomach. I knew that he was gone.

I was hiccupping now. There were tears streaming down my face, as I walked behind the bobby, pushing my pram with only its parcel of groceries in it. I saw that the blanket was gone. It was a red, woollen blanket which I'd knitted in squares in the evenings, beside the fire in Tubular's house.

'The blanket,' I said half shouting at the policeman. 'It's gone, they took the blanket too.'

He turned and nodded at me and kept walking. I felt like we were walking the wrong way. That we were going away from Oliver. But I'd no choice only to follow him. It seemed like it took hours to get to the station, that we would never get there, wading through the crowds of people going about their business and none of their faces, Oliver's.

A policeman looked up from a desk, his face white, his moustache bushy. It took me an age to manoeuvre the pram into the small waiting area of the police station. I saw the policeman who'd led me there look at the pram, as if to say, sure, leave it outside, but I wasn't leaving it outside again. It was the only connection I had to my baby.

'Name,' said the policeman at the desk. And I told him. But then I said I had given all my information to the first policeman and we needed to do something quick.

The desk sergeant looked up and he saw my face and my eyes and my panic.

'It'll just take a few minutes, love,' he says. 'And then when we have all the information, the full description, we'll get word out to all our stations. If there's no sign in a few hours, we'll get notices done up. Don't you worry, I'm sure he'll turn up,' he says.

I welcomed his kindness. I welcomed his explanation of what was happening and his reassurance that things would be al-

right. That somebody, even this minute, could walk in that door, clutching Oliver and say they'd made a terrible mistake.

I described Oliver, right down to the small balding patch on the back of his head.

'He has a little mark, on his leg, on the back of his right leg,' I tell the policeman.

He wrote it all down, carefully, in a big notebook.

And when he had all the wording down he told me I was free to go.

'Where?' I say, feeling my eyebrows raise up.

'Home,' he says. 'Go along now, home to your husband and if we find anything, we have your address.'

'I can't go home,' I said, shocked. I was ready to lead a search party, to walk right in front of a group of men and women and policemen and shopkeepers who would hunt down and find out who had taken my Oliver.

'What about the search?' I say.

'PC Devine will make some enquiries,' he says, pointing at the young bobby who was now hovering by a drunk who was shouting obscenities at the top of his voice in the waiting room.

'We need to search for him,' I say. 'Somebody's taken him. For themselves. We need to find them. Now!'

He shook his head.

'Mrs Cotton, I know this is a shock for you. PC Devine will take you home now. See that you're looked after. You leave the police work to us.'

'No,' I say. 'I can't go home, not without my baby.'

The desk sergeant looked over at PC Devine and   nodded. Devine came over, put his hand on my shoulder and gently turned me away.

This time he assisted with the pram and helped me get it outside.

'I'm going back to the shop,' I say and I started walking back the way we came. He went to protest, but then he followed, passing me out and walking straight ahead. Me, the pram and the policeman, marching up the road.

'Have you ever come across this before?' I ask him, trying to think of answers or questions that might help.

He nodded his head a bit.

'Aye,' he says. 'The odd case of child-stripping, where they take the baby, for the clothes,' he said. 'Oh, and there was a babe taken in the East End. A few years back.'

'Did they get it back?' I say.

'Oh yes,' he says. 'It was the father who'd taken it. Smothered the poor thing he had.'

I stopped, the wheels of the pram halting in their tracks, staring after the policeman and the stupid thing he'd said. He kept walking, not even noticing I was behind. I swallowed a load of air, told my mind that I had to keep going, that no one was going to harm Oliver and that most likely by the time I got back to the shop, he'd be in there with the shopkeeper, gooing and gaaing the way he'd been doing of late.

But when I got back to the shop, it was empty and the shopkeeper came out and he looked surprised to see me.

'Stolen?' he says, when I told him what I thought.

'Oh love, surely not,' he says. 'Must be a mistake. Couldn't be, surely.'

But surely, Oliver was gone.

Now that the policeman had me back at the scene of the crime, I watched him take out a notebook and stop people on the street, asking them if they'd seen anything suspicious in the area in the past hour. I thought he was doing it to have something to do, to not have to stand with me and talk about the horror of what was happening to me. And all the while I searched, looking at the arms of anyone coming towards me, eyeing up any prams being pushed on either side of the street.

That awful sense of foreboding loomed in the space where he should have been. The dip in the mattress where he lay. The end of the pram where his little toes would have kicked.

Because I wouldn't let him bring me home, the policeman moved off and said he would make enquiries door to door. I said it was houses we would need to check by now.

I couldn't leave the shop. I felt that if I left, he would be brought back and I would miss him.

I stood, my hands on the handle of the pram, looking left, then right, then left again.

I asked every single person who passed.

'Have you seen a baby, a little boy? He was taken from his pram, here, about an hour ago?'

People shook their heads, they side-stepped me, thinking I was begging. Some stopped and answered me and said, 'isn't that shocking?' but I wasn't sure if they believed me. If maybe they thought I was making it up and I was only a mad woman.

My legs were tired. The shopkeeper came out a few times, asking me if he could get me anything. The policeman came back. Said there had been no news, but that he'd made some enquiries, taken notes and he would call around to my house that evening. I watched him walk off towards the police station again.

One minute I was sobbing, the next I was wiping the tears away so that I could ask a woman walking towards me had she seen Oliver?

I felt the light dip. The sun, dropped behind the rooftops and the intense heat of the day waned. And somewhere out there, Oliver was due a feed.

My breasts ached. They were swollen with milk, one side larger than the other.

Tubular would be home from work now. He'd be sitting in the kitchen, his foot tapping, wondering where I was and where was his dinner? His meal was sitting in my pram. My hand on its handle, squeezing it tight.

When the light had faded even more, the shopkeeper came out and started moving items inside. Bright flowerpots. Two signs. A wheelbarrow with cabbages in it.

'You poor love,' he says. 'Why don't you head on home now to your husband, I'm sure he's wondering where you've got to. You never know, maybe someone will turn up on your doorstep with him tonight. Has to have been a mistake, I've never heard the like of it.'

I didn't want to go. But I didn't know what else to do. Part of me wanted to get home, to tell Tubular the news. To involve him in the search, a plan.

When the shopkeeper put his key in the door and turned it, he put his hand on my back and we pushed off, me rolling the pram and looking back as we walked away from the shop, from the street where I'd last seen him.

I babbled to the shopkeeper. About what a special boy he was. About a small dimple he had on the left side of his face. About how he was my whole world and I'd never loved anything like I'd loved that boy.

He nodded, quietly, as we walked along. It didn't take long to get to Tubular's house and when we reached it, I put my key in the door. It opened before I had fully turned the lock.

'Where the hell have you been?' says Tubular, his face like thunder, swinging it open, away from my hand still perched in the air.

He looked at me and then to the shopkeeper and then to the pram.

'She's had an awful shock,' said the shopkeeper.

I looked at Tubular and let a sob burst out, a spray of tears and snot shooting from my face. I pushed past him into the hall, letting him speak to the man, and I went into the small room at the front where I sat with Oliver when I wasn't cooking or working in the kitchen.

There were small things of his lying about. A muslin I used when feeding him. A blanket I used when gently rubbing his cheek to sleep. A small wooden rattle Tubular had produced when we'd first moved in. I took his blanket and his muslin and his rattle and I wrapped them round my face, sniffing and breathing deeply, smelling his scent,
feeling my breasts lunge forward with milk.

'He's gone,' I said when Tubular came into the room, standing in the door frame looking at me on the floor with the materials at my face, rocking back and forth. 'Somebody's taken him. He's gone.'

Chapter Two

MOLLY

Dowth, Co. Meath, Ireland, St Stephen's Day, 1894
10:20pm (Twenty months before)

If I could slit anyone's throat it would be Flann Montgomery's. Right here on the slabs of the kitchen floor. I'd take one of our kitchen knives, not even the sharpest one and I'd hold his chest with my knee and I'd drag it lightly across his windpipe. And when his beady eyes were scared enough, all popping out red, I'd do it again, only harder this time.

I picture him now, his tummy all big, his baldy head shiny, lying on our floor, the embers glowing on his rotten dirty face. I hate that man. I hate him with every single drop in my body, my blood, my sweat, the wet of my eyes, I hate him and he doesn't even have the decency to do the job himself. He sent the sheriff,

because he's a coward. Daddy always said so.

Michael is crying. Patrick is whimpering, hiding behind the settle bench, peeping out, shaking, his shoulders only reaching halfway up the box seat. I go to him and I stand beside him and I put my hand on his back and tell him to shush.

Daddy's outside now. He's been out there for a few minutes, the clock over the picture of Holy Jesus tick tock-ing, the only sound in the room as we strain and listen to the murmured words on our doorstep. There are four horses and a dozen men.

My mother is standing over by the basin, her hand up to her mouth, her thumb on her lips, her skin grey and I know she just cannot believe that they would come like this, now. We are still, waiting, waiting for what Daddy can do, to make these men go away, to send them out of our yard, back up the lane and down the road where they came from.

There's a shout from Daddy, an angry cry and we see him out the window marching back towards the house, away from the sheriff, his brow all knitted together in torment.

He slams the door, the hardest I've ever seen it close and he locks it, twisting the big black key. We wait for him to tell us what we are to do but he's marching over to where me and Patrick are and he grabs the settle bench and pulls it, hard across the slabs.

His hiding place gone, Patrick whimpers and steps back, clutching at my skirts and I step forward to let him know I'm there, but I'm frightened now. Daddy is dragging the box seat over towards the door. 'Help me,' he shouts.

Michael runs and starts pushing but he's only small, so I step forward to help and Mam says, 'Oliver, what are you doing?' He doesn't answer her, instead he rams the tall seat up against the door, and comes back to the table and he pulls that too, dragging it up against the seat.

Our front door is barricaded. We are inside our house, just me and my family and outside in the dark, there are men on horses and in uniform.

BAM!

The only thing that stands between us is our wooden door, our wooden seat and our wooden table. But they attack us with wood, a cut tree, all the men holding it, running with it at our house, at our door.

BAM!

Patrick lifts off the ground with the fright and shouts 'Mam!' and he leaves my skirts and runs to hers.

'Oliver,' shouts Mam. She hasn't moved from her spot

at the basin. 'Stop this,' she says, looking at Daddy, but he's not listening, instead, he's searching for more things to pile up against the door.

'The windows,' he says. 'Get away from the windows.'

And just as he says it, a man is at the window and he's breaking it with his baton and it shatters over the oil lamp that sits on the sill, making the flame flicker and dance. Glass flies at Mam and she steps back, horror on her face and she pushes Patrick back.

'Molly,' she roars over at me, 'take the boys upstairs.'

'No,' says Daddy. 'The windows.'

He's at the dresser now, the drawers open, filtering through Mam's cooking utensils, the fine bone china rattling where it sits and he shouts, 'Have we any nails, we need nails?'

I don't know what to do. I don't want the boys to be upset, to see all this, to hear the horrible frightening tone in Daddy's voice. I want to do what Mam says but I always listen to Daddy and anyway, how can we leave him on his own to face four horses and another twelve men?

BAM.

I catch Michael's eye. He has a knowing look about him. We both know. The last time they tried to evict us Daddy was calmer, there was none of this carrying on, looking for nails to hammer wood to the windows, dragging furniture across the floor, acting like the devil himself got inside and under his skin.

BAM.

I go over to Daddy, I put my hand on his arm and I say, 'Daddy, please stop.' His hands are flying through the drawer, banging the metal, whacking the spoons. It takes a while for the touch of my hand to travel through his body, to reach his thoughts and his brain, for him to stop, to look down at me, quietly.

For a moment there is no one else, only me and him, like our evening walks in the field, like the times in the tub trap, just the two of us, whistling going to town, the sun on our

17

backs, the day ahead.

BAM.

'It's over,' I say. And tears appear around his eyes, tipping over the edges, watering, and I think, *this is the first time in my sixteen years of life that I have ever seen my daddy cry.*

His head sinks, wilting like a flower into his neck, his jaw melting, the shame and the sadness and the surrender.

We watch him go over to Mam and he takes her in his arms and she stands there stiffly, letting him embrace her, her arms hanging limply by her sides.

BAM.

And when she realises he is crying, she puts her arms around him too and she holds him while his shoulders shake a little bit and I think this has to be the saddest thing I have ever seen in the whole world.

They have broken my daddy. Flann Montgomery has broken my daddy. And I wish I could slit his throat.

Chapter Three

MOLLY

Trinity Street, Drogheda, Ireland, June 1895
(Fourteen months before)

This house is the greyest house I've ever seen. It's drab grey. There's a pebbledash on the walls outside and when I run my hand over it, I feel the dust caked there from the hundreds of carts and cows that pass by here on their way to market or to the ships where they'll climb aboard and travel the seas to their slaughter in England or the Continent or beyond.

Every day I take a cloth to the windows. I pull it round the front door and I scrub at the corners where the dust gathers in tiny sandy triangles. And every morning when I come back out, there is it again, that film of fine dust, trafficked on to the walls, the steps, and the windows we look out of. There's no getting away from it.

Mam keeps reminding us of our good fortune. 'Don't you know how lucky you are?' she says, glaring at me, every time I complain or grumble, mostly about wanting to be back at home where our farmhouse is, where the fields are. When she says that I look at her, through her, seeking out that wistful glance, the one that she sometimes can't hide, the glance that says she's feeling it too, that she's sorry we're here, living with Mr McKenna, in this grey house, in this grey town.

Mr McKenna is a clever man. He needed a wife and he got one, ready-made with three half-grown children. He's wary of me and my tongue and what I might say. He calls me 'the wily one'. I've been watching him, learning his ways, getting to know this man who will be father to my two brothers.

He takes the strap to them when I'm not around. I'll come in from the yard where I've been scouring the washing and one of them will be there, all red-eyed and tearful, rubbing their backside. When it happened to Michael I thought maybe it was a one-off, Mr McKenna just finding his way, with him being new to being a stepfather. But when he strapped Patrick, his small legs all swollen and stripes of blood in parts, well that's when I knew. I knew my mother had married herself a bastard.

I remember Mr McKenna from before Mam married him. I'd seen him in his drapery shop and on the street, walking along, his head bobbing up and down with the queer hips he has. I never thought much of him - he looked like all the other menfolk who owned shops in the town. Big bushy moustache. Oiled back hair. A suit so spruced up, you'd think he was going to a wedding or a funeral every day of his life.

He got to my mother through the priest, the matchmaker. We'd been staying in the Brannigans' house up the road, the four of us stuck in one bed, shivering in the cold, not making any noise and not being any burden. And after a few weeks, when we knew there'd be no going back to our boarded-up house and Mam was struggling with managing the business and paying all the taxes and crying into her pillow every night, the smiles at the Brannigans' dropped and the breakfast cutlery was thrown around the table in front of us, and we got to know that we were overstaying our welcome and we needed to be going somewhere else and soon.

My mother was a thin woman, but over those weeks I watched the skirt shrink further on her hips. She took the needle to it, darting it and bringing in the band, tucking her blouse in further down her bony chest. She was looking into finding a place for us, a

cottage, where we could stay and put our things.

Then Mr McKenna appeared at the door one day, carrying a tulip flower. The tulip was bright yellow, like the buttercups that grew in the cowfields and he held it out to my mother and I saw her smile, the first time in months. They went off in a trap that Mr McKenna had borrowed and I helped Mrs Brannigan with the tea and kept the boys quiet and wondered why Mam was off out with that man, rolling round the country roads with the tulip and a smile on her face.

A few days later, Mam asked me to go for a walk with her and off we went down the road, the frost still in the air, the springtime coming in and the birds   twittering and lovemaking and readying their nests in the hedges and the trees.

'Molly, Mr McKenna and I are to be married,' Mam said, straight out, matter of fact, when we were half way up the road.

'Mr McKenna?' I said.

'He has a fine house and a business. He can support us.'

'But Mam,' I said, as we walked. 'You don't even know him.'

'I know enough,' she said.

'But we'll have to live in the town,' I said and I noticed there was a whine in my voice. Like a little girl.

'Yes,' said Mam.

'And what about school, for the boys?' I asked.

'They'll go to school in Mell,' she said.

She had an answer for everything. I couldn't think of anything else to say. I wanted to say, '*What about Daddy?*' But what was the point in that? Daddy couldn't do anything for us. Not anymore.

'When is the wedding?' I asked as we came to the crossroads.

'Next Tuesday,' she said. It was going to be in the morning, after morning mass at the Dominican church in town, not in our church, where she had married my father.

At least there was that.

I folded my arms and looked at the ground at the crossroads, noticing a caterpillar folding in and out across the gravel. He stuck out on the road all luminous, his skin velvety soft. I bent down to lift him and when I looked up, Mam held out her arms and I hugged her, the caterpillar rolling into a ball in my hand.

There were no tears. All our tears had been used up over Daddy. We went back to the Brannigans to let them know that soon we wouldn't be a burden to them anymore.

* * *

Town life was different to country life. There were always people around. And carts. And horses all saddled up. You never saw the sun set or rise, because it was lost behind the buildings looking in on us. The lanes were dirty, stinking of various pots emptied out at all times of the day. The washing hung across the street, bits of rags and bloomers and breeches for everyone to see.

I'd only ever known the green fields and the changing sky and the grass at my ankles as we walked every evening. I had only known the river and the roads, and my friends and familiar faces I'd known since I was a girl. Here I was surrounded by
strangers, close by to people at all hours of the day, but the loneliest I could ever remember being in my whole life.

I longed to sit atop of Dowth mound, the grassy Stone Age tomb that lay like an upside-down pudding bowl in our sheep field. I'd climbed there almost every day, looking out over the patchwork of green and yellow fields. In summer, I swatted at the flies and midges, in winter I blew on my hands to keep them warm. It was where I went to think, to look out, to get things straight in my head. There'd been a lot of straightening out to do after what happened to us.

In the weeks after the eviction, before we moved to the

grey house, I spent a lot of time sitting there, thinking about Flann Montgomery. I should have known how serious it was, the day Nora brought the paper, the day she called in and winked at me and said, 'Molly, let's go for a walk.' We were always sneaking out, her and I, skinny-dipping in the Mattock when it was hot, taking off our dresses and walking through the fields in our bloomers, ducking down if we heard anyone coming along the road.

'Yis are in the paper,' she said as we walked up behind the farmhouse, to the big tree where we always went when we had some gossip to discuss. She took an Argus out from under her shawl and handed it to me, folded and thick.

I remembered the man who came on horseback last week and said he wanted to speak to Daddy about 'the court case' but Daddy told him to get off our property, his face all white and annoyed. Daddy bought the Argus every Wednesday, taking it out after his tea, sitting, thumbing the pages, reading bits of news out to Mam, but that week, the week after the reporter had come on to our land, there was no more paper in the house.

Nora and I sat at the tree, our bottoms perched on the smooth roots poking from the hardened ground. And there it was, a whole square article on page three, about my daddy, about us.

'*Oliver Thomas, farmer and wool and linen wholesaler of Dowth Farmhouse will give evidence at a special sitting of Drogheda District Court in relation to an accusation of theft on Tuesday next. Mr Thomas has been embroiled in an ongoing dispute with the Brabazon Trust on the issue of the removal of stones from Dowth quarry for the building of outhouses at Dowth Farmhouse.*'

'Did you know about that?' asks Nora, when I stop reading for a moment and look at her.

'About what?' I say.

'The stones and the court case.'

I shook my head.

23

'No,' I said. 'Not really.'

It was true. I didn't *really* know what was happening. I knew that Daddy was very quiet these days and that he and Mam sat up talking into the early hours after I'd gone to bed. I guessed that it was to do with Flann Montgomery and a row going on about the farm, but I never really knew what. They didn't tell me the details. And I didn't ask - I was afraid to know.

'A recent meeting of the Drogheda Poor Law Board of Guardians debated the case and saw heated arguments between the elected guardians. Mr Thomas has been ordered to return all stones to the quarry with immediate effect to guard against the intention to cause a notice to quit to be served.'

Nora had her mouth open a little bit so that I could see her pink tongue inside. 'What does that mean, Molly?' she asks, 'A notice to quit?'

'I don't know,' I say, starting to get annoyed with her for bringing the paper over in the first place.

I was quiet. Taking it in. No wonder Daddy had been worried so many evenings. He never told me about Law Board meetings discussing our farm and our family. A notice to quit. I'd seen those words written before, in big black letters, on a fluttery piece of paper nailed to Widow Biddy's door. She'd missed so many rent payments the sheriff had come with his men to turn her out; we had all gathered, and made them go off, roaring and hissing at them. There was a collection and money was put in and the widow was still in her cottage, a sour tongue in her head.

'My daddy says they're going to evict you.'

Nora was looking at me, a hint of a smirk on her mouth.

'Is that so?' I say. 'And where did he hear that?'

'Molly, that's what it means. A notice to quit.'

I knew bloody well what it meant.

'And what else does your daddy say?' I ask. She looks

guilty and shakes her head, embarrassed that she and her family were sitting round the fireplace gossiping about us.

'No one's getting evicted,' I say, the words almost stinging my lips. 'Not if my daddy has anything to do with it. We won't be going anywhere, you watch.'

With that, I got up, threw the paper at her, and walked off with my arms folded. I didn't look back but I knew that she was looking after me, a shocked look on her face, as I left her by herself, at the ash tree.

When the bailiffs arrived for the eviction, the first time, they made a hames of the whole affair. My daddy refused to leave and to remove any of his belongings from the outhouses. When he asked for the warrant he found that they'd forgotten to bring it, in their haste to get to our farm to turf us out.

After that, we thought we'd won. We thought they'd see the error that it was, that the law guardians would stand up for us, that a new court case would set everything to rights. The whole parish had built their houses of the same stones my daddy had used on his land.

We never thought they'd come back, with more horses and more men, that they'd take us from our home and turn us on to the side of the road, in the middle of the night, on a cold St. Stephen's Day. We had underestimated Flann Montgomery, our neighbour and land agent for Brabazon House and Trust.

I knew that now. As I sat on Dowth mound in the weeks after the eviction and as I went about my work at the grey house, dusting and wiping and mopping and cleaning, it was clear that Flann Montgomery had gotten away with the biggest crime I'd ever borne witness to in my life. But his time was coming. I could feel it, somewhere in my stomach, right below my heart.

* * *

My tea cup has little pink and blue birds on the inside. They are staring at each other, all entwined in black brambles with green leaves. I take another slurp of tea, so that they are completely revealed, washed naked, baked into the porcelain, forever to look at each other until someone, some day, drops the china and breaks them in two.

I'm sitting with Mam in the White Horse Hotel, where she's brought me after our shopping trip in town. She's bought me a new dress, gingham cotton, ribbons sewn neatly along the collar and down the front. It lies in a brown package at my feet and I kick at it, under the white tablecloth. I feel agitated. This is too fancy for me. I prefer the tea shop cafe where there's bare tables and no linen cloth to spill crumbs and tea on.

'I'm glad I scrubbed my nails,' I say to my mother, looking down at my hands.

'You could be a lady,' she says.

'A lady?' I say. I snort and a bit of tea almost comes out my nose.

'Well you could learn to be one,' she says. 'You're clever enough.'

I look around me. Ladies are seated, perched, chatting, wearing hats with berries fastened to them. I wonder how they can enjoy their tea with the wide brims all over their faces. Preeners, I call them. Always preening - their hair, their clothes, their hats. I could never be a lady. I could never want to.

'I don't want to get married,' I say and I mean it, keeping a firm expression on my face so she knows I'm serious.

'Why not?' she asks, even though she's heard me say it before.

'Because Mam, I don't want to be a wife. I want to be free, like I am now. I don't see why I have to get married if I don't want to. I'm not like those ladies or Nora or,' and I pause, 'you.'

'Don't you think your father and I had a good marriage?' she says and I'm shocked that she would bring Daddy up. We've never spoken like this before. She rarely mentions him, rarely brings him into conversation or lets me talk about him at all.

'Yes,' I say, considering. 'You did. You had a wonderful marriage. You were kind to each other.'

I look at her and I see tears are welling in her eyes.

'I miss that,' I say.

I know she knows what I mean. That she and Daddy truly loved each other. That she could never love Mr McKenna the way she loved Daddy, not in a million years, no matter how hard she tried.

'I miss it too,' she says and I realise it's the first time that she's lifted the veil. It's the first time she's let me see the hurt and despair she feels over Daddy, the

predicament she's gotten herself into, the marriage of convenience with Mr McKenna and his bristly moustache.

'I'll never get married,' I say, making my voice as prim as possible. 'Never.'

Mam looks at me, almost sadly. 'Just because you think something when you are young, doesn't mean your circumstances won't change. You say you don't want to get married now, but that could all change in the future.'

She purses her lips.

I don't like this talk at all.

'I told you,' I say, my teeth gritting a little. 'I'm not getting married.'

She looks disappointed and sighs and then she strains her neck to look over at the waiter and puts her hand in the air and rubs her fingers, as if the first one has an itch, to get the bill.

We leave the hotel and I am glad to get out into the air outside. We walk the short distance home, up the street, past the shops and the people on their bicycles and the carts doing their evening deliveries and collections in the dimming light.

'One day it'll make sense,' she says.

As we near the house, I see her stiffen, and when we get inside she tells me to start peeling the potatoes for dinner. Mr McKenna will be home soon. We must never be late putting his food on the table. He told us that from the start. It's one of his rules. And you must never disobey Mr McKenna. That, we had learned.

* * *

For years we had farmed our small holding, not bothered by anyone. We had a milking cow and sheep, a hemp field and a vegetable field, potato beds and a little pond where ducks fed and watered and splashed and we harvested the reeds, making small baskets out of them and St Brigid's Crosses in spring.

The farm had been passed from Daddy's father and his father before him. It was rented from the Trust, but it had been in the family for so long and had so many improvements made over the years, that it always felt as though we owned it. The house was extended with a little pantry out the back. The sheds were renovated and a proper dairy put in, where I would be sent most days to swing back and forth on the churn.

I didn't like dairy work. Even in the summer, when the room was welcoming and cool, I longed to be out of it, playing in the fields. Sitting on top of the mound, my face to the sun, reading the Argus I'd stolen from the mantelpiece, looking at the advertisements for all
manner of items on sale in town. Bone manure. Indian tea. Blancmanges and biscuits and boots and boating shoes.

As well as the farm, we inherited a linen hall, a large warehouse along the quays in Drogheda, a bustling town of factories and shops and the biggest port this side of Ireland. Daddy spent most of his time working there, organising large shipments in and out of the port, supplying cities in England with giant bales of linen and wool.

Every day when Daddy returned home, pulling up in the tub trap, the horse foamy and thirsty, I'd run from the dairy and greet them and help him unload the horse into the stable. I'd go with him to the back hall where I'd bring a bowl of boiling water, his towel, and soap.

I'd watch as he scrubbed at his hands with the nail brush, splashing the water back and forth, waiting to see if he was in the mood for talking or not. I could judge my father like no other, even better than my mother. I felt I always knew what he was thinking, that really, we were more or less of the same thoughts, the same brain, him and I.

If he was in the mood for talking he'd tell me about the orders coming in, about the paperwork problems in Liverpool, about the suppliers, always cribbing,
looking for more. He'd tell me where they'd exported linen to, which ships were buying, problems with taxes and charges that sometimes wiped out the entire profit on a bale of linen in one swoop. I learned that being in business was a complicated thing, that you could work for weeks and still come out with not a lot to show for it. No wonder Daddy always looked worried.

The outhouses on our farm were built over a number of years. They were an investment, Daddy said, a place to store the linen if the prices were low. He built them himself, slowly, carting the large stones from the quarry at the Dowth mound, where an explosion years ago had sent tons of flat grey granite rock into the field.

I'd helped Daddy mix the render, watched as he lifted the stones and set them in the walls, stood back as the building went up around us. Instead of thatching the roofs he put flat, black slates on, protecting it from the weather, securing them for years to come.

He was proud when they were all finished,
extending out our yard, set against our lovely whitewashed house. Soon the stock built up in them, valuable linen and sometimes wool and he made sure to lock it all up so that it was safe at night.

'You can't be too careful,' he said.

He said the same thing about Flann Montgomery. 'You can't be too careful with that fella.' And he was right. It was Montgomery who was the biggest robber of them all.

'They're fine outhouses you've built there, Thomas.' He was sitting on his horse, in our yard, the poor mare squirming under the weight of him.

'Aye,' Daddy answered. 'A lot of work gone in.'

'Aye,' said Montgomery. 'Where did you get the stones?'

'From the quarry,' my daddy said.

Montgomery dismounted and walked over to the barns, feeling the stonework with his gloved hands. 'The quarry at Dowth that belongs to the Trust?' he asked, a slight smirk on his face, as he if he was trapping Daddy with his words.

'The quarry that every house and pier is built from on this road,' replied Daddy.

'That's interesting,' said Montgomery. 'Very interesting indeed.'

They stood, not saying anything, my daddy with his hands on his hips, Montgomery, still smirking, looking at Daddy like a cat spying the cream.

When he left, whipping at the bay's flank so hard I thought the skin might split, I asked Daddy what it was all about.

'Don't you worry,' he said. 'Just that bastard sticking his nose in again. Can't bear to see someone doing well for themselves. Wants everything for his own greedy little hands.'

I listened to the clip clop of his horse going back up the lane before I turned to go and do the butter in the dairy. I hoped swinging on the churn would take the worry from my mind. I needed something to distract me from the awful feeling of foreboding I got when thinking about Flann Montgomery.

Chapter Four

HENRY

Brabazon House, Co. Meath, Ireland, June 1895

Henry had hoped to have secured his place with Lewis, Clayton and Thornhills by now, but they were dragging their heels and not making any announcement as to their new recruits. Anxiously he watched the post, standing by the window every morning as the postman on his bicycle pushed up the driveway and delivered their post to the back door.

He'd wait for the footsteps of Mrs Johansson. He'd hear her open the door to his father's study and come back again. He waited for her to put her head round the door and announce there was a letter for him. But the only letters he had received were from the other students who he was friendly with and who had also applied for a position at the firm. *No news yet*, they wrote. *No news is good news.*

He toyed with the idea of travelling to London himself, calling to the offices again, letting them know he was keen. He could perhaps take the opportunity to meet with some other firms if Lewis, Clayton and Thornhills wasn't going to go his way. But, it was an incestuous business and he feared word would get back. He hated having his heart set on anything, it left him so vulnerable. The only thing he could do was wait.

Part of him had believed that he wouldn't have even needed to return to Ireland. He thought that if he could get the apprenticeship set up in London, straight after his exams, he could travel the short distance from Oxford to the capital and stay there. It would have pleased him to write the letter home to his father. '*Secured apprenticeship. Will visit at Christmas.*'

Instead, he was at Brabazon at the height of summer. And that meant summer garden parties and regattas. Weeks of his father trying to convince him to forget his apprenticeship and work locally.

'Why don't you try Faber's?' Seymour asked him one morning over breakfast.

'Faber's?' said Henry. 'Why would I want to work there?' He was scowling, a habit he was prone to around his father, thinking of the small solicitor's office housed above a hardware shop in the centre of Drogheda.

'Why wouldn't you?' said Seymour. 'Good a training as any.'

'Sheep theft and vagrants. Hardly the crime apprenticeship I'm aiming for,' said Henry.

'Crime? What about land law? Property rights? Why don't spend your time on the law that matters. Not fighting for petty criminals. Faber's would give you a grounding in the work that needs to be done locally. And what you learn, you could put into practice here.'

'Yes, always about here, isn't it, Father? Did you ever think that maybe I'd like to have something outside of here, something of my own?'

'Nonsense,' said Seymour. 'Some day you'll appreciate what you have here. You'll stop trying to turn your back on us.'

'I'm not turning my back on you,' said Henry, sighing into his black coffee. 'But I want to learn about the world. I'll spend the rest of my years at Brabazon. At least let me have some of my youth in the city.'

'You've had four years in the city, at Oxford,' said Seymour.

'Yes, but this is London, Father. London. I'm sure what I could pick up there could help the estate, eventually.'

'I don't see how,' said Seymour. 'You belong here. In Ireland. Why don't we meet with Faber and see what he has to say? I'm sure he'd open up a position for you.'

'I'm not interested in damn Faber's!' said Henry, his voice coming out in a shout.

His father put his paper up in front of his face and cleared his throat.

'I'd like you to meet with Montgomery today,' he said from behind the print.

'Today?' said Henry. 'But it's the regatta today.'

'Yes, it's not till noon, I'm sure you can fit in a meeting between now and then.'

'Can't it wait until tomorrow?' asked Henry.

'No, get it out of the way. He's been hounding me for days. You'll need to go up to his house, he wants to show us something.' Seymour poked his head out from behind the paper. 'Why, had you better plans?' he said.

'No,' said Henry, wishing that the bloody letter would come from London letting him know one way or the other what his future would be. The training he'd get in London would stand to him for the rest of his life. The thoughts of Faber's made him want to run down to the river, jump in and never surface. It was a pity he was a good swimmer. Drowning was never an option for him.

* * *

It was the first time he'd travelled these roads since the night of the eviction. It seemed shorter now, with the light and the sun, the greenery at the edges, birds flitting in and out. They sang loudly, chirping and twittering, their chorus peppering the sound of the flow of the river.

There was something about this land. Every time he

travelled along it, he felt like it was taking him in. It was what he thought of when he was away; the valley and the fields, the patchwork of yellow and greens, criss-crossed with hedge-rows up to the narrow horizontal sky.

He wondered what Montgomery could want. He had seen nothing of him since Christmas, heard nothing from him either. It was as though he had gone into hiding after the eviction, like a dog that had bitten a child. Today was to have been a good day, a day for sportsmanship at the regatta, a day for not thinking about London and his apprenticeship escape. Montgomery had not featured in that.

'Master Brabazon,' said the agent, his eyebrows raised in surprise. He was standing in the field which ran alongside the old Thomas property, three men working to dig a ditch out in front of him.

'I hadn't expected to see you,' he said. 'It was your father I was expecting.'

'He asked me to come,' said Henry. 'You wanted to show us something.'

'Well,' said Montgomery, clearing his throat and driving his foot into the ground a little. 'Yes. I did, actually. It's this.' He pointed at the three men digging the ditch.

'I don't follow,' said Henry, dropping down off his horse and walking over to where Montgomery stood.

'We're clearing out this ditch, making the field bigger and I wanted your father to check it over.'

'Why would this concern my father?' asked Henry, looking at the sweating red-faced men, who were throwing pick axes high over their heads and bringing them down with force at the base of the mud and trees. 'Isn't this your job, Montgomery, as agent. To manage ditch clearing?'

'Well it's just with the sensitivities involved,' he said quietly, looking at Henry's face, but not quite at his face. More like at his cheek.

'Is that the Thomas land?' Henry asked, the situation now dawning on him. 'Are you clearing the Thomas land for your own?'

'It's not Thomas land,' said Montgomery. 'It used to be Thomas land, but it's not any longer.'

'And since when is it yours?' asked Henry, an anger now building in his stomach.

'That's what I wanted to discuss with your father. To show him,' said Montgomery. 'It would make sense to expand this field and the next. To make the whole lot bigger. Plots are getting smaller and smaller, I'm making an investment here, improving the land overall.'

'I'd like to look at the Thomas property,' said Henry. He walked back to his horse, fixed her reins and led her by the bridle out of the field. Montgomery, half running, followed him.

'Oh, it's a grand bit of land,' said Montgomery, panting now. 'They say there's tombs there too,' he said as they passed by Dowth mound. 'Wouldn't you love to get a look inside, see if there's any treasure?'

Henry didn't answer. It was typical of Montgomery – he had an obsession with wealth and money. They walked down the lane towards the old Thomas house, Henry remembering how he'd passed by it on St Stephen's night with the silent girl, how she had looked away as the trap sailed by the darkened home, tears growing cold in her eyes. The boreen looked deserted now, the ditches on each side swollen into the gravel.

When they got to the house, Henry was surprised to see a thin line of grey smoke wisping from the chimney.

'Someone's living here?' said Henry, looking to Montgomery, to see if it was a shock to him too. For a moment Henry thought that maybe the girl and her family had returned.

'Yes,' the agent replied and he opened the gate to let Henry and the horse walk in.

The yard was fresh and clean looking, with a pile of logs against a wall, two hens pecking round the door. From the stable he heard a horse whinny.

'It's my son,' said Montgomery.

Henry paused. 'Does my father know about this?' he asked, flatly.

'I'm not sure,' said Montgomery.

'You're not sure?' said Henry.

'I don't report every little detail,' said the agent. 'My son's looking after the place. Till it's all fully decided. Can't let the place go to rack and ruin.'

Henry led his horse through the yard, past the outhouses and to the two large barns built by Oliver Thomas. The doors were open and inside he could see wood stacked to the ceiling. Henry walked over to the barn and touched the wall, fingering the smooth stones set in the render.

'These stones,' said Henry. 'Where did they come from?'

Montgomery was squirming now, wishing Seymour had come down as expected, and not his meddling son. 'I believe Oliver Thomas put them there,' he said.

'Yes,' said Henry. 'I remember.'

'They were stolen,' said Montgomery. 'Taken without consent and used to add value and profit to Mr Thomas's holding.'

'And now yours?' said Henry. Montgomery didn't answer, but shrugged, his wide shoulders hunching into this neck.

'This is justice?' said Henry.

Montgomery shrugged again.

'What's done is done. Nothing has been decided with this land yet. As agent, I am duty bound to make sure everything is looked after, maintained,' he said.

'Yes,' said Henry. 'Maintained for yourself.'

Henry marched from the barn, holding the horse's reins in the air and pulling her into a trot.

'I'll be speaking to my father about this,' said Henry. 'Tell those men digging that ditch to go home.'

As he passed through the yard a woman came to the

door, dusting white flour from her hands. She nodded her head at Henry but he ignored her, mounting his horse and kicking her in the flanks into a canter up the road. Maybe leaving for London was a bad idea after all. He would come home to find Montgomery had wheedled the entire estate out from under his father's very nose.

Chapter Five

MOLLY

Mr McKenna liked to take a drink on Saturday evenings when the week's work was finished and he had his day off, Sunday, to look forward to. He'd have me boil up a big pot of water and he'd stand bare-chested in the back hall, soaping down his body with a cloth.

I don't know why he got me to bring the water in to him instead of my mother. Part of me knew it was so that he could be there in front of me, his hairy chest out, half hoping my eyes would wander over his body in curiosity. But I never looked at him. I made a point of putting down the water not catching his eye or his face and turning my head so I couldn't see.

You would hear him shaving around his bushy moustache, the razor slicing over the stubble, the rinse of it in the water, like a small fish coming up and going back down under. And he'd sing, an old Irish air, his deep throaty voice filling the back hall alongside the splashes. When he was done with the shaving, he'd rinse his comb in the water and pull it back with some oil over his hair. He'd rinse the comb then and that would go in his jacket pocket, ready to be pulled back over his oily scalp throughout the night.

He always put a new collar on going out on Saturday nights. It rose like a white wall against his black stubbly neck, the bit of double chin coming down to meet it. The chain of his watch would be hanging out for everyone to see and before he put his bowler hat on his head, he ran the greasy comb back over his hair one last time.

When it was time to leave, he'd kiss my mother on the cheek and tell us not to wait up, and when the door closed behind him it was as though the very walls in the house breathed a sigh of relief. We were alone, just the children and my mother and it was always our happiest time of the week.

Sometimes Mam would pour a small glass of cooking sherry after the boys had gone to bed. She'd tell me not to tell Mr McKenna and I'd laugh and say, 'I wouldn't tell him anything.' And it's true. I wouldn't share the weather, never mind a secret, with Mr McKenna.

We'd play chess or draughts, or lay out the cards and dice and if Mam was feeling very tired, I would read the boys a story by the fire. We'd make up stories too and we'd talk about what they wanted to be when they grew up. Michael said he'd like to be a farmer, and Patrick said he wanted to sail the ships around the ocean. I don't know where he got that from, but I guess he wanted to be different to Michael, in some way. He used to love to watch the sailors clamber up the rigs, jumping like fleas among the ropes and sails at the port, with Daddy.

On these nights, I would sometimes think of the friends I used to have at Dowth and how the dances would be coming up or a ceili in someone's house. Here in town, I didn't have any friends to ask me to a dance. So, I'd take out the sewing that needed to be done or try to persuade Mam to let me have some of the sherry or I'd read the paper, cover to cover, because there wasn't much else to be doing.

With the sherry in her belly, Mam would start nodding off by the fire and I'd have to shake her by the shoulders and say, 'Mam, Mam,' until she woke up with a 'Hmmmm' and she'd get up groggily, and say she was off to bed because she couldn't keep her eyes open.

Because she wouldn't give me the sherry herself, when she had gone upstairs and I was there on my own, I'd sneak into the kitchen and pour myself a glass and take it back with me to the fire, sipping it like a bee might on nectar, tasting the bitterness, not liking it, but drinking it all the same.

Tonight, Mam had been later going to bed than normal and I was in the kitchen, my back to the door, just putting the stopper back into the sherry bottle when in walked Mr McKenna, earlier than he normally got back from the pub.

I spun round, startled; he seemed surprised to see me too.

'Molly, you're up,' he said.

'Yes,' I said, not daring to move, because behind my back was the glass and the sherry bottle.

'Put on the kettle, there's a good girl,' he says and he parks himself down at the table, with a big 'aaaaaaa' and reaches for the bread knife to cut the bread Mam's left out for him.

I turn back around to the counter and I hide the glass behind the bottle. I fill the kettle, but not too much so that it won't take long to boil. I want to get out of this kitchen and away from Mr McKenna. He's bad enough in the daytime, sober.

'Will you have a cup?' he asks, looking at me where I'm stood in front of the stove and I say no, that I was just going to bed and I'm thinking how can I get back over to the counter to empty the sherry glass? 'Ah sure you can stay up to have a cup with your stepfather,' he says. I hate that he is able to use the word father in a sentence pertaining to me.

'Alright,' I say, thinking I might be able to manoeuvre the glass into the dip of the sink if I shuffle over a bit, quietly.

He lifts up his leg and puts his boot on the chair, picking at the laces and untying them. 'That's better,' he says wiggling his toes in his socks and I wonder if his feet have black hair on them like the curly hair on his chest.

'You're settling in, Molly? You like it here?' he says.

'Yes, Mr McKenna,' I say.

'Because you know,' he says leaning in a bit, 'Sometimes

I wonder.'

'Wonder what?' says I, eyeing him up, not liking his tone at all.

'Well ...' he says. 'It must be hard on you, like. So young. Losing your father. Living here, with us.'

'I'm grand,' I say and I'm wondering how much drink he's had. Could I leave the sherry there till morning and get up early and get rid of it?

'Your mother'd be lost without ya,' he says. 'And you're turning into a fine young gersha. Any man would be glad to have ya.'

I don't say anything. Instead, I turn the gas up on the stove and tap my foot.

'Have you been thinking about it, Molly?'

'Thinking about what?' I ask. There's a glint in his eye and I don't know if it's the drink, or what.

'Getting married.'

'Getting married!' I say and a big pssst sound comes out of my mouth. 'Why would I be thinking about that?'

'Well why wouldn't you be?' he says. 'A fine girl like you. Are you telling me you've never thought about it? About what it would be like to be with a man?'

I don't like where Mr McKenna is going at all.

'No,' says I. 'I haven't.'

'Ach,' he says and he goes silent, watching me pour out the water into the pot and sit down at the table to stir it and make it draw faster.

'You'd make a grand wife,' he says and he puts his hand across the table and puts it on mine. I draw it back, feeling as though a rat has run across my knuckles.

'Are you worried you won't make a good wife?' he says and he has a grin on his face as if this is all a big joke.

'No,' I say. 'I'm not.'

'Because if you're anything like your mother,' he says and I stand up, the chair shooting back, making a loud scratching sound on the tiled floor.

'I think it's time for bed,' I say and he holds out the palm of his hands and he says, 'Don't go, you haven't even had your tea.'

'I'm tired,' I say and I walk over to the sink, pouring my full cup of hot tea down the drain and reaching for the sherry glass, not caring if he sees. I chuck the sherry into the sink, watching the red and brown mix together, like the blood from a steak on milky pepper sauce.

'Ah, don't go, Molly,' he says, looking at me all forlornly as I walk past him towards the door.

'Goodnight, Mr McKenna,' I say and I feel a big sense of relief as I get out of the kitchen and up the stairs.

Next Saturday, I think, I'm not taking any chances. I'm going to be in bed early, asleep, the lock turned in my door, just like it is tonight.

I wonder if I should tell my mother.

But what is there to tell?

* * *

People keep saying that time will heal. But I can't understand that. If you put a big giant hole in your hand and it forms a scab and a scar, that's how time heals. When you tear someone out of your life, like Daddy was torn from ours, where's the healing in that? What can scab over to heal there? Nothing.

Mam is seeming to get on with things. She's up early making the breakfast, cleaning the fires, making the beds. She's bright and breezy, as if nothing ever happened to us. I think even Michael and Patrick don't miss Daddy like I do. They go to school and they play their games and go outside and walk down to the park. They talk about him sometimes, but I don't think he's in their thoughts the same way as he is in mine. I can't stop thinking about him.

Mr McKenna walks to his drapery shop every day, with a cane in his hand like a gentleman. I'd only been in the shop a few times before we came to live in the town and I remembered it as dark and stuffy, smelling of snuff and mothballs.

He stocks bowler hats and top hats, silk handkerchiefs and coloured braces. He sells flat caps with designer labels from London, keeping them down the back of the shop. At the front, near the doors, he arranges gaming hats for the gentry. He has notions about himself has Mr McKenna.

I was only in the house a few weeks, when he hauled me into the shop to help, saying I couldn't be rattling round at home all day with my mother. He was right in that there was less work to do in the grey house than there had been on the farm. There was no milking to be done, or butter to be made, there was no farm work to help out with, or crops to be sown, or weeded or harvested. But still, I would rather have stayed with my mother than spend hours in the shop with him.

The more time I spent with him, the more he sent spiders over my skin. I saw that look on him sometimes - the one he had on his face when he stood at the door with the tulip for my mother, a curly smile under his moustache. Wanting something.

He came in and out all day, standing close, sometimes in the doorway to the back office, trying to talk to me, to share a joke with me, to ask me to go fetch him a bar of soap or to leave a pair of shoes in the cobblers for him. I felt like he was thinking of things to come and talk to me about and he made me walk beside him on our way home, swinging his cane, pointing buildings out to me as if I was a tourist and not a native of this place at all.

On the days when I wasn't in the shop, I was helping Mam in the house. There was always cleaning to be done. It was a different type of work here, I felt. On the farm, it didn't matter if things were a bit dusty or black; in the grey house, everything had to be kept very clean, bare and white.

When we'd first arrived, Mam had done her best to make it homely for us and had bought some material and sewed new cushions for the parlour. But Mr McKenna said he didn't see the need for any *superfluous items* and he put her off so she went back to sewing up the sheets and socks and linens instead.

There were no more plans for pretty patterns. We had moved into a new life now. I thought that the tulip was a big falsehood of a flower. I had never seen so much as a daisy in the grey house. There were no petals, no vases, nothing of colour to brighten our day. There was only Mr McKenna and his routine and us fitting neatly into it, the way he wanted. And my mother might have chosen this life for herself, but I hadn't. I hadn't signed up to this at all.

* * *

Some days I walk up Mell, out the Slane Road and as far as Curley Hole, past the bridge and the weir at the Boyne. I go on Sundays mostly, after mass is done and the dinner cleared and Mr McKenna and Mam are going on their own march about town, which he likes to do to show her off on his arm. He nods his head at everyone who passes, tipping his hat and raising up the arm he's clamped across my mother's.

I like this bit of time to myself, the country air going up my nose and the birds twittering all the way with me as I walk, by the bushes, past all the cottages, the trees starting to forest in front of me. It's the one bit of time I start to feel like myself again. Like the old me. The country me.

Other people walk out here too. It's very scenic but I never really noticed because it was all I knew. Now I see it for what it is; the bend in the river, the blue sky, the calmness that this landscape cut into the earth brings. I don't look at anyone, I just keep walking, my head held high. I don't want to make idle chit-chat, to have anyone poke their noses into what I'm doing now, and how's my mother and isn't it terrible what happened to your father, you poor thing.

I'm feeling older. It's not just my figure, which is all developed into my dress - I know I look like a woman. It's my mind too. I don't think like I used to anymore. I'm not a child.

On these walks, I pretend that I am on a journey, that I am a woman setting out on a new life for herself, on an adventure.

Usually I sit at my favourite spot along the river, hidden from the road and home to a small nest of kingfishers who dart in and out of the bank, all whirr and snap of colour. When I sit in the grass and look at the water breaking in giant circles where the flow is quiet at the bank, I think of the days when Michael and Patrick and I would tramp across the field and cast our own lines out for the salmon.

The place where I sit is right across the road from the entrance to the Brabazon estate. I hear the carriages pulling up to turn and go up the long lane, the horses whinnying if they've come at speed from town. I find myself looking up the driveway wondering if Henry Brabazon remembers me and what happened to us or if we've already fallen from his mind.

He wasn't like I expected him to be, I realise. He was tall and skinny enough, nothing like his pot-bellied father or Flann Montgomery. He had jet black hair, so black it made his eyes pop, blue, the colour of the tiny cornflowers in the field. I remember him looking at me in the high-ceilinged hallway and outside in the giant archway of the front door, trying to calm me down, even though I was on fire on the inside and raging like a bull on the out.

That night, when my family were huddled, white-faced at the Brannigans', I left without my shawl, forgetting it on the back of a chair in my rush to get outside. I'd just upped and left as the people poured in, the whole parish on their way back from the dance, everyone out in support of us, coming from their homes with Christmas hams and bread and slices of apple tart.

'If we had've known,' they said. 'The snakey bastards.' They were sore and sorry. And when they heard about Daddy, their faces went white, tears springing to their eyes, the women wailing on the spot, going over to Mam and embracing her. It was easy to slip away from all that. Out on to the road.

People were shuffling in the dark, they passed by me

and I stepped into the ditch, trying to remain unseen. I didn't want anyone to stop and talk to me, to question me, to pass on their sympathies. I'd no time for sympathy. I wrapped my arms around myself, passing by Dowth mound, black against the sky, solid.

I wondered if myself and Turlough would have ended up there that night, after the dance, among all the other courting couples. He'd his hands all over me, touching my back and my bottom, running them up the inside of my ribcage, sending shivers through me with the hotness of his breath. I would have gone with him, I think. I would have climbed up there in the dark and found a spot and settled down to giggle and kiss and let him put his hands on me some more.

We were at the courting wall, a low cement structure behind the school hall, where the music could be heard pouring from the small open windows under the school roof; where couples were spread out, pawing at each other, when Stuttery Jack appeared, calling my name, in the dark.

At first, I was embarrassed to have been caught at the back of the school hall, but when I heard what Stuttery Jack had to say, that I had to get home quick, that the bailiffs were there, that the sheriff was there, that it was happening, again, and this time they had a warrant nailed to the door, the embarrassment turned to fear and then rage, as we ran, Turlough and I, hand in hand, from the school hall to my lane.

Poor Turlough. The face on him, what he must of thought, as I screamed and left his side and ran past the horses and the men, into the house to my brothers and my mam, who were standing there, watching the yard, the candles glowing against the firelight.

I breathed it in the frosty air, as I walked towards Brabazon House, feeling it go high into my head, past my nose, up behind my eyes, my boots crunching on the grass in the middle of the road. Hard then soft, road then crunch.

And there it was - all lit up, ablaze, standing out against the hill.

If I was crying the tears would have felt crisp on my skin. But there were no tears. It was as though I was saving them for the anger, for the power, for the strength I would need for what was to come. I probably should have been crying, great big gulping sobs - but I wasn't one for crying. It took an awful lot to make water come out of my eyes.

Mam said I should have been born a boy. Daddy said he was glad I wasn't, that I never cried because I had a power inside me. I was born on 21 December, a winter solstice baby, his December Girl.

'It's a special baby, born on the winter solstice in this part of the world,' he told me, every year on my birthday. It was our ancestors, you see, the people who came before us, the people who formed the mound up out of the ground, who built their temple to welcome the winter solstice sun into its chambers to awaken the dead.

I wondered if he was right. If I did have a power. If I did have something special about me on account of my birthday and the spirits inside me, breathed in from the tombs and the land.

It was no coincidence that they had come for Daddy, there, on that night. As we left our house, with a jennet cart of our belongings and we set out to walk into the black, it was right there in front of the mound that the spirits came for Daddy. There, at the tomb, they reached into his heart and stopped it and he fell on the road, a stack of pots falling from his basket and clanging, echoing against the backdrop of the sheriff's men hammering wood across our windows and hurling heavy stock from our sheds. Perhaps the spirits watched me as I ran to him and rolled him over to see the white in his face and the breath in his mouth evaporate into the sky.

A weak heart, they all said in the Brannigans' kitchen. *Sure, didn't his mother die of the same thing?*

And there he was in Mr and Mrs Brannigan's bed, a sheet up to his neck, coins on his eyes, in a bedroom where he'd never spent a single night before.

47

I'd seen it when I was hovering in the kitchen, wondering what to do - the bread knife was lying there, on a chopping block, the remnants of crispy soda bread all around it. I walked over and put my palm across it and looked around the Brannigans' kitchen. I stared straight ahead as I moved the knife from the board to the table and, in one swift movement, it was in the pocket of my dress, nestled with the handkerchief I'd wiped Daddy's face with. I sidled out, silent, keeping my head down, slipping away from the wailing and the commotion, out onto the road to walk the short distance to Brabazon House.

Now it loomed in front of me, around the corner of the hill, packed with revellers from the races, eating, drinking and being merry. It was hard to think that they had arranged it so, to pull us from our house on this night, while they celebrated and danced and drank their way into the small hours of the morning. Montgomery would be in the middle of it all, I knew it, talking and laughing and patting his big fat belly. I fingered the knife in my pocket, crouching down in the ditch at the gates, feeling the cold filtering up through my skirts. I just had to figure out how to get in and how to get to Montgomery.

The spirits would help me with the rest.

I closed my eyes and I saw the fear in Daddy's eyes, the whites looming in the dark, the anger gone, the hope put out, the same as when you blow out the oil lamp, the light extinguished, from bright to dark, in one split second.

My daddy would never celebrate another winter solstice with me.

Neither would Flann Montgomery if I had anything to do with it.

Chapter Six

HENRY

Brabazon House, Co. Meath, Ireland
St. Stephen's Day, 1894, Grand Ball

Amelia Aherne had changed from her riding skirt and jacket into a bright yellow dress. He thought how the colour suited her; sunny, like her personality, warm, like the hand she had placed on his arm when he'd picked her up, sodden from the ground, after she'd tumbled from her horse. The mare had startled at the noise of the starter's gun on the first race of the day, tossing Amelia into the air, and down, hard, on to the ground. The horse just missed the white barrier fence then ran around the Dowth racetrack, a large semi-circular course, spread out across two cleared fields in front of Brabazon House.

'Are you feeling quite alright?' He'd summoned the courage to approach and interrupt her conversation with a lady he did not recognise. Amelia smiled and blinked a little.

'No actually, I'm sore all over. But it was an excellent race meet, don't you think?'

'Oh yes, excellent. Did you have any winners?'

'No,' she said. 'Donkeys, the whole lot of them.' They both laughed. The St Stephen's Day race meet at Dowth and the Grand Ball afterwards was the highlight of the Christmas season. It attracted guests from as far as Dublin and Wicklow, who left their town houses and settled into their villas and country houses nearby for the festive celebrations. Henry found it all exhausting, but it did throw up the opportunity to look and now, speak to, the lovely Amelia Aherne.

'He does so love a meet,' said Amelia, looking over at Henry's father, Seymour, who was dressed in a black tuxedo and had a fat cigar in his hands. 'Do you think he misses it, racing?'

Seymour had been a renowned horseman in his day, having grown up on the track built on the estate by his grandfather. Henry's brother Arthur had inherited their father's desire and skill for speed, something that had completely bypassed Henry.

'I had money on your brother,' said Amelia. 'Second just isn't good enough.'

'No, Arthur hates to lose,' said Henry.

Musicians had set up in the corner of the great room, and were playing soft music to accompany the racegoers as they began to congregate in small groups on the sofas, at the fire, and near the large sideboard where the drinks were being served. Outside carriages were pulling up and dropping the guests off, wearing their winter finery. The scent of soap and cologne filled the air, but Henry couldn't shake the smell of wet earth in his nose.

Arthur looked like an animated school-boy, flitting from one guest to another. Henry knew by his movements and the grin on his face that he was already quite drunk. Amelia stood out in the room as though there were a halo around her. No matter where Henry moved, he always knew where she was, his eyes following her, staring at her back, or glancing at her face. He longed to stand by her all evening, to talk to her, to listen to her stories. But it was rude to ignore the other guests and reluctantly he bowed out of the conversation and moved off to mingle as he was obliged.

'Henry,' called Seymour as Henry made his way towards the drinks cabinet. His father was deep in conversation with Flann Montgomery.

'I was just saying to Montgomery here that you had some concerns about the Thomases.' He nodded to Montgomery, who looked at Henry.

'No need to have any concern,' said Montgomery. 'We have the full weight of the law behind us. We have proof. And we must make a stand.' He looked at Henry squarely.

Henry felt his pulse quicken. It always did when he felt he was stepping up to a debate.

'That may be,' said Henry. 'But for my taste, evicting a family at Christmas time is a poor show. I'm concerned it will reflect badly on us - on the Trust.'

Seymour looked to Montgomery, waiting for an answer. More and more he had been turning to Henry for his opinion on business matters, trusting his more modern judgment on certain matters.

'Eviction is a tasteless business, Master Brabazon,' said Montgomery. 'Nobody *wishes* to evict a family. But, this is about keeping the peace. If word got around, there would be three hundred people outside that house, protesting and maudlin' and causing ructions altogether.'

'Isn't there another way? Couldn't we have come to a more peaceful arrangement?' asked Henry, looking at a tiny cauliflower boil nestled on the side of Montgomery's face.

'We have tried everything, Sir. Given many a chance to right the wrongs. But they haven't taken those chances; they've only themselves to blame. He's a shockin' stubborn man is Oliver Thomas.'

'Indeed,' said Henry. Montgomery was hardly the most surrendering of men himself. 'Well, Mr Montgomery, it is my opinion that this will come back to bite us. I really hope that you can manage this situation.'

'Mounted troops have been drafted in,' said Montgomery. 'Everything is being done by the book. Best to do it tonight, no fuss, in one sweep. You'll see.'

'I suppose I will,' said Henry, his eyes still focused on the boil, past which Miss Amelia, with her hair piled high on her head, had just come into view.

* * *

Charity Eustace sat beside Henry for the entire length of supper that night and for each and every minute when she wasn't lifting her fork, knife or spoon to her mouth, she sat and picked at her nails. Henry watched the tiny flakes of skin fall from her hands on to the red tablecloth, creating their own snow storm at the dinner table. His stomach turned each time he caught sight of her hands. He imagined her lying in bed beside him and running her picked-at nails across his stomach and up to his face.

Seymour sat at the head of the table, raising his glass to several toasts throughout the meal, telling jokes, guffawing and leaning forward to shout down the table at guests who were too far away to join in the fun.

Henry started to drink his wine faster, hoping the liquid would seep into his blood and help him get through the evening. He thought how he would like to be at Oxford, the fire lit, a stack of books to read, the distant rumble of dorm-room arguments over cards the only disturbance.

'What are your plans after Oxford?' asked Charity.

'I suppose I shall come back here to the estate,' he said.

'You won't be travelling?' she asked. Henry thought it sounded more like an order than a question, but he answered, that no, it was unlikely.

'So many young men travel, it's such a waste,' she said. 'What could be so interesting about climbing on a filthy ship to cross the sea to visit countries that are stinking poor and riddled with disease? Lord knows what one could bring back.'

'The world is a book and those who do not travel read only one page,' said Henry, looking straight ahead and then turning to find Charity staring at him, her face contorted in confusion.

'What?' she said. 'Nonsense. I really don't understand the need to undertake such journeys. I often think those who wish to travel are running away from something.'

Commitment, thought Henry. Somebody had obviously taken a round the world trip simply to avoid having anything to do with this woman. Charity Eustace's family owned a land mass half the size of Leinster. It spread from Carlow in the south, up through the midlands and tipped their border at Meath.

His father thought that she would make a suitable match for marriage, despite Henry's protestations.

'I understand your concerns for the future,' Henry had told his father earlier, standing in front of the large mahogany desk in the study. 'But Charity Eustace is out of the question.'

Seymour's bald head was bent over a pile of parchment, documents that looked as though they were written in the previous century.

'Did I mention her?' said his father, looking up and holding out his hands, pleading innocence.

He had aged, his father. His jowls had grown droopy, sagging over his stiff white collar, his sideburns covering the descent a little. He looked tired, a puffiness under his eyes and he squinted at Henry, as though his eyesight was failing, as though he wasn't sure if it was indeed his son who was standing before him.

'You didn't have to,' said Henry.

'You could learn to love her,' said Seymour.

Henry shook his head and didn't respond. He couldn't find the words. He was tired of this pressure, of this subject that flared every time his father got him alone.

'Consider her,' said his father. 'At the ball, tonight - I want you to make an effort. Talk to her, look for her good attributes. I am sure she has many. I never took you for a shallow fellow, Henry. I thought you were beyond that.'

The jibe was meant to hurt. A tactic often used by his

father, when his direct requests were failing. And so, as Henry expected, he had been placed side by side with Charity at dinner and the evening stretched ahead into one long event that had to be endured.

'I've been thinking about India,' said Henry winding Charity up. 'It's a fascinating place. Such wonderful culture.'

He looked at her face, which was again gnarled into a puss. This is how he might pass the evening, he decided. Teasing and drinking. And watching Miss Aherne, who had been placed at the opposite end of the table, near to his father.

After supper, the table was cleared away and the floor opened up for dancing. The band started up loudly, Arthur standing in front of them waving sheets of music in the air.

'Come away,' hissed Henry and he grabbed Arthur by the elbow, leading him off to a nearby sofa. 'Grab a hold of yourself,' he said, sternly. He ordered a glass of water from one of the waiting staff and waited till Arthur sat and knocked it back. 'You've a long night ahead, pace yourself,' he warned.

'Ra, ra, ra,' said Arthur, lying right back against the sofa and shaking his head from side to side. 'Aren't you just the fine fellow, know-it-all Henry, never put a foot wrong, do-goody.'

Henry walloped Arthur on his arm, as discreetly as he could.

'Buck up, Arthur, or you'll have Father to answer to,' he said.

Henry grabbed another glass of water as a tray sailed by his head and forced his brother to drink it. 'You'll be sorry if you miss the evening,' he said, trying another tactic. Arthur looked at him through bloodshot eyes and said, 'Do you miss Mummy?'

Henry was silent, taken aback by Arthur's words, whose eyes were now starting to brim with tears.

'Of course, I do,' he said, and he put his hand on Arthur's shoulder and gently squeezed it. 'We all do. But she wouldn't be too happy to see you drunk as a skunk at the St Stephen's Day Grand Ball, now would she?'

'No,' said Arthur, looking off into the distance, dazed.

It was a topic that often came up when his brother was drunk. They had laid their holly wreath at her grave on Christmas morning, their tradition every year since she had died. But there was no conversation, no memories shared, just an acknowledgment that another year had passed without her in their lives.

Arthur stood up and pushed his brother in the stomach.

'Time to dance, brother!' he cried. Henry watched him stride across the room, wobbling a bit to each side and make straight for the lady in lilac who had been speaking with Miss Aherne earlier.

The lady smiled and accepted his hand and they took to the floor to waltz. He spun her around and around, making her laugh and Henry thought that even through Arthur's drink-addled mind, he would still charm the pants off any attractive lady. It was a gift, Henry felt, that he had simply not been blessed with.

* * *

It was after 1 a.m. when it happened. A few of the guests had left, their carriages summoned, the music finished. Henry had managed to wrangle a seat beside Miss Aherne and she was sitting propped up on the sofa, waving her fan at her face. She had been sipping wine and had moved on to a sweet champagne. He thought she got more beautiful the more she drank, her cheeks flushed, her laugh growing louder, her smile seeming to wrap all the way around her face.

She was asking him about Oxford and wanted him to describe some of the characters he studied with and he was enjoying rattling off tales of mischief and madness, feeling free to tell her some of the saucier stories that he wouldn't have attempted earlier. He was enjoying the effect the drink was having on him, too; he had finally settled into the evening, now that it was drawing to a close.

He heard the commotion in the distance at first, a shout and cry from the hall. He stopped talking to Miss Aherne and listened and as he went to stand, the doors of the great room burst open and in marched a young girl, dressed in a gingham dress, her face red. Her hair flew loose and there was something about her that seemed familiar to him but he couldn't think why.

She stopped and looked about the room, searching the faces of the guests. Behind her was Mrs Johansson and the butler, both making for her to try and grab her and haul her back.

'Montgomery!' roared the girl and a hush fell, only the faint clink of a glass to be heard. The crowds parted and there stood the agent, a round glass of port in his hand. As the girl stepped forward, making her way to Montgomery, Seymour appeared and held out his arms.

'What is the meaning of this?' he said, looking angrily at his housekeeper and butler over the girl's shoulders. 'How did she get in here?'

'You bastard!' cried the girl and an audible intake of breath filled the room. The butler reached the girl's arm but she lifted it with such force that he almost fell back.

'Get off me,' she cried, not looking behind her. 'You murdering bastard!' she said again, now almost reaching Montgomery himself.

Seymour stepped in front of her.

'You can't barge in here like this, young lady,' he said. A murmur worked its way around the edges of the room. What was going on? Who was this? How did she get in?

'Please, we can talk about this outside,' he said and Seymour placed his hands on her arms to lead her away. The girl pushed him roughly out of her way and he too staggered back. She had managed to get in front of Montgomery who was holding his glass up to his face, as if in protection.

'I hope you're happy now,' she screamed. 'You've got what you wanted.'

Montgomery took a step back and shook his head.

'Miss Thomas, this is most unexpected and most inappropriate. You must leave,' he said.

'You're nothing but a coward,' she said, her voice now dropping low, her eyes almost closing.

Henry had reached the girl and he moved in with the butler. They each grabbed an arm and managed to hoist her and drag her away from Montgomery, but not before she raised her legs and kicked out at him, narrowly missing his stomach.

'You murdering bastard!' she cried again. 'You won't get away with this.'

Henry and the butler dragged the girl from the room and Mrs Johansson closed the doors behind them.

The murmuring grew louder and broke into a babble, Montgomery swatting his brow and pulling at his collar.

'Who was she?' demanded Seymour, livid that the ball had been interrupted in such a manner.

'The Thomas girl,' said Montgomery in a quiet voice. 'The eviction was tonight.'

Seymour clapped his hands and cried out to his guests, 'Never a dull moment, is there? Carry on! The night's not over yet. More wine! Whiskey. This calls for a whiskey!'

Outside the great room, the girl had been bundled out the front door and had now broken down crying. The fight had left her and she stood, racked with sobs.

'You can't just barge your way in like that,' said Mrs Johansson, her arms folded. 'You had no right to do that. You should be ashamed of yourself. You should be arrested.'

The girl stopped crying and removed her hands from her face.

'They killed my daddy,' she said. 'My daddy's dead. He killed him. This is his doing.'

Henry ordered his carriage to be readied and said he would take the girl back home himself.

'There'll be no need for the police, Mrs Johansson,' said Henry and he turned to the girl. 'Can you tell me what happened. To your father? I don't understand.'

'His heart,' the girl muttered into her hands again. 'They broke his heart.'

Chapter Seven

MOLLY

I wouldn't look at, or speak to, Henry Brabazon, the whole journey in the trap down to the Brannigan's house the night of the eviction. There was holy murder going on and half the village out in support of us.

I stared off to the side, into the black bushes and shadowy lane way, the trees making eerie swishing noises as we drove. I didn't reply to the questions he asked me, I was rude and not caring, not one bit. I wanted to look at him, to take in his jaw and the dark sideburns that came part way down his face. I thought I might even want to sniff him, to see what a gentleman smelled like up close. But I sat as far as I could to the other side of the trap, hunching my legs up, turning my body away.

He told me he was very sorry for what had happened to me and my family and that he himself had no control over it and he was going to see what he could do to right the wrongs done to us.

But even Henry Brabazon with all his money and his power up in that big fancy house could not bring Daddy back. There was no righting the wrongs done to us. He could string Montgomery up and let us take sticks and knives and pierce his big yellow belly - give us Montgomery, I wanted to say - but it still wouldn't bring Daddy back.

Half way down the road, when he realised I wasn't for talking he stopped trying and we made our way down to Dowth, only the horse's hooves sparking off the ground to be heard. As we approached the Brannigans' house, the sound of people talking and murmuring came at us in the dark and we pulled up, the house all lit up, neighbours and other faces I knew standing about the yard.

They jeered at him when they saw who it was.

'Are ya happy now?' they said making low groaning and hissing noises at him as he stepped down out of the carriage and put his hand out for me. I ignored his open palm and jumped out, and folded my arms back around my body.

'Don't come in,' I said to him, the only words I'd spoken since I'd been put in the trap.

'I'd like to offer my condolences,' he said to the group, looking at them, his face all sincere.

'Don't come in,' I warned again, only this time my voice was lower and in a growl.

'I'd like to speak with your mother,' he said.

I didn't think Mam would want to speak to him. And as I looked into the yard and saw that there were people piling out the door now, when they'd heard that Henry Brabazon Esquire was standing outside, with me, I knew they were gunning for trouble. I felt we'd had enough upset for one night.

'Please,' I said. 'it's for the best.' And then I nodded into the yard at all the men standing around, some of them tapping sticks against their legs and I said, 'It's not safe.'

He gave me a bit of a slow look then, a sort of sorry stare and he climbed back up into the trap and I watched him man-oeuvre the horse out of there, back up the road, his head bent forward and down.

In all the pandemonium, it hadn't been noticed that I was gone and when I told them I'd gone up to the big house, to the grand ball, to find Montgomery, a load of the men shook their heads in disbelief and said, 'Holy God' and 'Her father'd be proud.'

My mother told me I'd done a stupid thing but then she took me in her arms and held me tight and whispered, 'What are we going to do?' into my hair.

I didn't know what we were going to do. I had done what I thought was the right thing - to let Montgomery know that he needed to pay for what he did to us. But now I was back here in the Brannigans', a load of people from the dance standing around, Turlough, looking white as a sheet and my daddy, being laid out in the Brannigans' bedroom, just off the full and heaving kitchen.

* * *

It was June and all Mr McKenna talked about was the Boyne Regatta. Before, we didn't pay much attention to the regatta. Daddy said it was an excuse for people to get drunk and dance and make fools of themselves all day. We'd only been twice that I could remember and after that, Daddy stopped bringing us, saying he'd better things to be doing on the farm.

This year, Mr McKenna wouldn't shut up about it. On and on he went – about so and so who'd be there, about how fine we'd all look. We were going to be on the other side of the river this year, where they had a big seating stand and a stage with a roof on it. It was where the rowers climbed off their boats after the race and where the band played.

Mr McKenna stocked straw hats with black and cream striped ribbon in the shop and put out his finest silk socks and coloured dicky bows for his regatta display. He himself would be wearing purple on the day; a shimmery velvet jacket with black down the lapels. He showed it to me in the shop and made me run my fingers up and down it.

'Feel it,' he insisted. 'Can't you feel the quality? Doesn't it feel lovely in your hands?'

'Mmm,' I said. Not wanting to feel anything Mr McKenna asked me to.

I thought he looked like a gombeen; a big purple

gombeen when he put that jacket on. I thought, he looks exactly like the people my daddy stopped going to the regatta because of and now, here he was, leading Daddy's family down the street, the cane still over his arm, my mother dolled up like some sort of lady, with make-up on and everything.

I'd never seen so many folks making their way down the town, filling the streets, their good mass clothes on, the chatter and atmosphere building. There were bonnets floating on heads, fresh flowers tucked into them, and coloured ribbons fluttering on the breeze. Small children clutched at their parents' hands, waving little flags.

I put my hand on my head, feeling the bonnet Mam had fixed there this morning. It was nice to be part of the occasion, I supposed, even if we were there with Mr McKenna.

The crowds grew into a throng at the bridge, bicycles queuing up, pony and traps stuck in the middle, trying to get through. The police were there waving and shouting at people to move along but it was like pouring corn into a funnel - you just had to give it time, let it stack up and watch it trickle.

I liked the warm press of the bodies. I could smell soap and cigarette smoke and the stink of a pipe carried over our heads. Mam kept looking back, telling us to stay with her, but I didn't care if I got lost. I was happy to be out on my own, away from everybody and just milling, free.

We got over the bridge and moved down the Marsh Road, where the factories with their chimneys were quiet. Regatta Day and Christmas Day were the only days in the year when there was no black smoke billowing out over the rooftops and floating down the river out to sea.

You could see all the factory workers among the crowd, some of them with beautiful woollen shawls and coloured skirts, the women who could afford to dress themselves nice. Most of them were just a bit older than me, and I wondered if I could get a job there instead of slaving in the shop with Mr McKenna. At least I'd get my own money then, paid into my hand every Friday, mine to do with what I wanted.

On this side of the river, the crowds were less. You could feel the wealth as we moved down the road and approached the gate, where we were to go into the arena. I spotted all the ladies now, the colours and feathers moving and gently swaying in front of us.

My eyes stuck to their bustled rumps, taking in their waists, smaller than a child's, their pin stripe brollies held aloft. I wondered how they got their hair to curl like that, all piled up under hats that seemed as though they could fall off their heads at any minute. They were so refined, so beautiful; they were nothing like Mam and me. I looked at Mam and felt sorry for her. She was gripping Mr McKenna's arm and he was leading her round like a horse, stopping to say hello to everyone he met.

'Congratulations,' I heard everyone say. 'What a fine family you have now, Mr McKenna.'

I looked around at the arena, the first time I had ever been in it and thought how small it was. From the other side of the river it looked giant, with the big green stand for everyone to sit on. I noticed a group of rowers standing together, their muscled shoulders stretched out under striped cotton shirts.

I let myself look at their bottoms, my eyes dropping to waist level, taking in the shape of their behinds in the tight, white cotton. I couldn't help but wonder what it might feel like to run my hand over those breeches, to feel the shape under my palm.

I was telling myself to look away, when I saw the bottom I'd been staring at turn around and when I looked past the waist and up to the face, I recoiled. It was Henry Brabazon. I'd forgotten that he might be here. I thought he lived in England most of the time. And if he was here, well that could mean Montgomery was here too. I felt sick and giddy all at once. How was this day going to turn out now? Henry turned his head and I looked away, moving to the side a bit, so I wouldn't have to look at him. I hoped he didn't see us and then I thought, he wouldn't know us anyway.

An announcement came over the tannoy system. The races would be starting in a quarter of an hour. Mr McKenna took the cue to lead us over to the catering tent where they were serving tea and plated sandwiches with ham and pickled onion, and cheese and cucumber.

'Isn't this a spectacle?' Mam said to me, her eyes all aglint.

There was a table on the stage with seven silver cups on it, all as tall as a small child. Engravements curled round the cups between the half-heart handles, all the previous years' winners' names scraped into the metal. Mr McKenna had sponsored a race, it was to be the third one and he was going to present the cup to the winning team. He couldn't wait to get on stage and have everyone look at him. The band was set up to the back of the stage, playing marches and upbeat numbers for the crowds. The music carried across the river to the other side, over the warm air and smell of tidal water.

'Look, Molly, a parrot,' said Michael and I looked to where he pointed at a blue bird with green and yellow feathers. He ran over and the man holding the bird gave him some seeds to lay flat on his hand and Michael didn't even flinch as the parrot put its big, strong beak on his clammy palm. I noticed there was hardly anything for children to do on this side of the arena. Over on the other side were the hurdy-gurdys, sweet stalls, and even a big tower spiral slide that had been especially built for the day.

The band made a trumpeting sound to mark the first race. We clambered up the green stand and took our seats and waited. It didn't take long, within minutes you could hear the crowds up the river roaring, the noise distant at first and then growing closer and closer.

We all looked left, straining our heads to see and I realised what a vantage point we had, compared to the crowds across the river who could only jump up and down. Then they appeared, two boats, like long darts, thrusting along the top of the water, quick as blades on ice. We leapt to our feet, shouting and cheering now, competing with the crowds across the river who were roaring and screaming in excitement too. It was Drogheda Rowing Club and then Dublin University Rowing Club. Ahead, then back. In front, then not in front. I gave a big roar too, enjoying that I could scream like that and nobody could say anything to me.

We held our breaths between the squeals, focusing our eyes on the flag that marked the finish line. The two boats shot past the stand, and we strained forward to watch as Drogheda Rowing Club nudged a margin ahead of its rival, right on the last stroke before the line.

The crowds leapt even higher, whooping, cheering, and screaming for our local winning team. I roared too, caught in up in the excitement, clapping and feeling pure joy in my heart.

And when the rowers climbed on shore, when they pulled their boat up on to the wet muck and silt, I looked down at the heaving chests and red faces as they recovered from the exertion. I realised then that I, my mam, and my brothers had been roaring in support of Henry Brabazon, the man whose family had overseen the theft of our home and the death of my father. I felt like a traitor and I sat down in my seat and between all the commotion and the shouting and the noise, said a quiet prayer to God and asked him to ask my father to forgive me.

* * *

Henry Brabazon caught me unawares when I was leaving the arena to take the two boys over the bridge to see if they could find at least a little fun. Patrick was antsy at the thoughts that he might get on a hurdy-gurdy and he was sure he'd seen a man with a monkey.

'Do you think I could hold him?' he said, looking up at me through a smattering of square freckles.

'I'm sure you could,' I said, smiling. It was nice to be

with just the boys among the crowds, looking at everything, getting excited.

'Hullo, there,' said a voice. I'd been looking at a beautiful woman with a bright blue dress on and a parasol over her head. Her skin was like white glass, no colour in it at all and I thought, if I could look like anyone, if God said, Molly, you can take the looks of anyone in the wide world, I would have said her.

Patrick tugged on my hand. 'Molly,' he said. I looked to where he was pointing. And there he was, Henry Brabazon, stood right in my path and I hadn't even seen him because I was looking at the beautiful lady.

'Hello,' I said, stepping back a bit, because by not looking I'd nearly walked right into him.

His black hair curled into a point at the front. He looked sweaty, from the rowing I suppose. He was still in his cotton shirt, not dressed yet in his summer suit like the other gentlemen.

'It's lovely to see you,' he said, in his ever so grand voice. 'I didn't expect to see you here.'

No, well, you wouldn't, would you? I thought. But I didn't say that. Instead I told him that my mother was remarried now. To Mr McKenna. Who owned the drapery on West Street and who had sponsored the third race. Which his rowing team had won.

'Oh, Mr McKenna, yes, I know of him,' he said. 'I've been in the shop. Well, that's nice,' he said. 'That you're settled.'

'Yes,' I said, noticing my heart going into a buzz in my chest.

'Are you enjoying the regatta?' he asks.

'Yes,' I say. 'You were very good. In the race.'

Why am I offering compliments to Henry Brabazon? I feel ashamed as soon as the words are out of my mouth and I want to let go of Patrick's hand and tell him to go to the railings and wait for me. I don't want anyone to hear me. I look around. Are people watching?

'A fabulous day for it. One of my favourite rivers, this. That includes the Isis,' he says. I don't have a clue what he's talking about.

'At Oxford,' he says, explaining.

'Oh,' says I. A girl walks by licking the air around a large wad of candy floss. I scan the moving crowds. No eyes catch mine.

'Such a coincidence bumping into you,' he says and he flicks back his head and the black curl at the front flops up and down. 'I was actually up at your old house today. At Dowth.'

He watches my face for a reaction but I don't know what to say to him. I haven't been back to the house since the eviction. I can't bear to imagine it and the ghost of Daddy moving round the yard.

'Right,' says I.

'It's in good repair,' he says.

'Is it?'

Why is he telling me this? Referring to it as 'ours' as if we still have a claim to it. I know I should be walking away from him by now, giving him the cold shoulder, letting him know that Montgomery and him did nothing but ruin our lives but I'm still stood there, looking at his blue cornflower eyes. Patrick tugs on my hand, because he wants to go.

'We're going to see the hurdy-gurdys,' I say to him.

He bends down and puts out his hand for Patrick to shake. But Patrick's shy and he goes behind my skirts and all of a sudden I think of that day, when his little hands were on the back of my thighs the same, gripping through my underskirt, pinching the skin with fear, the eviction men outside, and my daddy like a lunatic in the dark.

Brabazon stands back and says, 'Lovely to see you, Miss Thomas.'

Thomas. It's been so long since I heard that name. All I ever hear these days is McKenna.

'And if I have any news I know where to contact you, now,' he says.

'What do you mean?' I ask, not understanding.

'About the agent's son in your house. It's not something I'm happy about.'

The world goes silent for a second. I'm sure there's a whistling in my ears.

'Montgomery?' I say, his name like ash in my mouth.

'Yes,' he says. 'I saw his son there this morning. I don't think the board of The Trust would be too happy about it.'

My mouth's opening and closing like a trout's. I'm not sure if I heard him right and I repeat the words in my mind, trying to make sense of what he's just said. Agent. Son. House. Montgomery's put his son, that big, bumbling son, the image of him with his rounded tummy and hair all receding, into our house.

'Yes,' I say, the only word that will come out. And I'm walking away from Brabazon now, clutching Patrick's hand so tight he tells me I'm hurting him. I know Brabazon is probably standing there looking after us, hands on his hips, his rowing arse clutched tight, wondering why I just walked away like that as though I was in a daze, but I am in a daze. The people are in front of me and all I can feel are those feelings, the same I felt on the night that it happened; that I need to find a knife, that I need to go and find Montgomery and slice him and watch him bleed till he's cold and gone.

'Who was that man?' asks Michael as we're walking out of the arena and down the Marsh Road.

'That was Mr Brabazon,' I say, looking ahead, my mind fifteen miles up the river, back in our house, my knees on Brabazon's puffy chest.

'From the big house?' he says.

'Yes,' I say, my voice snippy.

'Why were you talking to him?' he asks. And I know he's thinking of all the bad things he's heard, the name scattered about, insults in the air.

'He was just saying hello,' I say.

'What were you talking about?' he asks.

'Never you mind,' and I point down the bridge and tell Patrick I think I can see the monkey man. They're so innocent, the boys. They don't remember things like I do. They've taken to McKenna's house, with his strap and his ways, like they always lived there. Like there was never a before. They don't talk about Daddy, they don't talk about the countryside. They're only interested in the today and tomorrow, in the boats they can make out of wood and go sailing in the park. I watch them run ahead, all smiles, running right up to the monkey man and giggling when the creature runs across their necks and down their arms, like a funny looking cat. I give the man the pennies and they stand stroking the monkey; making noises for him and feeding him the little nuts the man gives them.

It's only me who is sad, walking around with them, with the weight of the news of Montgomery and his son upon me. When we've gone through the crowds and watched the hurdy-gurdys and gotten some barley sugar and laughed at a man with a white face and black marks on it putting his hands all in the air like he's climbing a wall, I tell the boys that I'm feeling very tired and that if they run back to Mam and Mr McKenna, I'm going to go back to home for a while.

Chapter Eight

MOLLY

I need to be on my own. The crowds are too much, the spectacle is gone for me now. People block my path every step I take and I can smell the stink of summer sweat and tobacco. I watch the boys walking over the bridge, back to the Marsh Road and slowly I walk up the street, past all the revellers, who are shouting now and full of the drink. A man calls out to me and makes to grab for my shoulder but I'm quick and step out of his way and scowl at him as I walk away.

I always knew it was Montgomery who was behind the court case and the eviction. That he wanted what my daddy had and he wasn't going to stop till he got it. Now he had it; his own son living in our house, in our yard, on our farm.

I walk slowly, all the thoughts going through my head, up and down off the footpath, out of the way of the traps trying to pass by through the crowds and the young boys with the handcarts saying they were selling papers, but you knew they had a bottle of whiskey hidden beneath. I'm going home to try and get a bit of peace, to be all alone, to think.

When I get to the house and in the back door, my thoughts are still tumbling over each other and I stand in the kitchen, poking at the stove, not hearing the door open behind me. I turn around and Mr McKenna is there on his own, the boys and Mam left behind at the regatta.

'Oh?' I say, wishing he hadn't come back and that I had the house to myself like I planned. 'Where is everyone?'

'I wanted to catch you on your own,' he says. 'There's something I want to show you.'

I say nothing but listen to him as he tells me he's been at something in the shed and if I come with him, he'll show me - I'm not to tell my mother because it's a surprise. I'm a bit intrigued. I haven't seen him do anything for my mother. Not since the yellow tulip.

I don't really want to go out to the shed with him but he takes off out the back door. I pause for a moment and then follow him. I realise as I go through the green shed door that Mr McKenna *has* been spending time out here lately. He says it's the only place he can give his head some peace, but I never acknowledge him when he says that because he means it as an insult to us and my family and I think, *well why did you take us on then, if you don't like the noise or the company?*

The smell of fresh wood shavings fills the air. It reminds me of the barns at Dowth, musty and earthy. The shed has a big bench along one side, where he has all his tools spread out and he tells me that if he didn't own the shop, which his daddy passed to him, then he would have been a carpenter.

He's bent over, rummaging in a box on the floor, his bony arse sticking up, black trousers to match the purple jacket he's so proud of. I think that it's strange that he's back here with me, at home in his shed, when the regatta is still going on and there are plenty of snobs for him to be hanging around with.

'Come in,' he says. 'Close that door behind you.'

I don't know why he wants me to close the door, there's nobody here, but I do anyway, considering it's a big secret he's going to show me. I move inside and watch him pull out a small wooden crate covered with a rag. From under the rag he takes five little pieces of wood. They're shaped like figurines, like people.

'What are they?' I say, holding the one he gives me to look at.

'Russian dolls,' he says. 'I wanted to make your mother a gift, something nice.'

I'm holding these pieces of wood not really understanding. I think my mother is a bit old for dolls.

'Open it,' he says. I don't know what he's talking about.

He takes the doll from my hand and he twists it so that it splits in half. It cuts open as though somebody chopped it right around the middle. Then I watch him open up all the dolls and pop them all into each other and before I know it, he's holding only one doll, when before there were five.

'I want it ready for her birthday, Molly,' he says. 'But I need to paint them. Could you help me with that?'

I think this is a very nice thing Mr McKenna is doing, I didn't think he had it in him, but I tell him of course, I'll help him paint them.

'I've only ever whitewashed, though,' I tell him. 'What kind of painting do you mean?'

He takes a piece of paper out of the crate, torn from a periodical, a picture of a Russian doll on it, in full colour. The biggest doll has a small, red, rosebud mouth and a yellow face. She peeks out from a painted shawl, draped in delicate dots and swirls. I really don't think I could paint like that, but I tell him I'll try.

'Why don't you try a bit now,' he says. I don't want to start now. But he's so insistent.

'I think your mother would really appreciate it.'

I sigh, take the paintbrush he gives me and I watch him prise open a small tin with a flat screwdriver and reveal a gloop of red paint.

I dip the tip of the brush into the tin and I paint a few strokes on the wood, watching it soak in, feeling the pull of the bristles as they go up and down the smooth surface. He's done a good job on this, Mr McKenna. I never knew that he was capable like this with wood, but there they are, laid out in front of me, these perfect miniature dolls. I get to thinking that if he's so good with the carving, why did he not make the boys some toys? Like the wooden boats they're so fond of or a Noah's Ark, or any of the wooden animals we see on the toy shelves at Duffy's Hardware Store in West Street, that they're always wanting but never get.

When I'm thinking about this, I notice that Mr McKenna has moved behind me, that he's not beside me anymore. And he has his hand on my arm, moving it down to my wrist as he says, 'not like this, like this,' and he's trying to show me, but I don't like it, it doesn't feel right. I go to move to the right, away from him, but he just steps in closer, still holding my wrist, moving his body real close, so that I can feel his legs up against mine.

I'm going to have to go and paint later, because I can smell the drink on him now and I didn't know he had drink on him and I don't like being around him when he's like this.

'Mr McKenna,' I say and I go to sidestep to the left this time, but it's like he was expecting it and his foot is there and I can't move.

I say his name again, 'Mr McKenna,' only firmer now, like I mean what I say, that I'm going to have to go now because this just isn't right.

Then my head is down. Crack. I realise that he used his other foot to swipe my legs out from under me and I'm pushed forward, his hand on the back of my head. He's holding it now, his whole weight on my neck and head, my face right on the work bench with the smell of wood shavings and the doll, still in my hand with its paint all wet, and I'm looking at it right up at my eyes.

I don't think I can breathe. My neck is blocked. I don't know if it's his weight or his wrist or his arm that's taking the breath from my body, but there's no air and I can't scream.

And then I feel it.

The draught on my skin. My skirts, pulled all the way up from behind, the backs of my legs exposed.

He grunts and he leans even harder on me and he's pawing right inside my knickers now, pulling them to the side and his hands going at me, his fingers hurting me and inside me and I wonder if I'm really here at all.

And then there's a pain like I've never experienced before.

A sensation so shocking I feel as though my very soul has left my body and is raised right above and is looking down on me and Mr McKenna as he goes at me, grunting and grinding and hurting me so bad that I think he's murdering me there on the bench in his dark green shed.

He rattles me forever and then his breathing gets real heavy and his body jerks and I feel that he is done. He withdraws and he's muttering now, telling me not to tell my mother and if I do, that he'll take a knife to her throat in the middle of the night.

Then he leaves the shed and I notice there are tears in my eyes, and on my face and when I step back from the bench there's blood, all over the floor and down my leg and it's the exact same colour as the paint on the tips of the brush, on the body of the Russian doll that I'm still holding in my hand and was painting only moments ago.

Drogheda Argus, June 1895

The shocking murder has taken place of Mr Flann Mont-gomery at his home at Dowth, Co. Meath. The following are the par-ticulars as they have been ascertained. On Monday last, the night of the Boyne Regatta, Mr Montgomery was attending to some matters at his home in Co. Meath, whereby his son did find him, laid out in the yard, with his throat cut. A search of the area did reveal no intruders or suspects. An inquest, the result of which was that Mr Montgomery came to his death in consequence of the stab wound to his throat, was assisted and aided by his son to no avail. The Royal Irish Constabulary has made appeals for any witnesses or persons with information to come forward. Mr Montgomery was formerly the agent for Brabazon estate, Dowth. Co. Meath.

Part Two

Chapter Nine

GLADYS

England, Southwest London, June 1895

Every day Gladys made her husband, Albert, a boiled egg and soldiers for breakfast. She trimmed the bread nice and neat and waited until the toast was a little cooled to butter it. Albert wasn't a fussy eater but she knew he liked his toast with the butter sitting on top - so he could see it. She made sure to order the butter in every week from the grocers. To have everything just so. To please him.

They were in a lovely house now. It was redbrick, with white window frames, the parlour window a sash, jutting out on to a very respectable street.

She had never expected that Albert would rise through the council ranks like he had. When they'd married at sixteen, he'd been a simple road sweeper, but with his way of managing people, with his talent for getting things done quickly, without fuss, he'd risen to be head of maintenance services, and for that, she was proud.

She never thought they would afford a house with high ceilings, four bedrooms and the kitchen in the basement, like a posh house she had dreamed of when she was a child.

When Albert had eaten his breakfast, wiped the crumbs from his moustache, put on his overcoat and got up on his bike for work, she would close the door, pad back to the table and sit for a few minutes. She liked her tea hot, boiling so that it scorched her throat.

It made her feel alive.

After her tea, she would start the housework, taking water from the boiling vat, starting with the black and white mosaic tiles that led to the front door, scouring the steps and then changing the water to wash down the door. Their house was one of the neatest on Louisville Road. Even the leaves on the green plants outside got a wash if they looked dusty.

With the front door sparkling, ready to greet anyone who might knock on it that day, she started on the kitchen before working her way through every room in the house. She went over the bedrooms daily, even though they were un-touched and not a soul had gone in or out since she'd last run her cloth round the skirtings and patted down the eiderdown.

She changed the laundry good and regular to keep it fresh and free from damp. She hated the mould that had puck-ered the walls of her house when she was young, growing mucus on her chest, making her wheeze. She had promised herself that when she got married there would be no mould in a house of hers. She would wipe it away every day if she had to. Maybe that was how she got into her cleaning routine.

She couldn't leave the house until it was done. She wouldn't have been able to - her body would not have let her past the front door unless every single job had been com-pleted.

Monday was laundry day, and she would spend the day soaking and rinsing, scrubbing at the washboard, swirling the sheets with the pole. They could afford to send it out to laun-der but she wouldn't have it. She needed the work, the rou-tine, the feeling of getting things clean. Instead, Albert bought her a mangle and she enjoyed turning the handle and watching the sheets come out, ready to dry on the line. It really was a miracle machine.

She never left the house on Mondays, but every other

afternoon of the week she would put on her coat and place her hat carefully on her head. She'd walk to the shops to pick up whatever they needed. Mostly, they didn't need for much and there were meat men and bread men knocking on the door each day, but she liked walking to the shops with her basket over her arm.

Before she did the groceries, she'd walk up to the common, breathing the fresh air into her lungs, taking the same route every day, counting the trees as she'd go. One winter, after a lightning storm, four of the trees were felled and she felt uncomfortable knowing that they had been struck down like that and she'd have to change her counting. She hated change. It unsettled her.

After her walk, it was home to make the tea. Every day had a designated dish. There was no breaking her routine, except for Easter and Christmas Day. Sometimes, she knew by the slump of Albert's shoulders, when she poured the lamb stew on to his plate on a Wednesday, that he'd like something different, a break from her routine. But he knew by now that this was her way.

It was the only way.

Lately, however, an idea had come into her head. It had started when she'd gone through a bit of a shock. She had been feeling a little sick and a tiredness had washed over her, more than the normal fatigue the cleaning brought on. She thought her stomach felt a bit taut and sure enough her monthly never came.

For weeks, she watched her underclothes, waiting for its arrival, dashing to the toilet in the morning to make sure it hadn't started to seep away from her unbeknownst in her sleep.

And when it had been enough time, when she was certain that she could feel the swelling low, under her belly button, a flickering even inside her, she sat Albert down on a Friday evening after he came in from work.

'I've something to tell you, Albert,' she said, her hands

twitching as they clasped each other on the kitchen table.

A pained expression crossed his face, as though she was about to deliver bad news.

'I'm with child,' she said quietly, not looking him in the eye, something she'd never really been able to do with anyone. She preferred to look at a person's chin, or ear while she was talking to them - it unsettled her to catch their gaze.

He had stood up straight and hugged her, and when she glanced at his face she could see tears in his eyes.

'Have you been to see the doctor?' he said. She told him she hadn't. That she wanted to tell him first.

Albert reached in his pocket and pulled out a bundle of notes. He told Gladys to make an appointment first thing in the morning.

'I'm so happy, my love,' he said. 'You've made me the happiest man in London.'

When she got up the next day, an excitement brewing in her stomach, the affection Albert was showing her filling her with joy, she forgot to check her underclothes when she went about her morning toilet visit and it was only later, at lunchtime when she was making preparations to leave the house and walk to the doctors, that she felt it; that familiar twinge in her pelvis.

In a panic, she lifted her skirts, right there in the hallway. And there it was; the dark shadow, staining her cotton, knifing her heart.

There would be no need for the doctor.

There would be no examination.

She was as she always was.

She tucked the pound notes into a pillow case at the back of her wardrobe, thinking that all this excitement and breaking her routine had caused it to come. She'd forgotten herself, gone outside herself, not doing the things that made her feel safe, that had to be done to make things right.

She vowed that she would go back to herself, to the rules and that somehow, in some way, she would fix it for

Albert.

He deserved a child.

And at forty-two, her last chance now extinguished in her body, it was time to do something new, something that would guarantee their happiness, no waiting or wondering or panicking at the stab of a cramp.

It was time to put her plan into action.

All she had to do was choose.

Chapter Ten

MOLLY

London, June 1896

The mind is a wonderful thing. It has the power to take you completely away from yourself, up out of your body, floating on clouds, over people's heads, soaring through the sky like a big, black crow, looking down, ahead - only more clouds. I have become very good at leaving my body.

I understand now why Mam did what she did. It wasn't about her at all. It was about us. Sometimes a smile creeps on my face and I think, we're not that different my mam and me. We both sold ourselves for our children.

Mr Tubular is here now. That's not his real name, but it's what I call him. He reminds me of the tubes on the church organ back home. Tall and empty, making long, drone noises. He goes on a bit. So, I rise above him, and I stay in the air, outside of here, looking down on the streets and cobbles and the flower sellers, pushing my way through the smog and the smoke, tiny flits of black soot nestling in my hair.

When I brush my hair every evening and the black flits fall out, that's what I think of. I don't think of the men that have run their fingers through it, or held on to it as they've held on to me, pushing with all their might as if they want to break me. I think of the flights I had today, of all I've seen, in the air, in my mind.

Mr Tubular has taken a shine to me. It might be my accent or because I'm quiet. He tells me he could look into my eyes all day. He's not the worst, but he's coming to see me regularly now. Madame Camille is pleased; she says he's hooked.

He gets off me after he's finished and he starts dressing, standing on one foot, hopping up and down into his trousers. I sit up and attend to myself, over to the bowl for washing, the cloth for wiping, the powder to make me fresh again and ready for whoever's next. He starts asking questions, being all personal, wanting to get to know me.

'What part of Ireland did you say you're from?' he says.

'Dowth,' I say. 'It's in County Meath. North of Dublin.'

'Doubt?' he says.

'Dowth,' I say again, emphasising the end part of the word.

'Oh,' he says and laughs.

Why had I told Mr Tubular? Why had I broken my rule of never telling people where I was from?

'Not been to Ireland,' he says. 'Maybe someday I'll go.'

I turn my back away from him, pulling on the scratchy chemise Madame Camille gave me. It has holes at the front, near the crotch. If I ask, she might give me a new one, but what do I care if there's holes? There's no looking respectable here anyways.

I wasn't in the mood for small talk with Mr Tubular. He was done, and he'd paid. I stood facing the corner, looking at the peeling paper above my head. Mottled damp crept from the ceiling down the wall. The room smelled of sweat and semen. I folded my arms and waited.

He asked me another question but I didn't respond. Instead I sighed, to let him know our time was up and he was to leave.

'I'd like to see you again,' he says.

'I'm always here,' I say, my voice as flat as I could make it.

'You're too good for this place,' he says and I remain motionless.

I watch a solitary drop of water travel from the ceiling joint, along the sharp edge of the folded falling paper. It moves along the edge and then plops on to the floor, splattering on to the lino below.

I hear the door close and when I look around, Mr Tubular is gone.

* * *

It was as though the notice had been sent by God himself, a small, yellow card, *Help Wanted, Apply Within*. I'd walked the streets, in and out of little shops, speaking to the keepers, watching them shake their heads. One felt sorry for me and gave me a hard end of bread. I was still limping a bit, finding it difficult to walk.

I climbed the grey steps of the house and pulled back the heavy iron knocker. A housekeeper answered, small, wispy bits of hair poking out of her cap.

'Yes?' she said and she didn't look too pleased to see me.

'You're looking for help?' I said, pointing to the card displayed in the window.

'The service entrance,' she said, spitting the words at me. She slammed the heavy door closed. I peered over the edge of the steps and could see a basement below. Slowly I climbed back down the steps and through the small gate to allow me down to the service entrance. That was stupid of me I suppose, knocking on the front door.

I rapped on the service door, looking at the flakes of paint that had chipped off around the glass. It was a few minutes before the same housekeeper appeared again, a scowl still on her face.

'Have you references?' she said. And I shook my head.

'Can't help you, then,' she said and she went to close the door. I stuck my foot in it and stopped it with my hand.

'Please,' I said. 'If I could just talk to you. If I told you about myself. You might …'

My voice trailed off. I sounded desperate.

'Where are you from?' she said, looking me up and down now.

'Ireland,' I said.

'What part?' I picked up on her Irish lilt.

I told her I was just off the boat, that I'd come by train from Liverpool, that I was on my own and that I was a hard worker. She stood back and the space behind the door revealed a large kitchen, a puff of hot air hitting my frame on the doorstep.

Two girls stood in the kitchen chopping vegetables. They looked up when I came in, no expression on their faces, white caps on their heads. The housekeeper led me past them and into a small pantry at the back.

'We don't usually take anyone on without references,' she says.

'I'm a good worker,' I say. 'I was reared on a farm. I can cook and sew. I'll do anything you want.'

It felt as though my insides had been turned inside-out - the pain travelled up to my stomach. I put my hand below my belly button, soothing myself.

'You can have a trial,' she said. 'You'll be starting at the bottom, but if you're good you can work your way up.'

She told me to come back that evening and I could start in the morning. When I did come back, I sat with all the staff and we had our tea and the relief washed over me that I wouldn't have to spend another night in the hostel, sleeping with my hand on my bag, hoping the pain between my legs would finally ebb away.

Everyone went to bed early ready for another day of work and it felt so good to know that I was safe for the night, that I had managed to secure myself a place with bread and board and a purse full of shillings to be paid into my hand at the end of the month.

I was put in a room with Martha, a girl from Scotland with red hair and she lent me her hairbrush that night and told me she didn't mind at all. I listened to her gentle snores filling our attic room and when I was sure she was asleep, that her breathing was that of someone dreaming, I let the tears come out. Crying because I was settled, crying for the pain in my stomach and between my legs and crying for all that I had lost.

He'd taken everything from me, had Mr McKenna.

* * *

I was still bleeding and every time I got up from my hunkers, after sweeping out the fire place, I felt as though I might pass out with the rush to my head.

Mrs Harrington, the housekeeper, told me I looked pale and for a minute I wanted to tell her what happened to me. But I didn't have the words - how could I tell anyone that? That I was dirty? Destroyed? She told me to take a spoon of tonic after tea and I did, feeling its oil trickle down my throat, tasting of blood. I took a gulp of cold tea to get rid of it.

Mrs Harrington was right when she said the work was hard, but after the first week, when I was getting my bearings and finding my way round the house, I eased into it and did everything she told me and everything I could to please her. I wanted to be kept. I wanted to get my wages at the end of the month and start saving for myself. I was on my own now and I was going to make my own way.

Martha asked me one of the evenings if I'd like to take a walk with her. We left through the servant entrance, out on to the street, chattering about where we were from and how the house wasn't too bad to work in at all. I didn't tell her the truth, that I'd left behind a mother and brothers that I loved very much. I told her I didn't have any family, that they'd died and that's why I'd come to London, on my own.

Her red hair glinted in the autumn sun and I thought how pretty she was, with skin the colour of milk and long lashes catching your eye every time she blinked.

'Look at yer one over there,' she said as we walked.

I looked to where she'd nodded her head and saw a woman standing under a lamp post, her face painted in make-up, a frilly bonnet and blouse on her, coloured, mismatched, standing out.

'You know what she is, don't you?'

I looked harder, at how she leaned against the post, a smirk on her face, as though she knew a secret none of us did.

'No,' I said. She looked a bit unusual, but I didn't see anything too wrong with her.

'She's on the game,' said Martha. 'A whore.'

'What?' I said, whipping my head round to look at her again.

I'd never seen a prostitute before.

Martha laughed and told me I was very innocent and that I was in London now and this was city life.

I did feel innocent, having only ever been to Dublin a handful of times, travelling there with Daddy to the horse fair or to meet a merchant. I'd heard about prostitutes, but I'd never seen a real one.

'Dirty whore,' Martha said and she wrinkled up her nose like she'd a bad taste in her mouth.

As I looked, a gentleman walked past the woman and she tipped her bonnet at him as she curtsied. He stopped, smiled and began talking to her and she moved in closer, as though she knew him well, as though he were familiar to her.

'You'd want to be desperate to end up like her,' said Martha, as we walked on, past the evening strollers who were out on the streets like us, taking a break from their jobs as domestics in the large houses all along this street.

* * *

A few weeks after I arrived at the house, after I'd gotten to know Martha a bit, I started noticing a sickly feeling creeping into my stomach. It came after I ate, like a rash inside my tummy, and then it would disappear and come back at bedtime. One morning I got up and I spilled my stomach into the pot under the bed, just about making it.

'What's wrong with you?' said Martha, who was pulling the pinny over her head. Her hair was sticking out in great, big, red bunches.

'I don't know,' I said.

The sickness came and went. I ignored it, because it usually went away. I thought it might be something to do with Mr McKenna and what had happened, an infection maybe. I started getting up earlier than Martha, so I could be sick in peace and not have her asking what was wrong, and annoying me. When the smells were strong in the kitchen, or when one of the footmen walked by, stinking of sweat having carried heavy cases up the stairs, I pulled my sleeve over my nose and closed my eyes and told my stomach to behave itself and make the sickness go away.

And it did. After a few weeks, it wasn't as bad anymore and one morning I woke up and it was gone completely. I was pleased and that evening had an extra helping of bread and butter at the table, feeling for the first time in weeks that I wanted to eat and be full.

I leaned back in my chair at the kitchen table, listening to the banter back and forth. I liked living here with the mix of accents and the jokes and no one poking their noses into each other's past.

I put my hand on my stomach and rubbed it, feeling satisfied for the first time in a long time. Then I noticed it. A firmness. A hard ball where my soft tummy had been.

I wondered if I could have an infection that made me swell, after what Mr McKenna had done to me, after all that sickness, something might have been causing it.

A slow horror wiped itself across my mind. It had been weeks since my monthlies had come. I'd been in England three months now and not once had I bled.

I patted my stomach again, feeling how hard my insides were.

The sounds of the staff chatting faded in my ears, as hairs stood on the back of my neck.

I leaned forward, the two front legs of the chair hitting the ground hard.

It wasn't an infection Mr McKenna had given me.

It was a baby.

Chapter Eleven

HENRY

The letter came on the very last day of summer. He had given up hope completely. He had gone from watching the postman every day, to some days, to not at all. He had gone through feelings of despair and desperation, to raised spirits, followed by frustration again. And all the while, his father got it into his head that staying on the estate was the best thing for him to do.

Arthur had no opinion on the matter. He was looking forward to his own college life starting and he made the most of his summer. There were evening gatherings and lake fishing trips, long days at the summer races and shopping excursions to Dublin. Arthur was amassing a fine array of suits, hats and cravats, while Henry was happy to live in his wide breeches and open necked shirt.

Henry took to walking the land, marching through the woods and pushing his thoughts round and round in his mind. This had been one of the most frustrating years he could remember; university was finishing, his romantic future looked dim to say the least and London seemed to be off the cards now. And all the while he had the problems of the estate being pushed on to his plate by his father.

Montgomery's murder had shaken Seymour badly. He had tightened security on the estate, barricading the gates to the house and employing extra footmen to guard the house at night. He began to speak of the famine times, when landlords were found murdered on the roads.

'I never thought I would see a day like this,' he said, after Montgomery's funeral, his face drained of colour, dark dashes under his eyes.

Henry understood his father's fears but did not feel the same himself. He refused to bring a chaperon with him and shook off his father's demands to stop walking in the woods by himself.

'You'll turn up swinging from a tree,' said Seymour.

'Maybe,' said Henry. 'I've been thinking about it.'

He was prodding his father to pick up on his melancholy, half joking in frustration at the way the year was panning out. He'd never truly considered taking his life, but on some of the days, on some of the bleakest, he wondered what it would be like to throw a rope across one of the trees in Townley Hall woods.

Henry had come to understand, as he'd gotten older, that their mother had most likely ended her own life. It was not something that was ever discussed and the tentative questions he did put to Mrs Johansson and more rarely, to his father, were always shrugged off.

He remembered her funeral, which was small and late in the evening and he realised that the whole event had carried a shame about it, whispers, white faces, silence. He thought of the final glimpse he had of his mother, a quick flash as the door of her bedroom was opened and closed as he passed. She was laid out as if she were sleeping, but the sound of sobbing came from her room. He knew it was their father.

He had not been allowed in to see her. He couldn't even remember the last time he'd seen her properly. She hadn't said goodbye. She had been there and then she was gone. And it wasn't a subject Seymour wished to ever discuss.

A detective was put on Montgomery's case and five local men were arrested. All five had either been at the regatta or the pub in the village that evening and with too many alibis, they were let go, one by one.

The murder was a mystery.

Amelia Aherne had shown up at one of the summer parties at Brabazon. Henry had smiled, kissed her cheek, and tried to avoid contact for the remainder of the evening. But, just as he'd forgotten she was there, when he was engrossed in a conversation about the harvest or tenant tensions or Montgomery's murder, she'd appear in his line of sight again, slighting his mood, sending an ache right through his chest. How had she slipped through his fingers?

In the previous semesters at Oxford, Henry had spent most of his evenings penning letters to Amelia. Some he had taken, scrunched in his hand and tossed in the waste paper basket, embarrassed that he had ever put such emotion to paper. But this semester, her letters back had been rare. It was as though she had stopped wanting to write. He still sent his own letters, even if he had not received a reply. He knew that each one he wrote was growing increasingly desperate.

In the final days of college, in the week where he was sitting back to back exams, staying up late into night, crushing black coffee beans and forcing the hot brew he made down his throat, a manilla coloured envelope arrived. It was addressed to him in Amelia's writing, her long loops on the letters, the tiny mark she made on the 'z' in his name. He cut it open with a knife, pawing at the letter, his heart racing now that he had finally heard from her. What joy that she had written, particularly in this week, when he needed something good to think about outside of study.

His eyes raced over the words, scanning, getting to the bottom of the page, the message not going in. He reread the letter, but still did not understand it. When he read it a third time, he let the letter fall, right on to his plate, the remains of the ketchup on his kippers soaking into the paper. The letter absorbed the sauce in little pink spots, covering the words she had written in a dark brown ink.

'I know this may surprise you and I hope that we can remain friends. I wish you the very best in your study, and with your future. You will make a fine man of law, I have no doubt. Sincerely and with kindest of thoughts, always, Amelia.'

She was to be married. To an earl in Carlow. Henry stood, pushing the chair back with force, a lump building inside his throat. He should have asked her to marry him at Christmas, it had been on his mind to, but his father's chatter about Charity Eustace had put him off the whole thing.

He had walked over to the wall, stared at the wood panel and considered punching it to feel the pain shoot through his wrist. But if he broke his hand, he could not write and he would not pass the exams he needed to pass to make a new life for himself. Instead, he walked over to the bed, picked up his pinstripe pillow and pushed his face into it, feeling his teeth grip and grind against the heady stuffing. He roared, as loud as he could, screaming from his stomach and lungs, putting all his frustration into the soft fibres against his nose.

And then he returned to the table, pushed the plate with the dirtied letter aside and started reading the book with the dense text again. He had lost Amelia, but he swore it would be the last time he would lose anything again.

Now that she had appeared back at Brabazon for the summer party, he wondered if there was still time to rekindle their friendship, to bring things back to where they had been. He considered writing her another letter, from the heart. In it he would tell her how ridiculous he had been, that he should have, could have, proposed last year and if she'd only find it in herself to forgive him, cease her current engagement and form a new engagement with him, they could live happily together, he was sure of it. He could slip the letter into her hand, pass it to her when no one was looking.

But as the evening wore on, the time slipped away and he couldn't bring himself to go through with it. He felt like a coward. He was a coward. He watched her take off in the carriage, turning to flutter her handkerchief, flicking her wrist delicately at him.

The summer was ending on a depressive note. Everything felt like it was slipping away. He watched the evenings get shorter and the sun set earlier each day. He sat by the river as the tops of the trees cast shadows on the flowing water below. He wished that he were a fly or a fish, something without a brain, with no thoughts or emotions, no worldly pressure on his head. If only he were like Arthur. Wild. Drunk. And second born.

Then the letter arrived, brought in by Mrs Johansson, placed on a silver tray at breakfast, an envelope crisp and clean and neatly scribed to Henry Brabazon Esq.

We are delighted to offer you an apprenticeship at Lewis, Clayton and Thornhills.

He would start the second week of September. He would need to travel to London immediately to make plans. He was going to be a criminal lawyer. Whether his father liked it or not.

* * *

London was very different to Oxford. The sheer size of it overwhelmed him. He missed the atmosphere of the boy's club that he had in university, the rowing practice twice a week, the smoking room and the taverns they used to visit.

It was vast and grey and filled with planted parks. He spent as much time as he could sitting in them, pretending he was back on the estate, at the river, in the woods, trying to remember what the mulchy air felt like in his nose.

The irony was not lost on him - that he'd longed to leave the estate and come here to make a career for himself and now that he was here making a career for himself, he wished to sail home and sit in the country for the rest of the day.

Lewis, Clayton and Thornhills had put him to work on thousands of pages of documents. The words crossed over before his eyes and his neck and shoulders were tired from hunching over the files. It was not the work he had imagined and he had yet to see the inside of a courtroom. He was at the bottom rung of a very long ladder.

In the evenings, he went drinking with the other apprentices in the practice. There were two he formed a quick kinship with; Malcolm Greene from Hertfordshire, who was short and stocky and quick to laugh, and a spectacled scribe of a man called Cecil Conyngham. It was Malcolm who led the drinking, his stomach an empty alcohol pit and he forced both Henry and Cecil to increase their tolerance within days.

'Where to tonight, chaps?' he'd say as they left the office.

'I can't tonight,' Cecil would say.

'Let's try that new place, on the Green.'

He was forceful and fun, and the unlikely trio became familiar faces on the gentleman's scene, drinking, laughing and being merry.

Cecil became the butt of the jokes. He was quiet and shy, and grew red in the face when Malcolm brought up, as he did most nights, his virginal status.

'Tell him what it's like, Henry,' said Malcolm, nodding over, flicking his head up in the air. 'Go on, describe it.'

'Describe what?' said Henry. He hadn't really been listening. He'd been looking at the whiskey in his glass, wondering if he could stomach another night of drinking and how his head had been feeling so muddled lately. Was it the drink? Or the books?

'What it's like. To be with a woman.'

'Oh, not this again,' said Henry. 'Honestly, Malcolm, you're like the man that doth protest too much. Do you ever stop talking about it?'

'I like to see my chums happy,' said Malcolm.

'I am happy,' said Cecil.

'I think you should treat yourself, for Christmas,' said Malcolm.

Cecil slunk further into his seat, his shoulders drooping, and put the glass to his lips, slugging on the whiskey.

'You could always offer your services,' said Henry drily, looking at Malcolm.

'I have, but he won't hear of it.'

They laughed, and gathered round the billiards table, ready for another game. Henry knew Malcolm was serious. It wouldn't be long before all three of them found themselves stood in a knocking shop, egging Cecil on. He hoped Malcolm would at least pick a decent one.

* * *

In December, Henry was beginning to think that the apprenticeship was a big mistake. The study he'd completed in college had not prepared him for the realities of the law practice. He couldn't concentrate on the work he had been given - his mind drifting off every few minutes, requiring all his will to coax it back to the words on the page.

The law documents held no interest for him. He was lifelessly bored. And always hungover. He had received a letter from Mrs Johansson that said their father had been unwell. He had worried a little and then worried even more when a letter arrived from Arthur in Oxford that said: *'Do you think we should go home?'*

Henry considered sending a telegram home but instead decided, without thinking about it too much, to book a train from London to Oxford to pick Arthur up and travel back to Ireland. He sent a telegram to Arthur telling him he'd meet him in the morning. He immediately felt better. The thoughts of getting out of London raised his spirits and the lifting of the shackles of Lewis, Clayton and Thornhills made him want to celebrate.

'You are asking *me* if we should go for drinks later?' said Malcolm.

'Yes, I don't know why but I would murder a gin,' said Henry.

'I know just the place,' said Malcolm. 'Would you like a swifty?'

Henry watched as Malcolm took out a small, silver flask from under his desk. He threw his head back and necked the liquid, his eyes filling up red.

'Want some?'

'No thanks,' said Henry, shaking his head at Malcolm drinking on the job. 'Don't you get enough in the evenings?'

'This is to take the edge off. It's what keeps me going. How else could you stay awake through this?' Malcolm pointed at the document he was reading and collapsed his head on top of it making a snoring sound.

Henry laughed and then quietened. 'I have to go home.'

'Home?' asked Malcolm.

'My father's not well. And it's coming up to Christmas. If Messrs Lewis, Clayton and Thornhill have an issue, they'll have to deal with me in the New Year.'

'They won't like it,' said Malcolm.

'No,' said Henry, 'That's why I have a craving for gin.'

'Gin it is then,' said Malcolm, holding the flask high up in the air and feeling the last of the liquid trickle down his gullet.

Chapter Twelve

MOLLY

Every night I excused myself early and went upstairs to bed to cry. I pulled the thin blanket that smelled musty over my head and I let great sobs come out, all down my face and into the pillow. I cried till there was nothing left, no water and no salt and then I lay awake and then half asleep, drifting in and out till Martha came into the room and there was no chance to cry anymore.

I used to take pride in being a girl that didn't cry. I used to say that it was hard to make the water come out of *my* eyes. This baby was already changing me; how I felt, my emotions, my person.

I was going to start showing soon and they wouldn't have it. I didn't have enough money to rent somewhere on my own. And who could I tell? Martha would be sympathetic at first but then she wouldn't want to know me, in case it was catching.

One evening I felt as though the walls were toppling in on me. I couldn't stand going to bed early to cry again so I left, out the service door, for a walk along the cobbled streets. The cold had come in now, swirling round my ankles, light gusts of leaves hovering over the path.

I prayed as I walked, not because I thought it might help, but because I didn't know what else to do. I prayed that

God would show me a sign, that he would send something my way that would help me. And in way he did - in a way he didn't.

'Alright, love?'

It was a woman with yellowed hair, parted in the middle, black showing at the roots.

'You look like you've the weight of the world on your shoulders,' she says.

'I do,' I say. And I wasn't lying. She hugged herself with the cold, thin leather gloves wrapped around her fingers.

'Where you from then?' she says.

'Dublin,' I lie.

'By it's a cold one, innit?'

She had an Irish accent but it was all muddled, like some of the words had been replaced with English accented ones. She was standing in front of a lamppost, in and out of the shadows.

'I'm Clara,' she says. And I stand, looking at her, not even saying my name.

'Anything I can help you with, love?' she says and my eyes came back from the glaze they'd gone into. Clara was looking at me, waiting for an answer. I realise this woman could probably help more than most. This was a problem she might just have the answer to. Clara was the woman in the coloured clothes that Martha had pointed out to me on our walk. Clara was a prostitute.

'It's very delicate,' I say. 'It's not something I can say out loud. On the street.'

'Oh,' says she, looking me up and down. I have my coat on over my dress but I wonder if my stomach is showing and if she can see it.

She looks behind her, looking for someone and then she walks off and I see she's speaking to a man who's on the other side of the road and then she's back and she's says, 'Come with me.'

I follow her and we're walking side by side and I can't help but notice she has lovely slip-on shoes with gold buckles on them. They look new, not like the boots with the nails hammered through them that I wear.

While we're walking she asks me my name and where I'm working and tells me she's originally from Kerry but she left a long time ago and I think that's why her accent is funny. We stop at a cafe, one that opens late and we go inside and it's cosy but there's an atmosphere in the air too, as though a fight could break out at any time.

'Sit yourself down, love,' she says. 'Tea?'

I say yes, and I'm relieved to be away from the house and its closing-in walls and with this woman who looks like she wants to help me, probably sent by God himself after all. She comes back with hot sausages, bread and dripping. I make up the sandwich and start eating it because my appetite has been soaring these past few weeks.

'So ...' she says, leaning in close, her voice quiet and her eyes looking straight at me, daring me to tell the truth. 'What's been bothering you, my love. You can tell me.'

I'm chewing my sausage and bread, but she's so keen that I do a big swallow and I hold my stomach and lean into her.

'I'm ....' I say. And then I realise I can't say the words out loud. I just can't believe it about myself.

I lean back and then there's tears in my eyes, brimming over, threatening to come out and fall right down on to the bloody sandwich.

I hold my stomach and point to it and she says the words for me.

'In the family way?'

I nod and now the tears are flowing and not only that but there's sobbing noises coming out of my mouth and I have to cover my face. Clara leans in real close and pulls a hanky out of her pocket. I take it and rub my face. It smells of lavender.

'How long?' she says. I tell her five, nearly six months.

'You're sure?' she says.

'It only happened once,' I tell her. 'It was force.'

She looks sad and understanding all at once, like she knows about force.

She's patting my arm and telling me it'll be alright. And I feel better already, just talking to her and someone else knowing my secret, someone who's not in the house that would tell anyone I know.

'It's probably too late to get rid of it,' she says. 'But I know someone who might help, might take you in. I can arrange a meeting. If that's what you want?'

'Yes,' I say. 'That's what I want.'

She tells me to meet her at the lamppost at the same time tomorrow evening.

The tension that's been pulling at my back and my neck lifts away and I notice a smile on my face that I wasn't expecting. We get up to leave, and just as I'm reaching for my coat, I feel a kick on my insides, a big boot, like I used to give my brothers when they were annoying me.

* * *

She's a strange looking woman. I can't work out if she's lovely or not. At first glance, you might think she's the most glamorous woman you've ever seen. But now that I'm sat here, at the desk in front of her, I can't help but notice her nose is a strange shape, almost too big for her face. But she has a nice chin, no jowls at all, tight like a young girl's.

She's being nice to me. Pleasant. She says she keeps out of the way of coppers and constables, but they know what's going on and they let her at it. Because she's clean, she says. No trouble. She's very good at her job, she tells me.

All the girls call her Madame Camille but I know that's not her real name, not with the Liverpudlian accent she has. She lays it on the table for me. My options.

'The house where you're working won't have you for long,' she says. 'A girl in your position, unmarried, a big baby belly on her. It hardly represents a respectable house well, now does it?'

"No, it doesn't,' I reply.

'They'll throw you on to the street and that'll be that,' she says. 'There won't be any mercy, not in your position.'

I think of the face on Martha when she finds out. How she'll remember the sickness. How she'll look at my belly, how they'll all look at my belly, every time I go past, whispering and skulking about behind my back.

We're sitting in Madame Camille's room, it's cosy with white walls and small pictures of the countryside dotted around, hung up with string. In one of the pictures, there's a man in a red jacket on a horse, hunting hounds spilling all around him, some of them mid-jump over a ditch. The room was once a bedroom, its high ceilings punctured by two black windows looking out into the night.

'You could go to a mother and babies home,' she says. 'Actually, there's one just a few streets away from where you are now, you know the big yellow building on the corner?'

I think of it now, looming behind a set of poplar trees. I never knew that's what it was. London was so full of big buildings, carved out of different bricks and stone. How was I to know what was behind all those walls?

'Have you ever walked past there and seen a soul?' says Madame Camille, leaning towards me a little.

I shrug my shoulders. 'No,' I say.

'That's because when you go in there, you don't come out,' she says. 'It's a prison. A workhouse. They keep the women to do the laundry and sew and mend and iron and the babies are given away to rich people who can't have children of their own. You'd be a slave. And you'd be a slave, with no baby. You do want to keep the baby?'

I nod. I want to keep the baby. I told Clara this last night. It was an overwhelming feeling I had. That he was mine.

'If you come to work for me, I can help you,' she says. 'During your condition and your confinement, it'll be light work. Cleaning over the rooms and making over the place.

Some cooking maybe. You can keep the baby.' She waves her hand in the air as she says this, as if it's a notion I have.

'A few of the girls have children. There's lodgings and there's a shift rota and the girls take turns in minding each other's babies,' she says. 'Then, after that, when the baby is born, you'll be working for me proper, till you've paid off your debt.'

Outside Madame Camille's room, there's men passing by, girls dressed in stockings and chemises leading them up and down corridors to their rooms. They wear lipstick, the necks of their garments open so the men can look right down at their bosoms.

'Will I be able for it?' I ask, thinking about after my confinement when she really wants to put me to work, like the girls outside.

'Yes,' she says. 'You're a nice girl. You'd pick up some regulars. Pay well. You'd probably work off your debt quick enough.'

I look at the porcelain cup and saucer on her desk, settled on a ledger book and papers. It has a pink rose on the outside and I remember the day myself and Mam had tea in porcelain cups in the White Horse Hotel in town.

'Alright,' I say. 'I'll hand in my notice at the house this week.'

'Good,' she says. 'Now what can we call you? Molly is so very common.'

* * *

In all this horrible business, the one thing I'm glad of is being spared the embarrassment of revealing my condition to Mrs Harrington and to Martha. I tell them I need to go back home, that I have an aunt who is unwell.

'I thought you said you'd no family,' says Martha, looking at me all suspicious.

'I don't,' I say, snapping at her. 'Except my aunt.'

Mrs Harrington is disappointed and says she's sorry to see me go and that she'd thought I'd stay longer. I want to tell her that I did too.

I leave on a cold morning, making my way to the address Madame Camille scribbled out for me, passing by the yellow mother and baby home, making myself have a good look in. I wonder if I could go through the gates, past the poplar trees and up to the giant door and knock on it. Would they take me in? Would they protect me from what I was about to do?

But my legs walk past and I arrive at the small terraced house down a backstreet in Islington. The small step up to the front door is dirty and the windows have a fine film of grime on them, blacker than the dusty dirt I used to wash off at the grey house. Madame Camille has lots of kip houses in this part of London and she moves them on regular. She keeps some for boarding and some for working. This one is for boarding and there's a few girls here with babies.

One of them opens the door, her hair standing on end, like she's just shaken it from a sack. There's a baby suckling at her breast.

'I'm the new girl,' I say and she backs away from the door and starts back up the stairs, leaving me standing there, clutching my case, looking around at the cold, musty interior.

'Upstairs,' she says, half waving her hand and she's gone, the door to her room slamming, making me jump.

There's a smell of burnt fat as I climb the creaky stairs. Three steps have boards almost fully missing and the rest look like they could go at any second. All the doors are shut upstairs except for one tiny room. It has a single bed with a thin, stripy mattress, a big saggy hole in the middle, old piss stains circling out from it. There's no pillow.

I put my case on the bed where the pillow should be and I lie on the dirty mattress. After a while I close my eyes and with my coat still on, I drift into a cloudy sleep, the first proper rest I've had since I left Ireland. I don't wake till near lunch time, when the girl with the scraggly hair is back standing in the doorway, the baby still in her arm, this time sleeping.

'You've to go to work now,' she says.

'Where?' I ask and she looks annoyed with me, as if she doesn't have time to be dealing with me at all.

'Madame Camille won't see you today, but you can go in and meet the house madam. She'll tell you what to do.'

She gives me the address of the kip-house and before I leave she tells me her name is Elizabeth, but I can call her Lizzie. 'There's a spare pillow and blankets in my room that you can have until Madame Camille buys you your own,' she says. 'And if you run away and take the sheets with you, I'll hunt you down and gouge your eyes out.'

She looks fierce, her pupils dilating as she speaks.

I think I'm going to like her.

The working house is bigger than our terraced boarding house. It has a large bay window facing the street, fancy brickwork and a small garden with a path up to the front door. The difference inside is stark. There are candles everywhere, and glasses, abandoned, half filled with drink. There's shimmery satin hanging down from the ceiling, making private nooks and crannies. Everywhere I look there's some sort of place to lie or sit or lean.

The house madam is made up in powder and rouge, but it's heavier than Madame Camille's, like she doesn't know how to put it on right. She puts me to sweeping and washing the floor straightaway and tells me the door and windows need doing too.

'We run a tight ship here,' she says, trying to sound exactly like Madame Camille. 'You'll do as I tell you. I'll not have Madame Camille dropping by here and having my guts for garters.'

I think it's a funny phrase, because just as she says it a girl appears in a chemise and stockings, garters wrapped around her thin thighs.

The curtains on every window are closed; thick velvet blocking out the light, making it feel like night time every minute of the day.

For the rest of the afternoon I work, wiping down the linoleum floors, washing and polishing the front door, cleaning the windows, fetching hot buckets of water and doing my best to keep out of the way of the customers that come through the door.

If any look at me, I turn away, squeezing the mop, and rubbing even harder at the surface I'm washing. I'm embarrassed to be seen here, that they think I'm like *them*, a fallen woman, filled right up with shame.

In the day, the customers are city gents and merchants, business men with grand suits and long, bushy moustaches. I hear them pawing at the women and slapping them round a bit. One of the girls tell me that the men are all married and have houses in the country, some have big townhouses in Kensington and Mayfair.

I think about their wives with their fancy furs and their airs and graces and I realise that things are always more complicated then they appear. Me and Nora always thought the ladies had the grand life. But what's grand about your husband going and pawing up a working girl and bringing himself home to you?

As the evening wears on, the factory workers come in, stacked with drink from the pub and feeling brave. They're usually quick, the girls tell me; tired and hungry after a long day, they don't stick around afterwards.

The girls dress their own beds, but in between customers I help with whatever they need, hauling down laundry for the cart and fetching new linens if they need them. I realise that I'm trying to learn, for when it's my time.

What I am learning is that whiskey helps. If the customer is too stingy to buy it for you, you can buy it for yourself and the house madam writes it down in a big ledger and it's taken out of your wages.

No one likes the house madam because she's Madame Camille's eyes and ears - she reports everything to her. I see one girl claim that whiskey has been added to her tab, drinks she never had, but as I watch them, I think all the girls are drunk; they've lost count of the whiskeys they've had and it's nothing to do with the house madam's accounting skills at all.

Then there's a lull. A bit of quiet, and some of the girls go out on to the street and this is the time where I give everything another good wipe down, the floors, the low coffee tables, the stands where the lamps and pot plants are, the trays with all the glasses. Slowly the girls trickle back in, their customers enticed and the house madam starts teaching me how to host and how to offer and serve drinks. She tells me I'm a natural - I don't know if this is a good or a bad thing but it's nice to get a compliment all the same.

Just before midnight, she tells me I can go and I feel relieved to get out of the kip house, away from its atmosphere of drink and lust, of cigarette smoke and musk. The streets are quiet as I walk, my boots clip clapping on the stones.

I watch everyone as they pass, servant girls and their beaus, men on their bicycles, shop workers finished their shifts. I think about the families they're going home to, their warm dinners and fireside naps, an evening of reading, their dignity and ethics all to themselves.

And here am I, walking home to my first night in a house of prostitutes, their poor children whimpering in raggedy beds, not knowing yet about the ways of the world around them. I feel very sorry for myself indeed. But I don't cry.

Because, it seems, I have no tears left.

Chapter Thirteen

HENRY

Half way between Oxford and Liverpool, while Henry and Arthur were playing cards at their table on the train, looking out at the rushing greenery, waiting each other's turn, their father Seymour, had a stroke. As one blood vessel after another burst, he fell to the ground and died on the carpet beside his bed, his mouth open, his hands clenched at his head, his last words unheard in the gloom of his room.

Mrs Johansson found him that evening, a coldness already swept through his body, his pallor pale.

When Henry and Arthur climbed off the steamer at Drogheda they knew immediately that their father was dead by the small cortege that had come to meet them. Mrs Johansson, dressed in black, holding a white rose; the footman; and Seymour's elder brother, Edward, old now, his skin so sagged he could hide marbles in it.

Shaking her head, Mrs Johansson clutched the boys and Henry was shocked at how Arthur broke down, giant sobs retching from his throat, openly crying and unable to contain himself.

'I'm so sorry,' said Mrs Johansson.

'We didn't get to say goodbye,' said Arthur.

They were silent in the carriage, only Mrs Johansson's plans for the funeral puncturing the quiet. They were expecting huge numbers and they would have to be catered for. Everyone thought it was a tragedy that the boys were travelling and no one able to tell them.

'But it was a blessing that you had already decided to come home. Otherwise we would be waiting longer. Just a pity it was too late,' said Mrs Johansson, sniffing.

Henry wondered if he had sensed that something would happen to their father. Was that why he had made the decision to come home, even though Mrs Johansson had only written of their father having a bad cold?

The carriage shook from side to side, laden down with its passengers, the two horses straining to pull it up the incline at Townley Hall. As they turned into the gates at Brabazon House, his Uncle Edward leaned forward, his blue eyes glowing in the light and whispered, 'It's your time now. Good luck, Henry.'

With the shock of the news, it had not yet occurred to Henry what his father's death really meant. Everything was now his; all decisions from here on in were his and his alone to make. The funeral, the burial, the send-off. The estate. The farms. The tenants. He was in charge, and there would be no going back to London. That was clear.

A single white rose hung from the pier at Brabazon Estate, identical to the one Mrs Johansson clasped in her gloved hands.

'The first rose was taken from the gate,' she said, pursing her lips together. 'I mean what class of tenant would do that, steal a funeral rose, for God's sake?'

Henry looked at the house as they drove up to the winding driveway. The sky was a watery December blue, wisps of white clouds high over Brabazon's roof.

Horses and carriages, with footmen at their heads, were lined up outside the house. The front doors were wide open, a trail of people coming in and out. There were faces he recognised and faces he didn't.

Arthur stepped out of the carriage and ran through the

doors. He raced up the stairs to his father's bedroom, where Seymour was laid out, looking as though he were asleep. Stepping aside, the handful of mourners who were in the room looked sorry, as Arthur broke down sobbing and threw his body across the coffin.

Henry stood at the door before entering the room quietly. He wished his brother would try to hold it together.

His father looked a bit thinner laid out, but he looked like himself all the same - there was that to be grateful for. He thought of the last time he had seen him, hunched over his desk, barely looking up as Henry bid his farewell. Would it have been such a burden for him to shake hands, to embrace him, to give his son a send-off?

Arthur's tears were getting worse. Henry placed a hand on his back and gently pulled him back from the coffin.

'Arthur,' said Henry, turning him to look at his face. But what could he say? No words could comfort him or bring their father back. He gripped his brother in a hug as the mourners left the room and closed the bedroom door quietly behind them.

Henry felt an overwhelming sense of guilt. Guilt that he didn't feel the same upset as Arthur. Guilt that he felt angry about the weight that was now on his shoulders. Arthur would go back to university, finish his degree and do whatever the bloody hell he wanted. It was Henry who would be left at Brabazon, carrying on the work of his father and his father before him.

He felt angry about that. He felt angry and sad and frustrated that the day he had always known would come was here so soon.

Damn Seymour. Damn him to hell anyway.

* * *

The funeral week passed in a blur. When Henry laid his head to rest at night, faces flashed before him. He was exhausted from the journey home and from the shock of his father's death. He was tired of holding everything together, making decisions, and answering all the questions that people were asking him. Particularly Mrs Johansson; she had gone from being a matronly mother figure to a woman he dreaded seeing approach. She would do nothing without his permission. It was tiresome.

Arthur had gone from long outbursts of crying to sitting, white faced among the mourners, a glass of whiskey in his hand. Henry knew he was numbing his feelings with alcohol, but at least it was occupying him. He couldn't cope with his dramatics any longer, it was adding more stress to the whole blasted thing.

Amelia Aherne had appeared in the great room among the crowds, holding out her arms and taking his cheek to kiss it, her perfume wafting up his nose and drawing him right back to another time. Her smell was a comfort and he wished that he could take her away and lay with her on a bed and just hold her in the quiet.

On the day of the funeral, cold showery clouds threw sleet down in angles, black umbrellas floating like lily pads on the sea of bowed heads.

Arthur had howled before they closed the coffin, draping his body across his father's, his shoulders shaking, his grief echoing through the house. Henry comforted him, before pulling him away so that they could get to the business of burying their father. He wondered if he should ask the doctor for something to give to Arthur, a tranquilliser, to help him.

They followed the funeral hearse on foot, walking down the avenue which led to the church, the same church they had walked to when their mother was buried. Then, he had clutched his father's hand and felt sad, looking around at the rows and rows of black trousers walking behind them. Now, he had no one to hold and felt nothing of the sadness he had felt then. He was empty, nothing.

After the service, they stood around the grave and

watched as his father was lowered into the ground, the ropes inching precariously till they reached the clawed-out earth. Henry thought not of his father, but of his mother, that this was the nearest he had come to her since. He wondered what was left of her, if he dropped down and dug through the earth with his fingers, could he touch her, smell her, feel her dust?

He stayed at the grave after everyone had gone, asking to be left alone for just a time. He told Arthur and his uncle Edward to go ahead, to send the carriage back for him. He needed a break from the sandwiches, from the handshaking, the mourning.

When the graveyard had cleared he bent and picked up some of the clay from the mound at the grave. He put it in his pocket, feeling the earth filter through his fingers. He was glad that it was raining. Laying his father to rest in the sunshine would not have felt right.

He stood, letting down the umbrella so that he could feel the sleet on his face. It fell past his head, down his neck, reaching the back of his shoulders, tiny, icy daggers on his skin. He felt like he should suffer, that he should, in some way, feel physical pain. .

When there were no more thoughts in his head, he turned and walked slowly from the grave, picturing his father, still sleeping in the box, now scattered with earth. He was leaving him behind, all on his own, not a thing he could do for him any longer.

As he came to the front of the graveyard, the woods in front of him, he saw a man approach out of the corner of his eye. He was small and elderly with a flat cap on his head.

'Grand day,' said the man, stopping to talk.

'Yes,' said Henry, not wishing to engage.

'It's not what he deserved,' said the man, peering at Henry through white bushy eyebrows.

'Sorry?' said Henry, unsure of what the man meant.

'To go like that, peacefully.'

'Sorry?' said Henry again.

'He should have got what Montgomery got.' The man looked at Henry and drew his forefinger across his wrinkled throat, dragging it slowly and deliberately and smiling. He cackled out his gubby mouth and shuffled past Henry, his right leg dragging a little, forcing him into a short hop each step he took.

'Do you know who I am?' Henry shouted after him, the man's gesture now dawning on him for the insult it was.

'Oh, surely I do,' said the man, not looking back. 'And I hope you're not as big a bastard as your father.'

Quelling the urge to run after the man and choke him from behind, Henry crossed the road and took off walking into the woods. The tenantry could insult him all they wanted. But he would prove in his own way, that he was not his father.

Chapter Fourteen

MOLLY

I was getting bigger. My stomach was hard and round and I could feel him squirming, moving up under my ribs. I had to let out my dress to allow for my big front. Things that I'd never given a second thought to before, like bending down to sweep or reaching to pull my stockings on, became difficult.

Soon the dress I had would be no good. Elizabeth said she had a smock dress that would do me, it belonged to one of the girls when they had come in. Now if they got in the family way, they were seen to quickly. Very sore and tender afterwards she said, but it got the job done.

I had started to get used to the kip house. The shock at the start with the noises coming from the rooms and the girls all spilling out of their chemises, white flesh everywhere, didn't bother me so much now. I just got on with what I had to do, cleaning and hosting, topping up the drinks, going out to get cigarettes or to the chemist or the confectionery.

I got into a routine, the same as when I was in the big townhouse. I was useful and strong and I tried not to let my belly get in the way.

There were things I was seeing that I didn't like though. Things that I thought, if that happened to me, I'm not sure what I'd do. I was learning that Madame Camille made out that she was the best in the business, that her girls were safe and well looked after, but in a kip house, things happened and there was nothing Madame Camille and her powdered face could do about it.

Some of the men were rough, too rough and you'd hear the girl call out for you and you'd have to come running because he might have her in a chokehold or have given her such a box in the eye that would mean she wouldn't be good for a week. There were some nasty men who liked horrible things and they hurt the girls. They were hard to spot, because they looked normal, but they weren't, not in the head.

One Tuesday morning, one of the girls called me into the room. She told me she was in a bad way and asked me would I go to the pharmacist for her, to old Joe, who knew the girls and made up poultices and powders and ointments for them, to help. She showed me her most intimate herself, just a glance and I recoiled when I saw what was there.

'Angela,' I said. It wasn't her real name either, but she had blonde hair and when she was young everyone said she looked like an angel. 'What are you going to do?'

'There's nothing I can do,' she said. 'It won't heal. I have to get on with it. Ask Joe for the best he's got, the strongest stuff. Here's the money.'

She pushed the coin into my palm and all the way to the pharmacist I thought of the red and the pus and the pain and how Angela was doing that day in day out and Madame Camille didn't give a damn.

I thought about it happening to me. Because it could.

In the board house, I helped out a bit with the children, but they were mostly in bed when I got back. I usually worked the day shift and the girls who were mothers would work the nights, so that they could tend to the children in the day. Not one of us ever spoke about the fathers of our children or why we had come to be here. We didn't need to know and in a way, I was happy to be with them, in my condition. They were the only people who couldn't judge me.

Coming up to Christmas, there was a raid on the kip

house. I had just left for the evening and the constables came thundering in, all charging with their batons, smashing the place up and pulling the girls outside in all manner of undress, arresting them and throwing them in jail for the night. The men scarpered, not one of them in trouble.

The next morning, we were surprised to get a knock on the door of the board house from Madame Camille herself and she came in all business like and told us we were setting up a new shop and we all had to help. She said the girls would have to take on extra shifts and I saw her eyeing me up, taking in my stomach.

I met her eyes and folded my arms. Our agreement was after. I wasn't doing anything that would harm this baby.

I minded the children that day, playing tic-tac-toe on the floor with a bit of chalk I found, tickling them and telling them stories like my daddy used to tell me. In the evening, one of the girls told me I had to go in for the evening shift at the new place.

I set out in the cold, wrapping my old coat around me, it was so thin it felt like a sheet of paper. The streets were busy. She's a clever one, Madame Camille, she'd set up in a place closer to town, with more people about. She knew how to find the right places, with the right punters around.

I thought the new place looked cheap. There was no linoleum or velvet curtains, just a plain old house with beds that had been put in that day, there were no lamps or plants yet, just the bare trays, glasses and enough whiskey to keep us going. Madame Camille wasn't going to miss out on the Christmas trade, police or no police.

I did my best, flying around cleaning, trying to get things in proper order. It was still in the back of my mind that I might be put to work. We were short and the men were starting to gather in the hosting room, some looking shy, the rest, drunk and fondling anything that went past.

I had just brought a man up to a room, when I came back to find three men standing, blinking in the lights of the hosting room. One of the men was broad shouldered and all confidence and he reached out to one of the girls and pinched her bottom. Beside him was a skinny fella, red spots on his cheeks, his first time in a kip-house by the looks of it.

Then I saw him, the jaw nearly dropping right out of my skull, the sight of him shocking me white. Henry Brabazon. In London. In my kip house. And me with my big belly on me.

I whipped around and scuttled straight back to the corridor. He couldn't see me here. I didn't want to look at him. I didn't want anyone to know about my condition or where I was.

Then I remembered Montgomery. About his murder. About me.

Angela came walking out of her room. I grabbed her.

'There's a man,' I said, my eyes like saucers. 'I can't go out.'

'What?' she said, startled.

'There's someone out there, I can't be seen.'

'Oh,' she says and she walks out to the front room to take a look.

'Your man?' she says and I know she means the man with the shoulders.

'No,' says I, 'the taller one.'

'Oh,' she says. And then she points at my belly and says, 'Is he ...'

'No,' I say. 'No, he's not. But he can't see me, I can't be here.'

My heart is racing in my chest. I cannot believe that he is here, walking in off the street like that. In London. Why this kip house? He had to have come to find me - those two men with him could be secret police officers.

Seeing my face, Angela leads me down the short flight of stairs to the kitchen.

'Wait here,' she suggests. 'Or outside maybe?'

She points to the back door, where the bottom of an iron fire escape screwed to the wall. I decide that's what I'll do.

I don't want to be anywhere near upstairs or him. I open the door, go out and close it behind me, the December air swirling all round me. It's fresh and nice for a minute.

The thoughts are flashing all through my mind. He could come down those kitchen stairs and arrest me and take me to a jail cell and then bring me with him on a train and a boat all the way back to Ireland.

Because only he knows. Only he could connect me to Montgomery and Dowth that day. In London, I'd pushed all that from my mind, even in the black of the night when Martha had been snoring in her bed, I could crush the thoughts one by one, stopping them from creeping in.

I hadn't ever expected to see Henry Brabazon again. Now he was here and so too were my memories. I try to push them out of mind again and think about something else, about the cold, about the baby, about the girls - anything else.

It *is* cold. The freshness I felt at first has gone now and all I can feel is the freezing air around my head and neck, up through my nose as I breathe in and out, hitting the back of my throat like wet ice.

I hug myself to keep warm. It's not working. I stay there, shivering now, peering out into the dark, making out an overgrown garden, bushes black against black. I hunker down. There's nothing to sit on, apart from the cold, hard mud and I don't fancy it much. Instead, I rock on my heels till my knees get sore and I get back up, looking at the yellow squares of light in the walls, of the shadows moving behind them, of the people in the buildings all around.

I can hear laughter and shouting coming from the streets where the Gentleman's Clubs are. Somewhere, there's a baby crying, a sharp painful cry and I think, how will I ever get used to that?

I consider going back in. Maybe just to wait in the kitchen. I look at the fire escape, the rickety, old, metal ladder. I could climb it and hide up there either but then I think I might fall in my condition and I should probably just wait. So, I do.

When I can't feel my legs or feet anymore, when the sensation has gone out of my hands and my nose feels like there's a red-hot lance going up it, Angela sticks her head out the door and says, 'Molly, fucking hell, get back in here.'

I put one foot in front of the other but I can't really feel what's in my shoes and when I get into the kitchen I sit on a small chair and think I might be dying of the cold.

'You really didn't want him to see you, did you?' she says and I think, *of course I didn't, I bloody told you that.*

'He's gone,' she says.

'Is he?' I say, although my lips feel like they're swollen and my teeth are chattering bad. It's hard to talk.

'He went not long after he arrived actually. Just said he was going home.'

Now I know. He came to look for me. Because if he came to be with a girl, then he would have done that, but he didn't.

'And what about the other two?' I ask.

'Just gone,' she said. 'I had the spectacles. Poor sod.'

'Did he say anything?'

'About what?'

'About me?'

'Who, Spectacles?'

'No,' I say, 'the man who left. The tall man. Did he mention me?'

'No,' she says. 'Does he know you're here?'

'I don't know. I think he's looking for me.'

'Well he never mentioned you,' she says. 'Honestly love, he wasn't here long enough. He scarpered as soon as he caught sight of the place. Sobered up, I reckon.'

'OK,' I say. I wonder how I'm going to get through the rest of my shift for the worrying. I'm so cold. And so tired.

* * *

I take to bed with the fever. It folds over me after I come home that night. It creeps through my body, a sweeping mass of chills and heat, icicles and roaring fires in my limbs all at once. My arms and legs feel as though weights have been laid down in the bones and when I try to lift my head, my neck is a jelly with no power left at all.

I pass in and out, coming back to the room and going again. At first the girls poke me and tell me to get up, Madame Camille won't be too happy if I don't get to my shift, but then they are gone again and I can hear murmuring voices at the door. *Should they call the doctor?*

I watch a big shape on the wall. It's grey and white and black and it moves like a kaleidoscope I'd seen once in Duffy's hardware in town. Over and over it turns, changing shape, coming at me big and small. I wonder if it is a spirit or a devil, here to take me away, everything catching up with me, making me pay for what I've done. I'm frightened, especially as I can't stay awake and the fire still burns and the spirit won't go away, watching me, from the wall.

One of the girls is at my head, cupping it, holding out a warm cup of tea for me to drink. But I can't and as she holds it to my lips, it burns the dry skin that has formed there, cracked with the fever and the consciousness I was falling in and out of.

I dream of my baby, that he is dying inside me. That the big black and white spirit on the wall is coming down to take him away from me, killing him in my belly and filtering him away in a big ghostly breath.

I want to cry for him, to tell the spirit to leave me alone, to leave the innocent child, he has done no harm to anyone, but no sound will come out. Only sleep, hazy, fretful, sweating, and then there are people in the room, and I'm being lifted out of the bed, my weight supported by two people, my bump hard as they give me a Queen's chair out of the room and into some class of carriage outside.

There's a blanket around me and more voices and then nothing else.

Until I wake in a yellow room. The paint is cracked on

the wall. My eyes focus on it, going in and out and I put my hand on my belly and it's still there. The mound is there.

I turn over a bit, my limbs sore as though they're swollen, and I feel him kick me, hard behind the belly button. He's still alive. And so am I.

'Miss Thomas,' says the nurse when she comes into the room some time later. I haven't moved. I don't have the energy to. My head is still sore, but not like it has been.

'You're awake,' she says. And she's over feeling my forehead, all gentle, and taking my pulse, holding a big silver watch that's hanging on a chain on her pinny.

'I'll fetch the doctor,' she says, before I've had a chance to ask her anything.

'Influenza,' the doctor tells me, when he comes in, breathing heavily as he takes my pulse too. 'You are very lucky. It was touch and go for a while.'

They tell me I've been sick for five days, and yesterday, the fourth day, the priest had been called to say the last rites over me and my big belly. They thought I was going to die and I didn't even know a thing about it.

They help me up and give me some watery soup and as soon as I eat it my energy levels come back up and I begin to feel better. But my body is weakened, my muscles feel as though they've been torn at by dogs, every knot of my spine poking and hurting through my skin. Still the baby moves, twisting and turning, drinking the very life from inside me.

That evening the nurse gives me a sponge bath and I feel soothed after she's washed down my face and neck and hands. My hair is matted from the salt and sweat, and she helps me tie it all up and rinse the cloth around my hair line. She gives me a cotton smock to change into and I'm just settled back in the bed when the door opens. It's Madame Camille.

'You're on the mend,' she says and she's smiling.

'Yes,' I say, eying her suspiciously. I knew by now that Madame Camille only came around when there was something of interest to her. If there was business involved.

'I was just passing and I said I'd drop in to check on you,' she says. 'You're feeling better?'

'Much better,' I say.

'The girls were very worried. I was worried,' she says.

'Yes,' I say. I feel a bit vulnerable, wasted away in this hospital bed, her with her made up face and hair piled up high.

'But I'm delighted to see you're better.'

'Yes,' I say. *What does she want?*

'Well I'm sure you'll be back to the house and back to work in the next few days?'

I can't imagine getting up yet. Dragging my body back to the house and back to work were not what I was thinking about, not yet.

'I might have to rest a bit,' I say, trying to think of what the doctor said to me. But my brain is muddled, as though I haven't slept for a week, even though they told me that's all I've done.

'Another day in here,' she says. 'Then another day at home then back to work. I'll be adding this to the slate.'

She stands up.

'I look after all my girls,' she says holding out her long fingers and pushing them into dainty leather gloves. 'Didn't you receive the best care?'

I nod.

'You wouldn't have gotten that on the streets, now would you?' she says.

I nod again. Because she's right. If I was on the streets, I'd be dead by now. Deader than this, anyway.

Chapter Fifteen

GLADYS

It was the happiest Christmas she could remember. Albert had a smile that he couldn't seem to rid himself of. He whistled as he cleaned out the fire, sweeping the ash into a bucket, to help her. He carried baskets and helped her fold out the big sheets for changing the bed. The laundry was going out to a washer woman now on a Monday. She was to do no heavy lifting.

It was difficult to break her routine - to let go of some of the practices she did without fail each day. But she found she could replace some of the heavier tasks with lighter ones to keep her patterns going, the ones that made her feel safe.

He brought home a goose and she enjoyed stuffing it and basting it all Christmas morning, getting it nice and crispy, just the way he liked it. She paused while stirring the gravy, touching her stomach and looked across at Albert and smiled.

'Kicking, is he?' he asked.

'Little bugger,' she replied.

Her hand rested on her corset. Between the corset and chemise was a flat cushion she'd cut and stitched to the front of the undergarment.

'Do you think, could I touch him?' said Albert.

'No,' said Gladys, shaking her head. 'I can't bear to be touched. My skin is crawling.'

He looked disappointed, but she turned her back, watching the brown bubbles burst on the skin of the gravy.

'I've a surprise for you, after dinner,' he said.

She smiled again, to herself this time. How happy she'd made him.

They sat to a meal of sweetbreads and pate, salmon and goose. Albert had told her to create a feast; they were celebrating.

'This'll be the last Christmas, just the two of us,' he said as he held his knife and fork up, ready to cut into the brown flesh of the goose. After dinner, Albert went out to the back yard and came back in, pushing the door open with his foot.

'Look what I got,' he said, smiling.

It was a white painted cradle carved from oak, heavy, on a rocker and with blue edging all around.

'I just know it's going to be a boy,' he said, kissing Gladys on the cheek.

'It's beautiful,' she said, tears in the corner of her eyes. She bent down and ran her fingers along the edge of the wood.

Yes.

They were going to have a boy.

* * *

To clothe the baby, she had started to make binders and shirts from the softest cotton she could find. She carefully folded the shirts when they were finished, wrapping them in tissue paper and lavender and storing them in the nursery wardrobe; the baby's room. She had picked a pretty wallpaper with tiny brown dots through it for putting on the walls.

She had never seen Albert so happy or proud. He went off to work whistling and came back with an embrace for her in the evening. She was careful not to let him brush near the bump too much and he was happy to leave her alone, respecting her wishes to remain untouched. Most evenings he talked of nothing else but the baby.

'I'm the proudest man in England,' he told her.

As part of her baby shopping, visiting haberdasheries in central London and general stores for all of the things she would need, she took to sitting in secluded parks, watching nannies and other mothers with their babies. She observed their behaviour, their smiles as they held babies in the air or cradled them in their arms. She looked forward to when she could take her own little boy to the park, to toss him in the air and catch him again, giggling.

'Isn't he lovely?' she would say, as she sat beside a young nanny.

'Yes, he is.'

'How old is he?'

'Four months. A good feeder. A lovely baby.'

'Yes,' she'd say and lean in real close and tickle the baby on the cheek.

'Could I hold him? I'm expecting my own in a few months.'

The nanny would look to Gladys's stomach and then hand the baby over, and watch as Gladys stared at the baby's face, holding it tight and swaying it gently up and down.

'Is it your first baby?' they'd ask, noticing her grey hair and deep lines around her eyes.

'Yes, I'm very lucky,' Gladys would say while bouncing the child. 'A miracle baby.'

The nanny would smile and wait for Gladys to hand the baby back, which she would do slowly... reluctantly. Soon it would be time to find her own baby, a baby she wouldn't have to hand back. She hadn't decided where she would find him yet, but it pleased her to know that her baby was out there already. He was somewhere right now, growing, waiting to be born. She couldn't wait to meet him. Whoever he was.

Chapter Sixteen

MOLLY

I didn't know what to expect for Christmas. I half thought Madame Camille would give the girls some time off, or at least a break on the day itself. But she didn't and we were busy and after we had our lunch, which was a chicken and some boiled potatoes with gravy, the working house was opened up and a trail of men started to come through. They sickened me, those men. Especially the ones with the families.

I couldn't help but think of my own family. I thought of Mam and Mr McKenna and the two boys, sat at the table, my chair empty. Would they say a prayer for me? Would they be thinking of me too?

I longed to write a letter, addressed to Mam, to tell her where I was, to let her know that I was living. All she knew was that I'd left the regatta and never been seen again.

But how could I tell them where I was, of the awful immoral place I was living, the things I was seeing, and the baby growing inside me, bringing shame to every moment I sucked in my breath? I thought of the Virgin Mary giving birth to the baby, Jesus, in the stable on Christmas Day and how she hadn't been married. Maybe I could be forgiven after all if I just prayed hard enough?

I was getting very tired with the late nights and hauling the laundry and all the cleaning. There was always work to be done in our board house too, dinners to be made, groceries to be bought, the children to be washed and the water boiled to wash them. I felt like my stomach was yanking the life out of me, pulling the blood from my bones, the muscles from my skin. When it was time to get up in the mornings, I thought I might die of the tiredness.

The new kip-house near the Gentleman Clubs was working well for Madame Camille. She added her usual touches to the place, making it welcoming and setting it apart as more exclusive than some of the more down-standard houses around us.

Every evening I was afraid Henry Brabazon would walk back in the door and catch me. I never knew if he would and it meant I spent my whole shift watching the door, waiting for him and his moustache and his lovely black hair.

He hadn't so far and I could only hope he would not. Because next time, I knew, he would walk in and have me arrested there and then. And where would that leave me? With a judge waiting to send me to jail and have me hung by my neck on a rope? I thought if I could just get through the next few months without being seen then I could leave here; run away or do something to free myself. Anything at all, to save me.

* * *

I was still watching the girls and learning the tricks of the trade. They told me bits and pieces, how to finish the men quickly, to try and get a nice regular - maybe one who would be kind and sometimes just want the company and to talk.

I didn't see much because the doors were mostly closed, but I could hear and if I asked a question the girls would tell me. I was educating myself. I knew when it was my turn I would just have to bear it. There was no other way.

London was freezing. The cold had swept in before Christmas, bringing icy winds and biting air. I arrived at the kip-house every day with my nose glowing red. I had been given a new coat after my flu, a green wool coat, a hand-me-down from one of the girls but it was warm and I was glad of it.

One day we heard that Maggie, a northern girl who had been at the kip-house for a few months had gone missing. She had been out on the street near the end of her shift and she hadn't come back. The house madam that night had let it pass, thinking she might have just gone home, broken her shift with tiredness or with drink. But Maggie never came back to the house and there was no sign of her the next day either.

Madame Camille was called and she arrived with a face like thunder, annoyed at being drafted in for another problem that couldn't be handled. But when she saw the fear on the girls' faces, she softened a bit. Maggie had been seen talking to a man, a gentlemanly looking sort and had walked down the street with him and hadn't been seen since.

'I'll speak to my sources,' she said, meaning the police and we all got back to what we were doing. That evening a meeting was called and for a few minutes, the doors were locked and all the girls, Madame Camille and I sat around the little coffee table in the hosting room. It was the first meeting we'd ever had, all of us, alone, no customers there at all.

'Girls you know I look after you,' says Madame Camille. She's standing in front of the fireplace and she seems so tall among us girls sat down on the sofas. She reminds me of my teacher in school, only she's glamorous and made-up, her cheeks growing rosy under all that white make-up from the light of the fire.

'I have some bad news and I want you to prepare yourselves.'

We look at each other, then lean in closer, waiting for her to go on.

'Is it Maggie?' asks one of the girls, her voice high-pitched, her tears already starting.

'Yes,' says Madame Camille, looking very sombre indeed. 'They found her this afternoon. I'm sorry girls. About a mile from here.'

The wailing starts. The type of wailing I used to hear when the cats were in heat and they'd be clawing and climbing all over each other, a horrible caterwauling.

Found where? I wonder. What are they crying over? Then I realise without it needing to be said. The girl is dead. Murdered. By a john, too.

I was told to go and make tea, I could hear banging on the door, fellas trying to get in. Madame Camille went to the door herself and told them in a firm voice to come back in an hour.

'They'll be ready for you, then,' she said.

A whole hour to grieve for Maggie.

I made the tea as quick as I could serving it up to the sniffling girls who were talking about the last time they spoke to Maggie and what she was like. But it wasn't just Maggie they were crying for. It was for themselves. Any one of them could have been Maggie.

Madame Camille tells us she's going to introduce some changes and that she won't be sending girls out on to the streets anymore. Everything would work from the kip-house, for the time being.

A few days later I got hold of the Evening Standard. I pick it up out of a bin, its edges sticking out, all dog-eared and damp. There were never any papers in the kip-house and I missed reading them, picking up the news, looking to hear of home.

I was scanning the pages for articles on Ireland when I saw a headline that drew me in.

MURDERED PROSTITUTE HAD EYES GOUGED OUT.

Maggie. She'd been found stabbed, her neck slashed, and her lovely green eyes gouged out. Her blood had pooled into a puddle where she'd been thrown under a bush in Hyde Park.

I think of her, of what was going through her mind as the knife was drawn and brought down upon her.

And then I think of Montgomery, of the knife that tore through his windpipe, pulling it open so that the blood and the flickering muscle could flow out.

Did Maggie cry out as her attacker ripped her open? Like Montgomery did? Like a baby, crying for his mother, a man like a bairn, like the coward that he was?

* * *

When the pains came in March I didn't know what they were. They felt a bit like my monthlies, an ache and pull, down low, like something was trying to drag me by my pelvis into the ground. They started out like that, but then they changed. And I knew.

I was at the kip-house and I told the house madam that I thought it was my time so she shooshed me out the door in case one of the customers saw me.

'Nothing like a labouring woman to put them off,' she said, handing me my coat and telling me she'd let the midwife know and have her come around.

I walk home, on my own, slowly, stopping to grip the wall. I was scared. And I felt tired already.

When I got home, the house was quiet but I found Elizabeth and told her I thought it was my time. She helped me up the stairs, got me changed and put me in the bed. She felt my stomach and the big, hard lock that was going across it when the pains came.

'How often are you getting them?' she asks.

'I don't know,' I said. 'Every few minutes, I think.'

'Oh, you've a way to go yet,' she says. And the words make me sad. Like I've just turned for the finish line in a race, but somebody has moved it and I see it getting further away, where the eye couldn't even see.

Elizabeth says she'll make me a cup of tea, put some water on to boil and get out the towels and strips of cloth the midwife would need. She tells me not to be counting on the midwife calling soon, that it was a busy neighbourhood with babies delivering, and we were nothing special in this house.

When she brought up the tea I didn't want to drink it. I felt sick. And when the wave would come, I was gripping the bed with the pain of it, till it passed.

I got up to pace around the room but nothing helped. I felt like I wanted to sit and when I sat I wanted to stand. There was no way to get comfortable and the waves just kept coming, sucking the energy from me and sweating my brow.

I was beginning to wail when the midwife came, hours later. The pains were coming fast now and I could hear a voice in the room crying out. It was only after the sound was gone that I realised it was mine.

She took a look with her big hand all the way up there and she said things were progressing but I still had a way to go.

I felt like I was dying. I wondered how they knew I wasn't. But when I told them that they just laughed at me and said, 'Poor pet.'

I wanted my mother. I wanted her there, to tell me it would be all right.

I don't know how long the pains came for, over and over, rendering me unable to talk or even breathe. They kept telling me to breathe, but I couldn't.

There was a big, soggy mess below and after that the pains got worse. I didn't think they could but they did. I was roaring, like the cows I used to hear when they were calving. Low and loud. It came from deep within my throat, noises I'd never heard come out of my body before.

Just before the baby moved down and I could feel him making me want to push, I got to take a little rest. It was as though he was saying sorry, for doing all this, to give me a little reprieve before I had to get him out.

I lay there, passing in and out of a sleep, a whiteness above my head. There were whispers in the distance. I thought I heard my mother's voice, an accent like hers.

I was lying by the banks of the Boyne, the butterflies

lighting on the grass, the river babbling and rushing by. I was there, just for a moment, with my brothers and the sun, but then I was back, in the musty room in the terrace house and now another pain ripping through me - it was time to push.

I flipped over, like a big heavy animal, grunting and roaring and all the while I could feel him moving down, coming out, making his way past me now, the burning tearing through me, a searing hot pain, stretching me inside out.

The midwife was shouting and I thought if they don't get this out of me, I'm going to truly die right here on this bed, in front of them, an agonising death.

I gave a big push, and he was out; I turned around and heard my voice, all high-pitched and yelping and I was taking him in my arms and looking at him, his face and flat nose all scrunched up, his cheeks fat and swollen.

'Congratulations,' says the midwife and Elizabeth was almost crying and telling me I did ever so well.

But I didn't hear either of them. I heard nothing but the mucousy cries of my baby. The midwife turned him upside down and clapped him on the back and stuck a little pipe in his nose and put her lips to him and sucked a bit and when she gave him back to me, his cries came, all piercing - the loveliest sound I'd ever heard.

I took my finger and held it in front of him and I watched as he stopped crying and looked at it, his two eyes almost cross-eyed in his head. I wiped it down his nose, around his chin and back around his head, feeling his wet skin and the soft bones beneath it.

This is who had been squirming inside me. It was these arms and legs that were kicking, these fingers and toes that were under my ribs. I couldn't believe that he had come from me, that I had grown him and here he was, like a real, live doll cradled in my arms. Had he really come out of me?

The midwife gave him a quick rub with the hot water and showed me how to put him on the breast and when everything was finished with, I lay back with him suckling, feeling a soaring in my blood like I'd never felt before.

I wanted to show my mam and my brothers and say, "Look what I made, isn't he beautiful?' And the worry that I had, that I'd be thinking of Mr McKenna when I looked at the baby, that I'd remember what he did and see him as a representation of something bad, was gone. I wasn't worried at all. I had my whole life ahead of me now with this little boy. And I felt very blessed indeed.

* * *

I called him Oliver. When I was expecting him, I thought about it and it crossed my mind that Daddy might not like to have a bastard called after him. But when I saw his little face, all squished and red and wet and crying, I knew he wouldn't mind. That he was part of me and that was good enough.

The first night passed on a high. I was shocked that something so perfect, so beautiful had been inside me all this time. That I had pushed him out. That he was mine. I held him, not sleeping at all, just nursing and holding, smelling him and feeling the warmth of his skin.

The midwife had looked round after he was delivered, washed, and on the breast and asked me where his things were.

I told her I had no things.

She looked annoyed.

She said she'd come back the next day with a few essentials but that somebody had to help me and find the things he needed.

'He's not a doll,' she said, all condescending. 'It's a baby, a shitting baby.'

I didn't like her using those words around my baby. He was an angel. I would get him the things he needed, whatever it took.

The girls in the house came in after their shift and congratulated me; said he was a stunner. And he was.

Just as dawn broke, I drifted off, falling into a greyish sleep, feeling his little heart beat against mine. When I woke up I felt sore and he was crying.

I stayed in bed all that day, sniffing and smelling him, swaddling him like the midwife told me to. She came back and washed me and said everything looked ok, but there was a lot of blood. I felt a bit weak.

She brought with her some worn looking smocks and binders and a couple of towels. 'I'll add these to the bill, but you need more,' she said. 'Usually a mother would sew these herself.'

I knew she was looking down her nose at me. That she thought I was too busy whoring to be sewing for my baby. But I had nothing. No money to buy anything. Nothing to trade. Only what Madame Camille gave to us in the house.

Just like she surprised me on my sick bed, Madame Camille made an appearance that evening, coming in all smiles and carrying a brown paper bag. She took out an orange, something I'd never had before.

'Now you eat this all up and get your strength back,' she said. 'And I've brought you a few things for the baby too.'

I was delighted when she pulled out two new snow-white smocks. She had towellings too and pins for the baby's nappy. She had ointment for his belly button and eyes and eyebrows. She knew exactly the things I needed.

She didn't offer to hold him. I knew she wouldn't want to, up against her beads and lace and her bony wrists. It would look wrong her taking him in her arms and swaddling him, nothing soft about her at all.

Then she came out with it. Something she needed to offer to me. Because we always had choices, she said.

'I know of a couple. A lovely couple. Catholic actually. He's a school teacher, grand tall man, very athletic. Anyway, they haven't been blessed with any children.'

I look at her, over the top of Oliver's head, his scalp alive with a smell I found intoxicating.

'Oh,' I say, as if she was just telling me a story, nothing to do with me.

'They're looking for a baby, Molly. A newborn. A good healthy baby. A boy actually.'

She looks down at Oliver's head.

'My baby is not for sale,' I say, as calm as I could. Was there nothing this woman wouldn't sell. Women. Babies?

'Oh, it's not a sale,' she says. 'Far from it. I was thinking of his future, Molly. The baby. They have a beautiful home, up near Streatham. He would have everything he needs; everything. An education. Food. They have a housemaid, Molly. He'd go to a Catholic school.'

Sounded like she had everything thought out.

'I'm keeping my baby,' I say and I feel my teeth gritted against each other.

'You don't need to make any decisions now,' she says. 'You've not even spent a day with him yet. He's beautiful. But in a few weeks' time Molly, when you've to go to work and you've your bills to pay and you're wondering what sort of life, what future you can offer him, I just want you to know, there are other options. For him.'

So, this was her game. Take in poor wretched souls like me, sell us into the business and take our babies away for more profit. Well I could see through her as though she were a pane of glass. She was not taking my baby off me.

I turned my head and stared at the brown wall. I watched a mouse scatter along the skirting board, a black thing, barely visible against the wood only for his quick darting movements. I thought how the mouse had more freedom than I had, running around wherever he wanted to go.

'Molly just think about it. It would do a lot for your slate too. Almost wipe it clean it would,' she said.

The slate. This magic slate I'd heard all the girls talking about.

'How much is on my slate?' I ask her, turning back from the wall.

'I record everything carefully,' she says, her forehead creasing a bit. 'Don't forget that I took you in. When you had nowhere to go. When you had that growing in your stomach and not a pot to piss in.' She stabs the air at Oliver, the corners of her mouth going up in disgust.

'It's not cheap to feed and clothe you and put a roof over your head,' she says. 'And you had a hospital stay and now a midwife to pay for. Let's say you've one of the heaviest slates I have.'

'How long will I have to work for you?' I ask. Straight out. It had been on my mind. I wanted to know what I owed her and how long it would take me to pay it off. I needed something to look forward to, something better for my baby.

'Well that all depends, doesn't it?' she says. 'On how happy you keep the customers. On who you keep happy. On how much more money I have to spend on you. And now with a bairn to pay for. Well it depends, love, doesn't it?'

I shut her out of my mind. Right there and then, I imagined her gone, evaporated, no longer sitting and polluting the air for my baby with her pungent perfume.

But I was scared. I'd heard rumours ever since Maggie had been killed. There'd been whisperings and when I leaned in closer, the girls told me that Maggie and Madame Camille had never gotten on. That they'd not seen eye to eye. That Maggie had stood up to Madame Camille and said she was leaving, that very week - the week she turned up dead.

And here I was, alone with Madame Camille, her sitting over me and telling me what a good idea it would be to give up my baby, for money, for a better future. Suddenly all the soaring my heart had been doing was gone. The baby started to cry and I looked down at his curled-up face. What sort of future was he facing at all?

Chapter Seventeen

GLADYS

The nursery was finished, the yellow paper with brown polka dots, carefully applied to the walls. Albert had hired a decorator from a few streets away and it had taken him two days to finish the room, brushing the paste on to the paper and hanging it with a pencil sticking out his mouth.

Gladys hated having him in the house, and she took to pacing the corridor outside as he worked, making sure he wasn't poking about in her things. Most of all she hated the break in routine, the disruption that it caused having a stranger in the house, having to take him tea and speak to him politely and see him create dirt and dust and not a care by him at all for the upset it caused her.

The wardrobe was filled with muslins and binders, all the baby's smocks and towellings laid out neat and pressed. Over and over she checked the things, feeling the cottony touch, smelling the material as though she were sniffing the baby himself.

She had padded out the cushions in her dress as far as it would go now and she knew that time was closing in.

Albert had asked her about when they might expect the baby to come but she had waved her hand at him and said the doctor couldn't be sure and there was a mix up with her dates and it would be at least the end of April. He hadn't questioned it too much, not knowing of these things.

She had decided that when the time came she would go away for a few days, and tell him that she was going into the hospital, where men were not allowed accompany their wives. It would be easy to keep him away - he was terrified of childbirth.

In March, she walked to the local primary school and said she wished to register her son for school.

'Name,' said the bored looking principal as he inscribed her details in a large ledger.

'Robert Eccles.'

'Date of birth?'

'Well he's not born yet.'

The principal looked up, his eyebrows coming together as he glanced over Gladys in her tight Alice bonnet. She was old-fashioned and prim, her large stomach a clue to the child she was discussing.

'Not born yet?' he said.

'No, he's due soon. I wanted everything in order.'

The principal closed the ledger and began wiping his pen down with a dirty rag.

'I think, Mrs Eccles, it will be safe for you to come back and register your son when he is born.'

'But I'd like things to be in order,' she said, an agitation creeping into her voice.

'I'm sorry,' he said, shaking his head. 'We don't register children until they are at least three years of age, it's simply not possible.'

She felt foolish that she did not know the rules, that he would think her stupid. She turned to leave, nodding at his advice, but still, it felt good to be putting these arrangements in place. It proved to the world what a good mother she was going to be and it brought everything a little closer. It was the first time she had said his name out loud.

Robert Eccles. A strong name. For a strong boy.

'How do you know you are having a son?' asked the

principal, still rubbing the pen with the rag as she opened the door.

'I just know,' she replied.

* * *

She feigned tiredness most days now. She stopped preparing some of the more time-consuming meals, telling Albert she wasn't up to standing over the stove. He touched her back and told her that was quite alright and that he would live on eggs and bread if he needed to while she looked after her health.

'And when it's time,' he said. 'Will the midwife come here?'

He had brought up the baby's birth many times but so far, she had managed to avoid discussing the issue.

'Well you know I am worried about it,' she said.

'Yes,' he said. 'I'm worried too love, especially with ...' and he paused. 'The age you're at.'

She looked down at her hands, clasped together on the kitchen table. They were raw from bleaching the steps which she was still doing every day, something she had to do, for her mind's ease. The skin around her nails was broken and bitten. Lately they'd been bleeding as she sat and chewed on them and made plans for what she had to do.

'I've decided on the Lying-In Hospital at Aldersgate. I've looked into it. They'll know exactly how to look after me, a woman like me. It will be costly, Albert, but it'll be worth it. It'll take the worry out of it. I thought of being here too and the midwife and all. But this could be our one chance. I don't want to risk it.'

Albert reached across the table and took her hand.

'My love, money is no issue, no issue at all. Whatever it is, I'll pay. I want you to have the best care. I'm glad you're going to the hospital. It's a relief , a big relief. Are there any signs? Of him coming?'

He looked down at her stomach. He didn't know much

about how she would know, only that there was pain in-volved. He'd been terrified about her giving birth in the house. Now, she'd be with doctors and nurses and all the midwives she would need.

'No,' she said. 'No signs at all. He's very comfortable in there he is. Could be weeks yet Albert.'

'Do you think so?' he asked.

'Oh yes,' she said. 'He's moving well, but I've no symp-toms yet.'

'Right,' said Albert. 'I am so looking forward to meeting him though.'

'Yes,' she said. 'He'll be a topper.'

That was the first part of her plan organised. She hoped the rest would be as plain sailing.

MOLLY

When I left him that morning I was sad for him.
That I would come back as something different.
That he would be drinking the milk of a whore.
I sat in the hosting room, in my new uniform of chemise and stockings, the neck opened low, my bare thighs showing.
The door knocked and in came a man, a small man with a cap pulled low - a shift worker from a glue factory up the road. His clothes smelled of burnt meat and bleach.
His lustful eyes wandering made me sick. I worried it would come up my throat as he kissed at my face and pawed at my stinging nipples.
He was breathing deep now, and he sucked in a breath with the shuffle of my dress to the floor.
Do what you have to do to make him finish quick. So, I did.
He wasn't interested in my body, only my hands and my mouth. They were enough for him. I was shocked when he finished, warm and all over me, after just a few minutes.
I now knew what the smell was in the kip-house.
The lingering smell that I could never describe before.
It was the traces they left in and on us, mixed with our sweat, with our wet.
'Good girl,' he said and he left the room, walking taller for such a small man.
The house madam said, 'Now that wasn't too bad, was it?'
But she was wrong. It was the worst thing that had ever hap-

pened to me in the whole world. What Mr McKenna did to me was force. What I was doing here was something else.

I wanted my mother so bad. I wanted her to hold me and tell me that she would take me away from all this and wipe my soul clean.

But all I could see was her face. Her sad eyes. Her disappointment in me.

I couldn't even think of my father.

That would have been just too much to bear.

Part Three

Chapter Eighteen

GLADYS

London, Louisville Road, 1900

Robert Eccles was a quiet boy. He ate his breakfast in silence, biting his toast all the way round the edges and nibbling at it, like a rabbit. Gladys felt her skin crawl as she sat holding her scalding tea, waiting for Albert to finish his breakfast, so she could hand him his lunch and kiss him on the cheek goodbye. Then she and the child could have their argument over finishing his food.

Motherhood was different to how she expected it. So much cleaning and washing and the added pressure of trying to keep the crumbs and crusts of dirt he seemed to drag with him everywhere. She had it now so that he would watch her and her hands, seeing where they were moving, wondering if they were coming near him for a short, sharp smack.

She'd found that surprising him with the back of her hand and never giving in on any of her strict rules, was starting to work. At four, he was calm most of the time, the boisterous running around that he was so fond of when he was younger, almost eliminated. He understood that if she found him with dirty hands, or bringing anything from outside into the house, he'd get what he deserved. The welts had healed. But he'd learned his lesson.

Still, it was difficult to keep to her routines with him in the way. He always seemed to be under her feet, or standing behind her, looking at her, wanting for something. Things had been calmer before he was here. More straight. Easier on her mind and her nerves. If she could go back to then, before he was here, well, yes, she probably would.

He was starting school in September, going to the small schoolhouse where she had tried to register him before he was born. She'd wondered if the school master would remember her, but he showed no flash of memory when he took the details and scribed them in the ledger. She expected the headmaster would make a good teacher - he'd take no nonsense. Robert could do with some proper discipline. Albert was far too soft on him, always cuddling up to him and patting him on the head and telling him he was a good boy. He never seemed to see what she saw - the impudence, the cheek, his thirst for dirt.

He'd pushed them apart, had Robert. During her pregnancy Albert had fawned after her, did everything for her, showed her how much he loved her. When she'd brought the baby home, Albert poured all that love into the boy. Something else he'd taken from her life.

The last time she could remember having all of Albert's affection was in those weeks when they waited for their baby to come home. She'd been too wound up to enjoy them, to wallow in his affection, to take pleasure in the last times they would spend together, just the two of them.

* * *

When Gladys Eccles could no longer keep up the pretence of pregnancy she carefully scribed a note to Albert. She told him that she had been having mild pains and that she was taking a horse tram to the hospital. She said she would send a telegram with news and details of when he could visit in the next day or two. She said she didn't want to hear that he had come to the hospital before the telegram, she wouldn't like that. She told him of her love for him and that she was looking forward to meeting their baby. 'I'm thinking the name Robert?' she signed off.

She left the house carrying the small brown case she had packed and repacked a thousand times with the baby's first clothes. Inside the case, the glass bottles rattled against the tin of formula and she thought about the guest house, how she would set everything up on the table, lined up, clean and ready. Albert would expect her to be giving the child the breast, but she would continue with her story that she couldn't bear to be touched. She would arrive home with the formula and that would be that. And it meant he could give the child a bottle or two himself. He'd like that, would Albert.

The tram took her most of the way to City Road and when she dismounted, she began to act as though she were in pain. She imagined the labour as taking hold in her body, her stomach sending great crashing cramps through her. The hospital loomed large and grey ahead, its pointed turrets and drab front unwelcoming. She was glad that Albert had agreed to the hospital. She had worried that he would insist on a midwife at home, where he could be near.

She passed through the front doors and into the hall, where the smell of disinfectant hit her. There were women leaving with their new babies and others with large, round stomachs coming in. It looked busy and with her head held high, she walked right past the desk at the front where a lady was writing and through a set of white doors. A sign pointed her in the direction of the labour ward. There were also the private rooms, a laundry room, and a resting room for husbands. She feared that Albert might come here after all, to enquire about her, his curiosity getting too much for him. She was relying on his weak stomach and the words she had been casually mentioning in the past few weeks. *Haemorrhage. Fever. Chaos.*

She climbed the stairwell, one step at a time acting as

though she herself were in labour. It was important that she kept up the act should anyone see her. In the corridor, there was a baby's washroom, six sinks all lined up, laundry drying on the piped radiators. A nurse had a small, screaming infant in the water. She was holding its red head above the water and soaping it down.

Past the wash room were the general wards, beds laid out in each, some with women already in, others empty. They had a crib beside each bed and a large table and armchair in the middle of the room. She could see why women were choosing to come here and why it cost so much. She had taken the money Albert had given her for her maternity stay and hidden it in the brown case she was now carrying. It would help pay for the next few days and she would save the rest. For whatever she wanted. For whatever the baby needed.

The general wards were no good to her. She could be seen. She turned back and walked straight into a nurse, her white cap perched high on her head. 'Can I help you?' she asked.

'I ...' said Gladys, panicking. 'I've ... I have some pains. I think it's labour. I'm in labour.'

'Didn't they take you to the labour ward?' said the nurse. 'This is the wrong part of the hospital dear. Only for women who've had their babies. Let me take you to the front desk.'

The nurse gripped her by the elbow to take her back down the corridor.

'No,' said Gladys. 'It's alright. I got mixed up, turned the wrong way. I'll go back to the desk now. So silly. But I'm demented with these pains.'

She stopped and put her palm flat on the wall, breathing deep as though she had a big pain coming.

'You're all right,' said the nurse kindly, rubbing her on the back. 'I'll help you back down the stairs.'

'No need,' said Gladys, puffing out her cheeks. 'Honestly, I know where I'm going. I'm sure you've got plenty of work to be doing.'

'Aye,' said the nurse, still rubbing her back. But when Gladys straightened up and said her pain was gone, the nurse let her walk off on her own, watching her shuffling, back down the corridor.

When she reached the stairwell again, Gladys ran up the steps to the next floor. She couldn't delay any longer, she'd been seen now. She had to get in and get out. And be quick about it.

The corridor she was on was much better. There were rows of doors ahead of her, a name holder at each one, telling which were occupied. The private rooms. The ones she needed. She made her way quickly along the doors, peering through the small windows, waiting to find one where the mother was asleep, just like she planned.

Voices sounded at the end of the corridor, nurses coming right towards her. Panicking again, she opened the door of the nearest room to her. She looked at the bed to find a woman with dark hair, asleep. Gladys stood to the side of the door and watched two nurses and a doctor pass. They went into the room of the patient next door. She had to be quiet. She had to get this done quickly.

A white crib, a drape from the ceiling over it, stood beside the bed. She tiptoed over to it and peered in but there was no baby in the cot. Looking closer at the mother she realised the baby was in the bed, tucked right under the woman's arm. She bent over them, holding her breath so as not to disturb the woman's bare skin and put her hands around the baby's shoulder and middle. She tugged and lifted the baby right from under its mother's arm.

She had a hold of the baby now and she pulled it right in close to her and backed out of the room.

As she left, she glimpsed the woman wake, their eyes locking for just a second. She turned and ran, rushing through the corridor, the infant cradled in her right arm, her suitcase swinging in the left.

She heard the woman scream as she reached the top of the stairwell and cursed herself. This was not how this was supposed to happen.

She had not even looked at the baby yet. She didn't have a good grip of it, clutching it with one arm, almost round its neck. When she reached the stairwell, she glanced back to see if anyone was following her. When she turned her head back, she saw the nurse she had met earlier climbing the stairs in front of her.

'You,' said the nurse, her eyes now falling on the baby. 'Stop!' she said.

Cornered on the stairwell, Gladys thought about pushing past the nurse and making a run for the bottom of the stairs. But she had no hands free. The nurse put out her arms and sidestepped her, blocking her way. The panic was real now. She wasn't going to escape.

With a scream of frustration Gladys thrust the baby at the nurse and pushed past her, holding on to the wall as she took the stairs two at a time, almost falling over the last steps. She ran through the front hall of the hospital, not looking at anyone, and past the front doors and into the midday air.

And then she ran, as fast as she could, away from the hospital and from anyone who might be following her. She ran all the way down the street and the next, racing to catch up with a horse tram ahead.

Anyone who saw her, a woman with a large, pregnant stomach, would have thought that she was a very fit lady to be able to run so. And when she got on the tram she sat and clutched her case and she couldn't help but weep. She had lost her baby, this time a real baby, not like the one before, which was only blood and not even a heart-beat.

She had let Albert down again. What an awful wife she was.

* * *

She'd hid in a run-down guest house after the hospital, not

daring to leave, curling handfuls of bread and margarine into her mouth, bought in a shop a few yards from the room she'd taken for two nights. She prayed Albert wouldn't go to the hospital to seek her out, that he'd stay at home, like she asked.

She spent the days pacing the floor, clenching and un-clenching her hands, scratching at her arms and her scalp. She thought about trying another hospital - the Lying-In wasn't the only building in London were babies were being delivered. But the thought of going back into the sterile wings, with the nurses and the sleeping, just birthed mothers, sent a dread through her. She couldn't do it. There had to be another way.

As dawn broke on the second morning of her stay at the guest house, the thought came to her - filtering in through the dark of the small single room.

It would buy her more time. It would give her time to think.

Carefully she packed up all her things, placing them back into the brown case, fighting a pain in the pit of her stomach as she wrapped up the baby's belongings again. It wasn't supposed to be like this. She shouldn't have been returning home without him.

She walked up Louisville Road slowly, taking her time, enjoying seeing the familiar cracks in the pavement that she could count and help calm herself.

She noticed the dust on the front door and how grimy the windows looked as she went to put her key in the door. Just two days and look what had happened while she was away.

Inside, the smell of home hit her nose, a smell she'd never really noticed before - it was comforting and she breathed it in, glad to be back on her territory, even though she could see that the whole place needed scrubbing down to get rid of all the germs that would have formed there since she'd been away.

Upstairs, she replaced her late pregnancy cushion with a half-way one, bringing her bulk down. She went to her dressing table and found her translucent powder at the back of a drawer. Carefully she applied it to her cheeks and mouth, making herself look as pale as possible.

Then, she went down to wait in the sitting room, on the ground, leaning against the sofa, her hand on her tummy. She would wait there till he came in, working on her story, on her emotions, so that she would be ready, to face him.

'My love,' said Albert, only his head visible, his body blocked by the door, as he stood peering round it. He had arrived home from work at the usual time, his key scratching in the front door lock.

He came in and leaned down, holding out his arms to embrace her, and as she got up and he pulled her close, she felt his head turn, searching the room for their baby.

'Why didn't you let me know you were getting out, I would have come to collect you?' he said into her hair.

He held her shoulders and scanned the whole room for the crib. 'Where's the baby?'

She let her face fall, as if she were in terrible pain.

'They wouldn't let me bring him home,' she said.

She sniffed and then let the tears come, a great sob coming from her throat. Shocked at his wife's upset, Albert put his arms around her again.

'He's so poorly, Albert, oh you should see him. So tiny. They said it could be weeks, weeks before we get him home.'

'Oh, my love,' he said, rubbing her back, holding her face against his torso. 'I've been worried sick. I got your note but all I wanted to do was go and see you.'

'He was too sickly for visitors Albert. He still is. Even I might not be let in to see him.'

'The poor mite,' said Albert and when she looked up, she saw that he too had tears in his eyes.

'And you?' he said. 'How are you feeling, shouldn't you be in bed? I thought they'd be keeping you, for two weeks at least.'

'I'm so tired,' she said. 'I feel weak. But I'm fine. I just want my baby.'

She let her shoulders shake, racks of sobs folding over each other, tears and clear snot cascading down her face.

Albert held her, comforting her, not asking any more questions.

And this was how she kept it for weeks.

The baby in hospital. Not able to be seen. Albert not able to ask questions, because he wouldn't know about such things and it upset his wife too much.

Chapter Nineteen

MOLLY

I'd learned a new skill. It was the ability to leave myself. To go away from my body and mind. I'd noticed it creeping in right at the start. After the first few days when I'd seen nearly thirty men. I found that I wasn't quite there. That as soon as they unbelted or pulled down their trousers or turned me round or even touched me, I was gone.

Most of the time I was still in the room. Still there, some part of me, my physical body maybe. I could see myself, just me and my blank face, no expression, doing what I had to do to get it over with. But my mind wasn't there. It was somewhere else. Up above me, floating near the ceiling, in the clouds.

I began to play a game - imagining the nicest thing that could ever happen to me, right there and then. Mostly I was at home. At the river. At the top of the mound at Dowth. Or with my mother. Never my father. I never brought him into my thoughts with the men that were here. I thought about Oliver and a lovely house we would have in the country. Just me and him. I thought of him growing big and strong, his fair hair growing long and bouncing as he ran in the sun.

I saw the flies and midges that kicked up out of the grass as he tottered. I felt the rays on my skin and I smelled the fresh, earth smell. I could float for as long as I needed to float, until they'd finished and then I had to get up and wipe myself and tidy the room and set about getting ready for the next customer.

I wondered how long I could go on for. Doing this and floating away. I feared I was damaging my mind, that I never knew which part of me was here and which part was there. I detested who I'd become.

The girls seemed to like me more now that I was one of them. I could see why they'd resented me being in the kip-house, cleaning and pouring drinks and never having to offer up my body like they had to. I was also taking trips to the pharmacist for the ointments and poultices they recommended to take away the soreness. The broken skin. The aching. I feared I would catch a disease - something awful like I'd seen on Angela that day. I prayed to God every night and every morning that he would protect me, get me through another day, and save me from the men with the venerals.

After a fortnight or so of working properly at the kip-house Madame Camille swept in, doing her checks, chatting and flirting with some of the punters. She got me aside and asked me how I was getting on.

'Fine,' I say, not really looking at her, more at the floor. And my feet.

'Good,' she says. 'Well, the reports are good Molly, you're doing well, I knew you would.'

Doing well. At being a prostitute. I didn't think it was a compliment.

'Madame Camille,' I say, looking up at her. 'My slate - can you tell me what's on it and what I've earned and maybe when I can start earning for myself? It's the baby you see, I want to be able to put something away for him, for the things he needs.'

'Don't you have what you need?' she says, her eyes darkening, her beautiful face creasing into a scowl.

'He's grand,' I say. 'I have his clothes now and that. But it's more for myself, to know that I have a bit for him.'

'Molly, I've told you already. You have a heavy slate. Haven't I put you up for the past six months for free? Paid for a hospital stay? A midwife? New coat. Baby things. Haven't you a cheek to be asking about payment when all I've done is fork out for you, hand over fist?'

A white spittle flies from her mouth and lands on my cheek, under my eye. It feels hot. I stem the urge to wipe at my face.

'Look around you, Molly. How long are these girls here? Do you see any of them starting to earn just a week after work? Seems you have a short memory, about all I've done for you.'

I was afraid she'd bring up about the couple again. The couple who wanted to buy my baby and that she'd tell me to consider it again. So, I told her I was sorry, that it was alright, I understood, and I wouldn't ask again.

Madame Camille had total control over me: where I lived, how my baby lived, and now how my body was bought and sold for the very roof over my head.

That was the first day that I had a whiskey and added it to my slate. Right after she was gone out of the kip-house; back to her life of grandeur and glamour. What difference did it make anyway? If I was going to be here for months, working off this slate, then what harm would a few whiskeys be to get me through it? That's what I told myself anyway.

* * *

Oliver was growing fast. He suckled on my milk at all hours of the day and when I had to go to work, he would cry so we had to start preparing glass bottles with formula and sugar in them for when I was gone. I hated leaving him in that house, in the care of a girl who had no care for him at all, who could never see the beauty of his eyelashes against his cheeks, the hollow of his temples, the way his little nostrils flared when he yawned or cried.

I was glad that I got breaks from the house to come back and feed him, to hold him. To smell his beautiful baby scent before I had to go back and smell the other smells I had come to hate. Sweat. Cigarettes. Coal dust. Semen.

I was having awful trouble getting my own family out of my mind. My mother was always in my thoughts. My brothers too. They came to me at night, in my dreams, their faces looming in front of me, never looking happy, as if they were crying. In the mornings when I'd wake, I'd think about them, and how lovely it would be to get out of bed, go downstairs and find them clattering round our old kitchen, making tea and buttering bread; getting ready for the day.

I thought how they might love to look at the baby, how they might hold him and coo after him and rub his little feathery head the way I liked to. It made me sad to think that he would never know his real family. That here and now, there was only one person who loved him in the world, and that was me.

As I got up and moved around and looked out the window at the cloudy sky, I thought about how I hadn't seen the sun in months. That the smog had covered everything up, making everything grey.

I felt grey too. The whiskey left me with headaches in the morning and I'd gulp down the glass of water beside my bed as soon as I woke. But it never got rid of the dull ache that was in the centre of my head, right in the middle, on the inside and when I got to work, I'd have a whiskey, just to get rid of that pain, because it always did.

I was drinking every day now. I knew each one was being added to the slate and I was afraid to add them up but I couldn't help getting the house madam to pour me another. I thought how I used to pity the drinking girls and think how silly they were. These things seemed to keep happening to me. Thoughts that I would never do such a thing, never become that. And yet I did.

In the summer, I started seeing a new man. He had a long face and hunched shoulders. He had been with a few of the girls in the house before, but he took a shining to me. It was my accent he said. He loved to hear me talk.

He was coming every week and always asked for me and after I'd done what he asked, he made me sit on the bed and he asked me questions about myself. I felt that he was wasting my time a bit, that talking wasn't getting any more money off my slate and so he began to offer more money, to spend some time with me.

Money for talking was good by me. I started telling him anything he wanted to hear. I buttered him up a bit, telling him what an interesting man he was, when really, he was no more interesting than the boot on my foot.

One day, as he was leaving, Elizabeth came past my room and looked in after he had left.

'That your regular?' she asked.

'Yes,' I say. 'He likes to talk.'

'I've a right pervert after me at the moment. Real disgusting,' she says, wrinkling her nose. 'I think I had him before,' she says, nodding after my regular. 'Does he make a noise like this?'

She starts honking, her voice soft at first, then getting louder. We both burst out laughing as she does a giant honk before making an exaggerated sigh and falling backwards on the bed.

'Like the church organ pipes, isn't he?' I nod because I'm giggling so much I can't talk. 'Mr Tubular!' she says and the two of us clutch our stomachs and laugh as loud as we can.

It felt good to make a joke over our pathetic situations. That we could find humour in this world we were living in. This world of never ending men, of our bodies not being our own, of our minds floating away so that we could get through it, one customer at a time.

'Mr Tubular,' I say and that was his new name. He'd been christened.

I could never have known then, the part that Mr Tubular was going to play in my life. That he, along with Mr McKenna, would change it forever. I could never have predicted that his shine for me was real. That he would, later that summer and with Madame Camille's agreement, make me his wife.

Chapter Twenty

HENRY

It wasn't something he expected. The interest. The letters. The gifts. The surrounding him at soirees and house parties.

The mothers were the worst. They pressed into him, their great big bosoms trussed up and in his face, lauding on and on about their daughter. Had he had the pleasure of meeting her yet? She really was a sight to behold. And so interesting!

He had learned that they were never interesting. That they were dull and some of them half-stupid, incapable of holding a conversation, no interest in the world outside of some dancing and light piano playing. They had nothing to offer him.

He stopped attending events, only going to gatherings that he absolutely had to. But this made him more of catch; the shy reclusive bachelor who was rarely seen.

Arthur attended everything he was invited to, bringing home tales of beautiful women and some not so beautiful, who he had kissed and fondled anyway.

'I think I had my way with her,' he would say, scratching his head at breakfast, his eyes bloodshot, his breath foul with drink. When he had had some tea and soda bread with butter, he would go back to bed, then get up late in the afternoon and start drinking again.

Henry looked forward to September when his brother would return to Oxford. He was tired of trying to control him. He wanted him gone, needed him away from the house and no longer in his worries. There was enough to be concerned about as it was. It had shocked him, the dire state the accounts had been left in.

The first boxes of papers had started arriving a month after his father's death. They had been with his father's solicitors, Faber & Sons, and on leafing through the first pages, he immediately made an appointment to go and see Faber himself. He'd sat in their offices, staring at the yellow walls, imagining himself working there. This is where his father had wanted him to intern.

'Are you serious?' he'd asked when Faber came into the room. 'Are you honestly telling me this is the state of affairs you left my father in? This?'

He pointed at some papers he'd spread out on the table, stabbing at the statements of the various bank accounts and savings bonds Seymour had invested in.

'Nothing? There's nothing left?' he said.

Faber, infuriatingly, shrugged his shoulders.

'Henry, you knew your father liked to gamble. It got out of control.'

'Out of control?' said Henry, surprising himself with the venom in his voice. 'There's nothing fucking left. Nothing.'

'We did offer advice that the stocks he was investing in could prove worthless. Which is what happened. Can I remind you, Henry, that we are executors of the will. We are not bankers.'

'No, but he trusted you,' said Henry. 'He was always running to you for financial advice. You were his confidante. All those meetings, bringing in his papers. I know he was paying you – to oversee things.'

Faber shrugged again.

'We offered advice where we could, Henry. We did try to warn your father. But he was insistent. He didn't listen to us. You know Seymour loved to gamble.'

'You, as legal guardians, had a duty to protect the estate and my father's interests. You allowed him to do this. I am laying the blame firmly at Faber & Sons' door.'

The anger felt like it might explode from Henry's throat. It was taking all his willpower to remain seated and hold some level of civility to his voice.

'What's done is done,' said Faber. 'Your father made the decisions. He knew the gamble hadn't paid off. And he was, right up to his death, trying to win back what he'd lost. He thought he could do it, and he might have too, had he not … well his death was very untimely. I'm sorry, Henry. I know you are upset. But it was your father's estate. And it was his decision.'

Things were making sense now. His father's demeanour each time he came home. His outbursts. His constant demands that Henry get involved in the legal paperwork. He knew he was losing the estate. And he thought that Henry, with all his legal learnings and experience, could help him. That's why he didn't want him going to London. He needed him at home, to fight his case.

'Is it really as bad as it looks? Is there anything I'm missing, accounts not outlined here, something to work with?'

'There's his insurance policy. There'll be a bit in that. And if we add up the remainder of what's in the accounts and bonds, there'll be a small sum. There is a possibility that some of the shares will rise again. Some are worth holding on to. And of course, there's the land, Henry. Prices are not at their best now, but maybe, if you held on to it for another six months, things could change.'

So, he could hold out and scrape the bottom of the accounts and hope for the best. He could watch the markets, like his father had done, praying for a gas or oil share to rise, hoping a fledgling company he'd invested in would hit gold and rocket. Or he could put plans in place to sell off the land to settle some of the bills and hope that he could save the house.

And what would they live on then?

Henry picked up the papers and angrily put them into the leather case he'd brought them in.

'Let me help you,' said the assistant, reaching across to lift the paperwork.

'You've done enough. I want every single paper, everything you have belonging to my estate boxed and sent to me today. Consider our account closed.'

In the carriage on the way home, Henry fumed, thinking over the meeting and the smug look on Faber's face. He always knew there was something crooked about him. Seymour didn't have the gumption to see it. Put too much trust in his old pals - exactly as he had done with Montgomery.

'A letter for you,' Mrs Johansson said when he came in the front door, pulling at his gloves and scarf, wearily.

He looked at the writing, a neat scrawl, not one he was familiar with.

'I'll be in my father's study,' he said, taking the letter with him. He still called it that. It would be a while before he would be able to call it 'his'.

When he got there, he poured a large Scotch, taken from the same cabinet his father had kept his drink hidden in. He debated whether to call Mrs Johansson for ice, before taking a gulp and deciding he could live with room temperature.

The letter was short, to the point. Charity Eustace wished to express her condolences and her deep upset at the death of Seymour. She would be travelling to the area in March and could visit if he so wished.

I do not want to intrude however. I know this is a difficult time for you.

Despite its similarity to the correspondence he had been receiving almost daily from a string of well-wishers, the letter warmed Henry. Charity's tone was genuine and she had been terribly upset at Seymour's funeral.

He sat and looked into the fire, sipping on his Scotch.

He rose to get a second drink, his last, he told himself, and as he passed by the books cabinet, he paused, pulled out a drawer and unearthed a piece of writing paper. He sat by the fire again and inked his pen. He thanked Charity for her kind letter and said that he would be delighted to welcome her in March.

He couldn't help but smirk at the ladies lining up to present themselves to him. They thought his wealth came before him, that they stood to gain a great deal by marrying him. If they only knew, they'd run, scuttling to the door.

Wasn't it funny too, he thought, that the situation he now found himself in was almost exactly the one he'd wished for. One, where he stood to be free, shaken from the shackles of this great house and the legacy of his ancestors before him.

But now... he was going to do everything in his power to hold on to it. To keep the lands and the estate that he had inherited, refusing to sell if he could help it.

It seemed his father had been right about one thing. Charity Eustace could, in fact, offer a great deal.

Of course, he would meet with her in March.

After all, he had everything to lose.

* * *

She had put on more weight, he thought. Her cheeks had filled out and it gave her a squirrel-like appearance. His heart sank when he saw her, standing in the great room, her hand aloft for him to kiss it.

'Henry. You poor darling.'

Her hand was doughy and soft, the skin white as porcelain. She smelled of perfume, an aroma of expense.

'So good to see you, Charity.'

'I'm ever so upset for you, how are you holding up? It must be so difficult. He was a great man, you must be missing him terribly.'

'Yes. I am'

Her words rang true - he was missing Seymour, something that surprised him. He missed being able to go to him, to talk, to consider things that were happening on the estate. He felt so alone, the responsibility bearing down on him, no one to share the burden of the decisions that had to be made. At least Charity would have a knowledge to talk things through. She had great experience from her own estate and was a confidante of her own father.

'My father was devastated,' she said. 'So sudden. We are all so sorry.'

'Yes.' he was touched by her sincerity. 'Would you like a drink?'

'Only if you're having one,' she smiled.

He wasn't planning on it, but now that she was stood here and he had the whole rest of the day to fill with entertaining her, a drink sounded like a good idea.

He poured her a brandy; she took it and licked her lips.

'I do love a drink during the day. It feels so wicked!'

'You should spend time with Arthur then. He's perpetually wicked.'

She laughed. 'How is he holding up?'

'He's not great, if I'm honest,' he said. 'He's taken it very badly. He's a softie really, is Arthur. He was very close to Father.'

'You weren't?'

Her words surprised him.

'No, I was too,' he said, even though he didn't quite mean it. 'I guess I'm just able to accept it better, if you understand.'

'You're a stronger fish. Poor Arthur. I always think of a little boy when I see him.'

It was funny she said that because he, too, thought the same. It was as though Arthur had never grown up - never lost his boyhood charm or senses.

'Where is he anyway?' she asked.

'Oh, he's away on a hunting trip. In Kerry.'

'Kerry, my... he'll be gone for weeks. So we have the

place to ourselves?'

She took a step towards him, a smile on her face.

'Indeed, we do,' he said and with every force in his body, he took a step towards her so that they were close enough for him to take a look at her cheeks. She had definitely put on weight, definitely.

* * *

Mrs Johansson took a shine to Charity. Henry found them laughing and joking anytime he came into a room and they were together. 'She's a hoot,' Mrs Johansson said.

He was starting to see a new side to Charity, one he'd not noticed before. It seems she had some fun in her after all, her own charm, in her own way.

They took their horses for long rides through the estate and beyond into the neighbouring ones. She was a good horse-woman and she didn't shy from high hedges or fences they had to cross.

He could see why his father thought they would be a good match. They did have things in common and her back-ground, though much wealthier, was not far removed from his.

In the evenings, they enjoyed hearty meals cooked by the chef and presented with great aplomb by Mrs Johansson. He'd ordered pheasant and duck and quail and on the last night, roast lamb. He wanted to ensure Charity enjoyed her-self. He wanted her to be comfortable at Brabazon, to feel that she could fit in there, that she could, possibly, be at home there.

She delved into the food with gusto, cleaning the plate with bread, complimenting the chef and the wine cellar.

'You must give me a bottle of this to take back to Daddy,' she said, smacking her lips after a gulp of red wine. They were seated beside each other and she reached across and touched his hand.

'Thank you for such a lovely few days.'

'You're most welcome. I must admit, you've been a very nice distraction.'

'Have I?' she said. Her mouth broke into a smile and he noticed the wine had turned her teeth black and placed a thin purple ridge around her lips.

'Yes...you have.'

He lifted her hand and kissed it, and he felt her shudder under his grip.

'Ticklish,' she smiled. But he knew she wasn't ticklish. He knew that she was in love with him, that she wanted nothing more than for him to lean over and kiss her.

He leaned across the table and was about to open his mouth to speak when she lunged at him and placed her mouth on top of his.

He almost pulled back from the force of her, but stopped himself as she worked her tongue against his, her hand yanking his head towards hers. Her breath was sour with wine but he went with it, not wanting to offend her and knowing that the kiss had been coming, obvious in the shine in her eyes and her gaze that followed him, wherever he went.

'I am so charmed by you, Henry Brabazon,' she said when she pulled back and looked at him. He forced a smile to his face.

'And I you,' he said.

She looked down at her plate and scooped up a forkful of meat, popping it in her mouth before taking another gulp of wine.

He wanted to leave, to get up from his chair and go straight to his bedroom, locking the door behind him. But years of entertaining, of having guests for dinner and being forced to stay at the table as Seymour expected, helped him to sit, to carry on the conversation and remain charming to his guest. Tomorrow she would be leaving. If he wanted to do the deed, then the opportunity was now.

'Would you like to walk in the woods before you leave

tomorrow?' he asked.

'Yes, I'd like that. I'll need to be on the road early though.'

'We'll go first thing.'

'I wish I could stay,' she said. 'I love it here.'

He loved it too. It was why he was doing what he was doing, against all his moral function, against the ethics he'd stood by for years. Sometimes you had to do things you didn't want to do for the greater good. At least that's what he told himself as Charity chattered and drank glass after glass of wine.

'Maybe you can,' he said, hinting at what was to come.

She raised her eyebrows and laughed, then pursed her lips and said no more.

He knew what she was thinking - tomorrow could well be the happiest day of her life.

How sad that made him feel.

* * *

It was cold when they set off down the lane; he, in his over-coat, she, wrapped in a wool shawl over her dress. She took his hand as they walked and he pushed on in a hurry, keen to get to the woods, to the spot he had chosen. He'd slept badly last night, knowing what was ahead of him and now that they were here, he wanted to get on with it.

She was in a good mood, pointing out things to him as they walked. A robin that seemed to be following them down the lane. Frost in a puddle the shape of a snowflake. An unusual curly fern, tucked in on the bank.

He was silent, lost in his thoughts, almost irritable as they walked to the end of the lane and turned left through a path at the gatekeeper's house, which led to a hilly nature walk. When they reached the top of the incline, a cliff face covered in trees, overhanging the River Boyne, they sat on the small wooden bench his father had installed soon after he married his mother. The view from the bench took in a sweeping bend in the river, looking out over beech and ash trees.

'This is breathtaking,' she said as she sat and clutched at his hand again.

They sat in silence for a few moments and his fingers touched the box he had in his jacket pocket, feeling the smooth shell of the walnut case. Taking a deep breath, he shunted from the bench on to one knee and turned to Charity.

'This may come as a surprise, but I think we should get married. Charity, would you do me the honour?'

He'd thought about extending his words, talking to her about how suited they were, how pleased her father would be, how it was his own father's wish. But in the end, he'd settled on spitting the words out and being done with it.

'Oh Henry!' Charity gasped and drew her hand to her mouth, tears filling her eyes. They spilled over and down her face as she repeated the word yes, over and over. 'My love,' she said. 'You sweetheart, I'm shocked, of course I'll marry you, Henry Brabazon!'

He held the walnut box open to her, an emerald ring that had belonged to his mother glinting in the dim spring light.

'It was my mother's,' he said. 'I trust you will take care of it.'

'I will!'

He took it from the box and went to put it on her finger but it was too small to fit. She took it and placed it on her little finger, pushing it down past the knuckle, where it hung, square and awkward looking.

'I know just the goldsmith who will fix it,' she said.

It pained him to think of the ring being dismantled, of a jeweller taking the ring and melting it and adding more gold. It was perfect the way it was, it had been perfect on his mother. Still, it would be Charity who would be wearing it now and there was no point comparing her to a woman long gone from his life. This was his future now.

'I always knew we would be married,' she said as they walked the final distance around the trail, her hand tight in his, her smile radiant.

'Did you?' he said looking ahead.

'You know I always had a fondness for you,' she said.

'Well yes,' he said. 'And I you.'

Fondness was easy. Love, was another matter.

She stopped and reached up to wrap her arms around his neck. She pulled him down to her mouth, invading his with her tongue. He resisted his urge to pull back, to push her away, to tell her to stop.

He had to learn to love her, to find, somewhere, a lust for her.

He promised himself that in the coming weeks, he would concentrate on small parts of her, areas that could be defined as attractive. He would start with her smile, with her happiness, with her good humour in what he had done for her. He would battle with his mind over his groin, willing himself to love, forcing an acceptance of the way things had to be.

This was his responsibility now. He would do anything to save the estate.

Chapter Twenty-One

MOLLY

The day I left the kip-house, a small holdall flung over my shoulder and Oliver in my arms, was the happiest day I could remember in my life. I felt as though I were walking to freedom, that my soul was being wiped clean, that the dirt stuck to my body from the hundreds of men I'd seen was dropping off, bit by bit.

It had all happened quickly - Mr Tubular was keen to get me out of there, to stop the clock on the men using my body now that he was going to use it for himself, alone. I didn't realise this is what he'd been building up to, that he had a plan to take me out of there, to marry me, to stop paying for what he needed from me and get it for free.

When I looked back, I could see that he had been hinting at it for a while. All those chats, cuddled up to me on the bed. Always asking me about the future. About my son.

'Molly, what would you say if I asked you marry me?' he finally said one night, his voice quiet, my skin bristling as he ran his finger over my arm.

I laughed. The girls had talked about this before. Keen johns - lonely customers who wanted to buy a wife.

'You don't want to marry me,' I say. 'You don't know me.'

'I want to know you.'

I wanted to say back to him, *but I don't want to know you, Mr Tubular*. I look at him, with his greying hair around his temples and behind his ears, bits of stubble all different lengths from different shaves. He's got big eyes in his long face. But he's no stature at all - he's probably the same height as me.

'I think you're lovely,' he says and now he's stroking my cheek and my whole body is prickling up in disgust. 'You're different to the girls here. You're innocent. You don't belong here, I want to take you away. To give you a home. I'd take on the bairn. I'd be a good father.'

I didn't like anyone knowing about Oliver. But Tubular was always questioning me, making out that he was interested in him. Now I knew why.

'He doesn't need a father,' I say but the words were defensive and I knew they weren't true.

'Every young lad needs a father,' he says. I look at him now in the face, placing him in a normal house where there were no half-dressed girls or silky sheets and curtains or the smell of sweat and drink and smoke. I see him sitting at a table, eating an egg, paper in hand, a little boy kicking his legs under the table.

'But how?' I ask.

'I'd buy you out. Whatever Madame Camille wants, I'd pay it.'

'I have a big slate,' I say. 'I was here for months before I could work and then I was sick. She's had to pay for me and the bairn too. I've never seen her a let a girl go.'

It's true. Madame Camille hated to give anyone up. She invested, she didn't sell. Our time could be bought. Not our freedom.

'If I spoke to her, would that be alright? If I struck an agreement with her, would you come with me then?' he says. He has the most earnest look on his face. I laugh.

'You're buying me,' I say.

'I wouldn't see it like that,' he says. 'I'd see it as taking you out of somewhere you shouldn't be. Think about it, my love. And next time, if you say yes, I'll talk to her.'

His words play on my mind. All that afternoon as I saw man after man, as I felt them rise up and collapse, enter and pull out, fondle and cradle, grab me and suffocate me, their arms around my mouth, my neck, my stomach, my legs, I thought about what he had said.

When I went home to Oliver, when I took his small body and held it against mine, as I let my breast into his mouth and saw him suckle and soothe, I thought, *the eyes and hands and mouths that have been on my breasts today and they should only be for you.*

I didn't want to marry Mr Tubular. But I didn't want to stay working in a kip-house either. I've no other choice, I thought. I have to say yes.

* * *

Madame Camille has a strange look on her face. A look of admiration I think, that I've done this, that I've managed to wrangle this situation for myself.

She's seated, all prim in one of her armchairs. We're in the room where I first met her. Georgian furniture is placed about the room, making it look homely. A decanter set sits on a table and a small fire flickers in the grate. The whole place smells of burning oils.

'Molly,' she says when I come into the room, my legs and arms sore from the last customer; he was heavy and he was rough. Mr Tubular is sat on the other armchair, one leg over the other, looking relaxed. He has a smile on his face, and he beams even more when he sees me. I sit on a hardbacked chair.

'Mr Cotton tells me he has proposed marriage,' says Madame Camille.

Cotton? I want to laugh. Is that going to be my new name?

I don't answer Madame Camille. I just nod. And I look straight at her, not at him at all.

'So,' she says.

I shrug.

'Well?'

I shrug again.

'Do you wish to accept?'

She is acting as though I have the power to. It's one of the games she plays. That our fate is in our hands. That we control it. Our slates. Our time. Our customers.

'Madame Camille, you know that decision is up to you.'

There's that look again, that one of half admiration, half contempt.

'Molly, I am quite happy to keep you here. To have you work out your slate. You're popular. Fresh. The men like you. You're good.'

I know this is a dig. This is a smarting comment to show my future husband, that I am good at being a whore.

'But, Mr Cotton is very keen. He has offered to clear your slate. And more.' She looks at him now and smiles. I wonder how much I am worth, how much money he is willing to part with to buy me. I remember the market at home in the Fairgreen, the great big cows, lowing and swaying, the farmers slapping their hinds, bargaining over the prices, and spitting in their hands to seal the deal. Here, I am the meat. And I want to know how much I am worth.

'How much is he paying?' I ask.

I look at him. Now it's his turn to shrug.

'It doesn't matter, Molly,' he says. 'What matters is that Madame Camille has agreed to let you go. If you are happy, you can finish work tonight and I'll arrange the wedding in the next few days. Then you can come to live with me.'

And it was as simple as that. There were no rows, no prolonged agonising from Madame Camille. I left the office, leaving the two of them to discuss business, the transaction that was me, and I went home to Oliver.

'I'm getting married.' I tell Elizabeth, as she's preparing to go in for her own shift.

'To who?' she asks, whipping her head around, red rouge on one of her lips.

'Mr Tubular.'

She throws her head back and laughs, opening her mouth all wide, 'Fair play, my love,' she says. 'I always said he had a thing for you.'

As she leaves to go out the door she sticks her head back around and makes a great big honking noise. I laugh too, then grow quiet, there by myself with the baby nestled in my arm.

I feel happier than I've felt in a long time.

I'm escaping.

And all I had to do was trade my body from many men to just one.

* * *

His house is bigger than I expected. It has a white front door and an ivy creeper curling round the front of it. I didn't think he'd be the type of man to grow plants, but the small garden at the front is filled with small shrubs and flowering petunias.

Inside, there's a smell of smoky coal. I can't wait to get out a scouring brush and scrub the whole place down, cleaning it for my baby, cleansing it for me. If this is to be my home, I want it to at least smell clean. Even if I still feel soiled.

The kitchen is a fair size with a black stove and an open fireplace. Above it, drying socks hang limply across a strung-up length of twine.

He tells me he cleaned up for me, but all around I see clutter, pans that could be put away, tin boxes and newspapers, bits of string and paper here and there. He's washed the floor but a thin film sticks to it, as though the mop was greasy.

'I thought we could have this,' he says. He stands at the table and points to a bottle of red wine with two glasses beside it. He's pushed aside a pile of newspapers to clear the space for it. A small handful of petunias sit in a drinking glass.

'Thank you,' I say.

This is our wedding celebration. That morning I had walked from the kip-house, hugging Elizabeth goodbye, and carried my meagre belongings and my son, to meet Tubular. He'd taken my bag with great pomp and ruffled Oliver's head.

He hopped from one foot to the other while he greeted me, like a schoolboy about to set off on an excursion. 'Can you believe we're getting married today, I couldn't sleep last night thinking about it!'

I had not slept either, although it wasn't excitement keeping me awake. Oliver had been burning up and I feared that he would catch a fever that I would not be able to treat. His health was my constant worry in the cold and draughty board house. I hoped now, with moving to Mr Tubular's, that he would at least keep warm at night.

We walked to his house, which was a well-built semi-detached property, inherited from his parents. They were both dead he told me, his mother only dying last year. He had one brother, who lived in Scotland. He was as alone as I was.

He held the baby, making a big fuss and being over the top in his chatter with him, while I went to his bedroom to leave my bag and put on the dress he'd laid out for me. He'd picked it up in a charity shop, telling me it wouldn't have been right to get married in any of the clothes I'd worn as a working girl.

I lifted the brown, speckled dress he'd left on the eider-down and examined the collar and cuffs. Under it, lay a black negligee, stockings, and a garter with a frill around the edges.

The sight of them made my stomach curl - it was clear he was setting out our arrangement from the start. I was used to seeing underwear in the kip-houses, the girls prancing round in half nothings like a uniform, but I'd hoped to escape it in my home, where Oliver was sleeping.

Sighing, I dropped the clothes I was wearing and dressed in what he had laid out for me. The stockings felt too big and loose around my thighs.

When I came downstairs, I was surprised to see a

woman sitting there. She smiled at me and stood to say hello.

'This is Mary,' said Tubular. 'She'll look after young Oliver for us.'

I'd presumed we'd be bringing him with us to the wedding and it pained me to hand him over to a stranger, in this smelly house and turn my back and walk away.

But I did. I could feel the resentment building in me already as Tubular took my hand in his on our walk to the register office.

'That dress looks lovely on your figure,' he said and he leaned into me as we walked, almost inhaling me.

It was warm outside and there were plenty of parasols about, stemming the rays of the sun. It was Tuesday and I was struck by the thought that my mother had married Mr McKenna on a Tuesday, another marriage of convenience, one which I never thought I would find myself in. I remembered how I once told my mother over tea that I would never get married. How foolish the young are, with no knowledge of life.

'Mary's a decent neighbour,' he told me as we walked. 'Never had children of her own. She'll be delighted to take care of little Oliver whenever we need.'

I didn't like him using the word 'we'. Oliver was mine, only mine. I didn't like that Tubular was considering pawning him off whenever he wanted, just like that. I would have liked him at the register office, today.

But I said nothing. I couldn't offend him, not yet. I had to find my way, work out how to behave with this man. I knew nearly every curve of his body and yet very little of his mind, of his ways, of his thinking.

There were three other couples getting married that day. We watched two go in ahead of us, their families and friends with them, the brides with flower arrangements in their hair and pretty bouquets in their hands. I should have snatched a bunch of flowers from Tubular's garden - I should have made an effort to look the part.

I felt plain, pale, the brown dress swimming on my figure. I'd never have chosen it to wear myself, it was something a much older woman would wear. There were bare patches under the arms and fraying around the cuffs. I couldn't help but think Tubular had borrowed it from his dead mother's wardrobe and the charity shop was just a lie.

We stood alone, no friends to welcome us, no family to bear witness. The registrar brought two council workers in while he read our vows in a monotone voice and they signed the register that legally declared us married.

There'd been no clapping, no ceremony, not even a kiss to seal the union, just the words and a nodding of our head, then the signing of the paperwork that meant we were now man and wife.

Marriage had never been something I'd thought about. Not when I was younger and Nora was chattering on about who she might marry and what her children would look like. I had always presumed it wasn't in my future, that marrying was for the weaker woman, a woman who couldn't make it on her own.

If I ever had imagined my wedding, it looked nothing like this. I closed my eyes for a moment as we left the council buildings and told myself I had done the right thing, by myself, by baby Oliver.

'What would you say to a wedding breakfast?' asked Tubular as he clutched my hand.

'That would be lovely.'

'Fish n' chips?'

I look at him to see if he's joking. I've had fish and chips before and sometimes, when I was coming home late from the kip-house and the whiskey was in my stomach, I'd stop and get a newspaper full of battered fish.

It was a treat, but not a wedding treat.

He looks ever so pleased with himself as he pulls my hand and takes me along a number of streets until we reach a row of cafes and small bistros. At the end is a fish and chip shop, with a small diner to the side. There are shiny emerald tiles on the outside and wooden slats as decoration on the inside.

We sit down and a burly waitress comes to take our order. I'm reading the small printed menu when I hear Tubular ordering two fish and chips, without asking me what I want.

I say nothing and sit back and tell myself to smile. This is married life now. I have to get used to it.

I watch him eat the chips. He uses his hands, not even picking up the fork - the grease coats his fingers and settles in his nails. He makes a slurping sound as he eats the battered fish, as though he's sucking the flesh from the batter, his tongue dashing outside his mouth to catch the remnants that fall.

I am married to a man and this is the first time I've ever seen him eat.

When we're finished, he pays the waitress and leaves a meagre tip under his plate. He puts his hand on the small of my back as we walk back home.

When we get inside, an acrid smell of burnt fat hits my nose in the hall. He points to the wine and tells me to sit at the table.

'We should go fetch Oliver,' I say. 'He'll need feeding.'

'Don't you worry,' he says, as he twists a corkscrew into the wine.

I watch him manoeuvre the cork out; it makes a light pop as he eases it from the bottle.

He pours two generous glasses and hands me one happily. We clink our glasses and he looks at me and smiles.

'To my wife,' he says and I look at his teeth which are yellowed from smoking.

'To my husband,' I say cordially, raising my glass.

I take a sip, then another and put the glass on the table. I'm anxious to see Oliver, to check that he's not making strange with Mary.

'Now,' says Tubular, I notice his eyebrows narrowing

and that he's looking below my face, to my breasts, which are full of milk. 'I think it's time we officially consummated the marriage, what do you think?'

The last thing I want to do is to go to bed with Tubular. It's half four in the afternoon and I can hear birds twittering outside.

He walks around the table and stands in front of me, reaching down to unbutton my dress. I don't move as he reaches the middle buttons and with a jerk, pulls down the shoulder. I feel the air on my skin and his touch on the strap of the negligee.

'You got my wedding present?' he asks and smiles, looking to my eyes and then back to the strap.

'Yes,' I say. 'Thank you,' and force a half smile to my face.

'Good,' he says. 'You make a lovely wife, Molly Thomas. You were born to it.'

I look over his shoulder at his socks hanging on the twine, as he kisses the skin around the strap, licking and darting with his tongue.

It will be over soon, I tell myself. Then I can bring Oliver home and start our new life, with our new family.

Chapter Twenty-Two

MOLLY

I often think about the night I murdered Flann Montgomery. I think about how he didn't expect it. How he never saw it coming. How I'd surprised him. How he never would have thought a girl like me would have the strength like that. Not that I knew I had a strength like that either. It seems I had a power hidden in my hands and a violence, lurking.

Never once did he appear in my dreams or the part of my consciousness where I found things wouldn't leave. The part that crept in just before I went to sleep at night. The part that was there like a lion in the room, when my eyes opened in the darkness to Tubular's breathing beside me.

No, I never thought about Montgomery in the dead of night when the shadows fell across the room. I only thought about him when I was awake. When my mind was clear. When I was fully conscious.

When I thought about that day, I thought how pathetic I must have looked. Lying there in Mr McKenna's shed, crying, the pain and stinging flowing from my pelvis to my legs, head still on the bench, letting the tears flow, sobbing, in shock at what had been done to me, in fear that he might come back and have a go at me again.

So, I'd pulled up my clothes, turned around and grabbed a little gardening fork that was lying on the bench. I held it out in front of me; a girl with a tiny pronged sword, listening for him to come back. But he was gone.

When I came out of the shed, snivelling and breathing fast, I opened the back door and looked in the kitchen. There was no sign of him, but I went straight to the drawer and pulled out the middling kitchen knife, the sharp one we peeled potatoes and cut the fat off the stewing meat with. I dropped the gardening fork on the counter and I held the knife out in front of me.

Quietly I opened the kitchen door and went up the stairs, waiting for him to jump out on the landing or something, but I knew by the silence in the house that I was on my own, that he was gone. In my bedroom, I took off my underwear, blood had seeped through. I ran a facecloth under the stream of water I poured from the jug stood in the enamel bowl and bathed myself with it, feeling the water against the stinging, willing the pain to be soothed by the cold, damp cloth. A sticky liquid ran down the inside of my thigh, something I'd never felt before, something so disgusting it made my stomach heave.

I dressed and picked up my spare dress, hairbrush, and undergarments, and I went to the boys' room to fetch the small travel case. On top of the clothes I placed the knife, tucking its small, brown handle into the folds of the clothes in the case.

Then I took a look around the boys' room and imagined them in their beds tonight and thought of how they might be missing me, looking for me, knowing I wasn't there, and wondering when I would come back. I didn't know when I would see them again. I walked carefully down the stairs and out the front door, slamming it good and hard, thinking how I wouldn't be rubbing it down for dust tomorrow.

Trinity Street was busy, the regatta stragglers now milling around, heading into their local for more drink. I kept my head down, not wanting anyone to see me. I was glad that the roads had people on them and I blended in; just another girl coming from town. Not to be looked at. Or noticed.

It was sore to walk, my legs aching and my insides hurting, but with each step I took, I felt a little more relief that I was getting away from him. That I was walking away. That I was escaping.

At the top of the hill, the crowds had petered out and the cottages were quiet. I felt the warmth of the sun on my neck but I kept going, through the sweat, through the small patch of damp blood I could feel soaking into me below.

On the Slane Road I had to rest, to sit down and take some breaths, I was dizzy and the pain was so bad I thought I might faint. I knew Mr McKenna would have gone back down to the regatta, making some excuse about having met someone very important. No one would put him and me together, or realise he'd had time to get back up to the house. He'd taken a chance, coming back like that. He didn't know I would be there for sure. He'd be sitting with my family now, smiling, an arm around my mother, satisfied with himself.

I closed my eyes in the dropping sun, breathing in and out and reassuring myself over and over. If I could just make it to the river, to Curley Hole to sit and think, it would be quiet there and I could rest.

Tell me what I should do, I don't know what to do, Daddy.

I made it to the river. It sparkled between the tiny gaps in the blackthorn hedges, glistening through the brambles like ice in the sun. I began to feel calmer as I walked beside it, something about the soft flow of the water, the fresher air, the feeling that I was going home.

When I got to Curley Hole, I went further than I normally would, past the path I would usually turn down, all the way to a deserted patch, half covered by the branches of a low hanging Alder tree. I put my case on the ground and I sat. Before I knew it, I was crying again.

This time I let myself cry. With no one to hear me other than the birds, I let it all come out. I couldn't go back there and live with him. I couldn't tell my mother and see her homeless again, not with the boys and her new dress and her new, fancier life. I was on my own. *And maybe*, I thought, *maybe it's all my own fault.*

I thought back on different things Mr McKenna had said to me. The way he looked at me, lingering sometimes. That night when he'd come home drunk in the kitchen. Had his idea formed then, that he was going to have me? What if I'd never had that sherry?

My eyes were bulging with the crying. I could taste salt on my lips. And all the while, the river flowed in front of me, louder here and rushing, nature continuing on, not giving a damn about what was going on at any part of its banks.

A wave of exhaustion swept through me. It came on suddenly, as though every drop of energy had been sucked from my body. I lay back on the grass, moving the case up behind my head, turning over like how I slept at home, curled up, my legs and arms tucked in. I closed my eyes and soon the sounds of the water were coming in and out of my ears and I was asleep.

I don't think I dreamt. I don't remember anything. The only thing I knew was that there was someone there, and I woke up, all crumpled, listening to the noise of the water, the smell of the grass and soil in my nose.

I looked up, my hands still clasped as though in prayer and it took me a few moments to recognise him. To bring him into focus. To see his dark hair and his moustache - he was bending down close, asking me if I was alright.

I sat up, rubbing my neck and nodding.

'I didn't know anyone else knew about this place,' he said. He was smiling, a nice smile, even though his eye teeth jutted out a bit.

'It's nice here,' I say quietly.

'Yes, I find it … relaxing.'

I didn't know whether to stand up or sit down. He sat down right beside me, close to my legs. Henry Brabazon, at this secret place, at the river I loved.

'Are you alright?' he asked me again. 'It's not often I find a sleeping girl with a suitcase under this tree.'

'I'm fine,' I say. 'I just fancied a walk.'

'Oh,' he says. I hoped he wouldn't pursue about the suitcase. What could I say, that I was delivering something, perhaps? It wasn't too far-fetched.

'Did you enjoy today?' he asks.

'Yes,' I said. It wasn't a lie. I did enjoy it right up until ... 'I did. It was a lovely day.' I wanted to tell him that I admired his team and their speed and how everyone had cheered them on. He had changed from his white sports clothes now. He was in dark slacks and a shirt, a cravat folded around his neck.

'This might seem exceptionally rude,' he says. 'But I have to be honest and tell you I am not quite sure of your first name. I know you're Miss Thomas. What is your first name?'

'Molly,' I say.

'Ah,' he says. 'It was playing on my mind.'

I wondered why such a thing would play on his mind. Why he would care what my name was or anything about me?

'Do you miss here?' he says, looking at my knees, which were tucked under my dress, making a triangle with the ground.

'Yes,' I say. 'I miss the river. I miss the fresh air. It can feel very cooped up in town.'

'I'm the same,' he says. 'I find cities stifling. When I'm home I walk as much as I can. In fact, I come here very often. It seems we both have a hiding place.' He was joking, but I couldn't laugh. We were not equal.

'Funny thing is,' he says, looking to me now, 'I'm waiting on a letter. About London. And I'll be frightfully disappointed if it doesn't come.'

And there it was. The word London. A word that dived right into my ear and nestled in the centre of my thinking.

We sat there in silence, listening to the water, me thinking how strange it was that I'd seen him twice in one day. But it felt different here. Here, he was alone, away from all the rich folk and their fine clothing and their delicately cut white bread sandwiches.

'I want you to know, Miss Thomas, that I do feel dreadfully sorry about what happened to your family.'

I didn't reply, but nodded my head.

'I think it is a shame. And I really am sorry for your loss, for your father. From what I've heard he was a good man.'

I hadn't heard anyone speak about my father in so long. It was always Mr McKenna this, Mr McKenna that, it was like Daddy's memory had been forgotten. And, of course, there were tears in my eyes again. I stared straight ahead, trying to blink them away, not wanting him to look at me and see me crying.

But he did. I could feel his eyes on me.

I turned my head and I looked at him.

'Mr Brabazon,' I say. 'I don't blame you. But your father could have stopped things. And your agent, Montgomery …' The word is like ash in my mouth again. Saying his name out loud bubbled bile in my stomach.

'This was his doing. I blame him for my father's death.'

He's looking at me, his forehead creased, his eyes thoughtful.

'I think there may be a way,' he says. 'A legal way. Of getting the land back.'

I don't know anything about legal ways. I only know that my father was in court and at meetings and had board after board look at the case and still they decided to send an eviction party to our house, twice, with their horses and their men and their batons and their white paper, fluttering on the front door.

'It's too late,' I say. Because it is. Daddy is gone. And Mam has made her choices.

'Thank you for trying, Mr Brabazon. I think you are a good man,' I say. I stand up, rub down my dress and lift up my case.

'Are you going somewhere?' he asks, eyeing up the case.

'I'm catching the train at Slane,' I tell him. 'I'm going to stay with my aunt in Dublin.'

'Oh, well, it was lovely speaking to you again. And if your mother does wish to pursue the issue, tell her to please write to me at Brabazon House. I wasn't involved in the previous court cases, but I feel if I was, this time round there would be a different outcome.'

A different outcome.

I smiled at him and dipped my head under the alder branches, setting out on the river path towards Slane.

'Goodbye, Molly,' he says and I turn back and give him a wave.

As I walk away I realise that he called me Molly and not Miss Thomas.

I turn left, making my way across the small bridge, on my way to Dowth, not going straight, like he would have expected to Slane. I peer back to make sure he can't see me.

I make sure that no one sees me, walking up that road, stepping into the ditch and going behind the hedgerows. My boots are muddy as I hide and walk, hide and walk.

When I arrive at Montgomery's farm, hunkering down in a blackberry bush, not six feet from his yard, a new feeling has entered my body. It's a powerful feeling, the one like I had the night that Daddy died, as if I'm soaring like the Holy Spirit.

The power stays with me while I watch. Children are playing in the yard, kicking up dust and throwing pebbles at each other and then their father, Montgomery's son, comes out and calls them and they leave, through the gate, following him like a string of little ducks.

A woman with a bonnet comes in and out of the yard, fetching things, carrying a bucket, throwing corn out for the chickens in a big arching skitter.

Then I see him, his big stomach and his bald head shining in the dying sun. Now all I had to do was wait for the sun to fall behind the hill, for him to come out and check on the horses and do his last visit to the yard.

I'd moved beside the stable, silent behind a tipped-up cart.

He didn't hear me or see me, not until I was right up in front of him, his eyes just catching a look of me long enough to know that it was me and long enough to know what I was going to do to him.

As I reached up with the brown handled knife I'd taken from Mr McKenna's kitchen and pressed it into his throat and pulled it from side to side, tearing at his windpipe, his gullet, I thought how the power was still with me, the power that gave me the strength to keep the knife in, to expose his throat and watch black blood flowing from the inside.

I watched the fight in his eyes, felt his hands grip my neck, the power letting me hold the knife there and keep it there long enough, inside the man who had taken everything from us. I could never come back home because of this man. I could never live with my mam or with the boys now, because of what happened. Mr McKenna had made sure of that. But Montgomery had put us there in the first place.

And when he fell forward and I pulled the knife back, the power was still with me and calmly, I picked up my case and walked out of the yard. When I was down the road a bit, I stopped behind a ditch and wiped the knife on the grass. I held it in my hand till I got to the river, and flung it, hard, watching it spin, jagged, right into the centre and land with a small splash and then slowly sink, the currents taking it away.

It was only when I was further down the road, walking on my way to Slane, still hiding in the hedgerows, that the power left me and I realised what a great thing I'd done.

I thought how Daddy would be ashamed, how Mam would be shocked, how the boys wouldn't understand. I thought that if I was caught, I would be taken to the prison, and surely to the gallows, where I would swing. I thought about Henry Brabazon, how he had seen me in the area, just before the murder, how he had spoken to me and could place me, if the police spoke to him at all.

But it was done now.

I learned that no one would suspect a young woman, with her neat hair in a summer bonnet, marching along with her suitcase in her hand. I found that I could walk right by the police and their horses and the alarm and panic as it was whispered through the village that there had been a killing that night. *There were criminals on the loose, a gang by the sounds of it.*

I also learned that no one would suspect a young woman who took her case and herself on to a steamer ship between Dublin and Liverpool and that all she needed to start again, were the coins in her bosom and her honest, hard-working face.

I thought of Flann and the knife and the power more and more lately. The thoughts came to my mind as I sat in Tubular's kitchen peeling potatoes, watching the muddy curls drop into a basin, feeling the knife slice through the starch.

Were you more likely to kill if you'd killed once before?

Would I find the power again, the one I'd found on that day, from the rage, with all the strength?

Could I do to Tubular what I'd done to Flann Montgomery?

But I didn't think I could. I couldn't do what I'd done in that yard, not again, here in London.

I wouldn't get away with it this time. I knew I wouldn't.

Chapter Twenty-Three

HENRY

Henry walked past Arthur, whose mouth had dropped open forming a round O. 'Don't follow me,' he said. Outside, he walked past the people who had gathered, chatting at the church gates and past the carriages that were parked along the roadway. He saw the Brabazon House carriage pass through the road gate and pictured the staff inside chattering happily, not noticing their master walking right by it, out of the church grounds and on to the road.

When he reached the woods, he broke into a run and ran all the way back to the stable yard, where he saddled his chestnut mare and climbed on her back, kicking her flanks until she was in a gallop, all the way down the driveway and out of the estate. He rode her past the river, through muddy fields, whipping her hind and shouting at her, hah, hah.

It was as though the horse could sense his distress and she drove her legs, the fastest, he felt, she had ever carried him. When he reached Dowth, he tied her by her foaming mouth at a Hawthorn tree and he climbed to the top of the mound, standing and surveying the lands around him. The lands he was going to lose. The lands he had been unable to save in the memory of his father. All because he could not face this marriage and the lie that it would have been.

But there was only one feeling now, one over-arching sense, where the nausea had been. And that was relief. The weight had been lifted. And he felt as though he could breathe again.

* * *

He had tried to go through with it. He had watched her and imagined very nice things about Charity Eustace. Her skin was soft. He had touched it when she'd placed her arm on his, pale like her lips. Thin lips. With a spattering of black hairs gathered in the corners. She had bright blue eyes. But they were wrinkled, lines that didn't disappear after she'd stopped laughing.

She'd been laughing in his company a lot. She took delight in his interest, touching him at every moment. He felt her eyes bore into him if he moved around a room. Her letters were incessant, scent poured on to the paper, her love declared over and over. He always wrote back that he loved her too.

Because it seemed like the right thing to do. He wanted to make her happy.

He visited her home in Carlow, making the long trek on invitation, taking in the manicured grounds of the sprawling estate her father had built.

Brabazon House was small in comparison. Charity's father owned so much land that he had a team of agents to assist him. It struck Henry that there would have been many suitors for Charity, her inheritance was so great. Yet she had taken a shine to him.

He had been treated to vast feasts during his stay in Carlow, dinners that lasted for hours, with guests arranged around him from both sides of Charity's family. They all warmed to him, telling him what a fine match he was for her, how happy she'd been lately, what a radiant bride she would make.

He smiled and told everyone how much he was looking forward to marrying her.

But it was all a lie.

Her father had taken him on a walk one morning, sensing perhaps that his intentions were not all to do with love.

'Do you know how many proposals she has turned down?' he asked.

'No,' said Henry, feeling himself squirm a little.

'I've lost count. She only wanted you, she was waiting for you.'

'How flattering.'

'Indeed,' said her father. He had a thick white moustache and a voice far more powerful than his short stature belied. 'And, Master Brabazon - I hope that you will make her happy.'

It was a warning. He knew her father could sense that he was not in love with Charity, not in a lustful way. Not in the way she held him in such high esteem.

With the wedding date now set, he started opening the invoices brought to him daily at breakfast by Mrs Johansson. He had been avoiding them, unable to tear open the envelopes to reveal more bills and carefully scribed details of the latest interest charges.

Now that he was to marry Charity, he felt the problem had been somewhat solved and whenever he felt a creeping feeling of dread about his upcoming marriage, he went and rifled through the paperwork in his study, reminding himself of why he was doing what he was doing.

Their wedding was set, a lavish affair to take place in the small Church of Ireland chapel where his parents had married, just off the estate. The wedding breakfast was to be held at the house, with a large marquee set up on the lawn. Charity's father insisted on a lengthy invitation list; she was his only daughter and she *would* marry in style. It was his idea to set up a marquee in the grounds estate but it was Charity's idea to install a mountain of glasses from which champagne would flow. Every time they met, Charity had added another layer of extravagance.

Henry began to despair. The money for the wedding would pay a large proportion of the debt he was battling. But he held his lip, instead, holding it out to her as she gently nibbled on it, thinking it was a lustful thing to do. He noticed her bottom teeth were crowded. Was there any part of her he could like?

*　*　*

His mood worsened as the wedding approached. When Arthur came home from Oxford on his break, he was shocked at Henry's appearance.

'I say Henry,' he said when they'd taken off their coats and sat down to a supper of fish and potatoes. 'Are you alright? You've lost weight. You're practically wasting away.'

Henry was surprised and looked down at his legs in the chair. He realised he was at the innermost notch on his belt. He'd been pulling it tighter and tighter and he'd need to take a penknife to the leather soon.

'Still engaged, then?' said Arthur, a soft smile on his face.

'Yes.'

'And, how is she?'

'She's fine. Absolutely fine. Counting down till the wedding day. There's a dressmaker in London sewing thousands of sequins on her dress as we speak. And now she's talking about chocolate rabbits because it'll be near Easter.'

'Chocolate rabbits?' said Arthur.

He watched Henry attempt a smile but could see that he was struggling.

'Dear brother, you know I love you. You know I support you. But there has to be another way. Are you seriously going to commit yourself to her for the rest of your life?'

It was refreshing to have Arthur home. To feel his presence and see his blond curls back at the table. He was the only one who would talk to Henry straight.

'I'm not losing the house,' said Henry. 'I will learn to love her. And I'm sure, if there are children, she will be occupied with that and I will be left alone, to pursue what I want to pursue.'

'Which is what?' asked Arthur. 'Country walks?'

'Peace and quiet,' said Henry. 'And the Brabazon legacy. Which, by the way, I hear you're doing a good job of thrashing.'

'Me?' said Arthur, pretending to look embarrassed. 'Nonsense. I'm just having fun. But by golly, Henry. The talent in Oxford. What a city. You never warned me!'

Henry had made peace with his brother's philandering. He had given up envying his freedom. He'd realised, with his father gone and Arthur away at university how alone he felt. He longed for his brother's upbeat company even if it did come with mischief and drinking.

'Henry,' said Arthur, looking serious. 'You don't have to go through with it if you don't want to. There are other ways.'

'This is the way,' said Henry, as he stabbed a potato with his fork and looked at the upturned mushroom on his plate. Black gills. Velvety soft. It reminded him of the dark hairs on Charity Eustace's lip.

* * *

The wedding came too fast. He'd spent the weeks in the lead-up to the day embroiled in negotiations on the final sale of Seymour's stock portfolio. He had held on to what he thought might offer some glimmer of an income, but the rest, he sold to an agent in London who bought up bad debt. With the small amount of cash he made, he repaired a large hole that had opened up in the roof of Brabazon, where the slates had been torn from the roof during a winter storm some years back. It wasn't until the water started seeping down into the first floor that they realised the damage had been done. He worried that one of the roof beams had rotted all the way through. But there was no money to replace that. He asked the carpenters to do the best they could with what they had.

The winter had eaten up the very last of his savings. Keeping the farm going, the staff, the stable yard, and the house itself were more than he could keep up with. It pained him to see Charity and her father organise and order expensive and frivolous niceties for the wedding. But he had to let her do it. It was her occasion after all.

On the morning of the wedding, Mrs Johansson shook him gently, leaning over him, whispering. 'Wake up, today's the day.'

He turned over and looked at the ceiling. The day was here. In a few hours, he would be married and Charity Eustace would become the new lady of the house.

He realised there hadn't been a lady of the house in twenty years. And as he pictured her sitting in the great room, organising staff rotas, and going over menus and accounts, the thought struck him that she was not a suitable successor to his mother. She had none of her charm, none of her graciousness. He thought about what his mother would think of her, and he knew, in his heart, what she would have felt.

The whole thing was wrong.

Mrs Johansson had brought breakfast on a tray, two yellow daffodils leaning in a slim glass, to brighten up his morning. He ate his food slowly, not wanting to get out of bed, thinking of the day ahead of him, of the ceremony, of the reception, of the well-wishers and faces and the people that would be filling the house for the evening. He wished that it were all over. That it was tomorrow and it was done with; *the deed* too.

He had been thinking about Amelia. Could he plant Amelia's face where Charity's was as he rutted in the martial bed? Or was that a sin?

Arthur came to shave him and help him get dressed. His hand shook a little and Henry angrily grabbed the stem of the razor and said he'd do it himself. 'I don't trust you with your hangover shakes,' he said and Arthur looked a little hurt.

'Sorry old boy,' he said. 'I think I'm just a bit nervous. It's a big day today.'

Henry said nothing but shaved his cheeks and neck himself.

'I know,' said Henry. 'It is a big day.'

When he came down the stairs, dressed in his wedding suit and sash, Mrs Johansson stopped mid-rush and looked at him.

'Oh Henry,' she said, tears welling in her eyes. 'You do look handsome.'

'Thank you,' he said. But he wished that he were looking handsome for someone else. That he could make Mrs Johansson proud, in a different way.

When it was time to go to the church, Henry watched his brother and his uncle Edward climb into the belly of the first carriage and a wave of nausea swept through the walls of his stomach. It had been there all morning, but now it had taken hold. He gripped the handle of the door and brought in his breath to try and steady himself.

'Are you alright?' asked Arthur, as Henry sat down opposite him with a sigh. 'You've gone white as a sheet.'

'Fine,' said Henry. But he didn't feel fine. He felt positively sick. The staff had lined up to wave him off, those who were going to the church were dressed in their Sunday clothes.

He looked at them lined up, waving, white frills on their sleeves fluttering in the breeze. What it would to be a domestic, free to marry for love.

Arthur and his uncle made conversation during the short journey to the church. Henry was silent, his sickness worsening, an aching thought warming his head.

'You do look rather nervous,' said Arthur, reaching over to touch Henry on the arm. His touch shocked him, a bolt, reaching through the deep thoughts he was absorbed in. 'We're here.'

Henry looked out the window. Guests had already gathered outside, most heading into the church, the early April weather too chilly to stand around in. He thought how ridiculous it was to have agreed to a marquee on the lawn.

'Alright?' asked Arthur again.

'Yes,' said Henry and he let Arthur open the door and help him down out of the carriage.

Spotting him, some cousins from his mother's side came over to clasp his hand and wish him well. He smiled, shook their hands, and worried that the nausea was going to spill over and he was actually going to retch, right here at the entrance to the church.

'Henry,' said Arthur, as they made their way inside.

Henry didn't answer, but strode on through the open door. Inside it took a few moments for his eyes to adjust to the dark. People had gathered near the top of the church, relations from both his mother and father's side, a landlord he recognised from another part of Meath. He walked up on to the altar, bowed and made for the sacristy off to the side, where he thought the vicar would be. The vicar wasn't there and Henry stood, leaning against a mahogany sideboard, holding his forehead with his hands.

'Henry,' said Arthur again, having followed him. 'Are you quite alright?'

Henry mumbled into his hands, shaking his head.

'What?' said Arthur. 'What did you say?'

'I can't do it,' said Henry, now audibly repeating what he'd been muttering into his palms. 'I can't do it.'

'Henry,' said Arthur. 'Everyone's here now. The bride will be here soon. You can't *not* do it.'

He put his hand on his arm, rubbing it a little.

'It's probably just the nerves,' he said. 'You'll be fine when you get out there.'

'No,' said Henry, shaking his head. 'I can't do it. Tell her I'm sorry. Tell them all I'm sorry.'

Henry told Arthur not to follow him and made his way

out of the church, past the guests who were still arriving for the service, and crossed on to the road. He took off into the woods that led to the back of Brabazon, his legs almost break-ing into a trot.

He was minutes away from catching a glimpse of the bride, who was arriving in an open top carriage, clasping her father's arm, the largest smile she had ever worn, shadowed under her veil.

Chapter Twenty-Four

MOLLY

Being a wife to a man you do not love is, in some ways, the same as being a whore. You must still make love. You must dress up and smile. You must be coquettish. You must pay off your debt. Most nights. Unless he's tired. Or angry enough not to touch you.

The table in his kitchen is varnished white, and I scrub it with a rough brush to keep the stains and the cup rings from seeping deep into the wood. There's a spot, where I sit, where the varnish has been wearing away. I dig at it with my butter knife and hope that he notices, that it causes a row and that he might stay angry for a while. I get a false sense of joy by provoking him.

I think I am going mad.

I wonder if we could have been happy, Tubular and I. If we could have grown a life together, formed a bond, organised a true marriage between us. We had exactly seven weeks where we got to try. Before it happened. Before everything changed forever.

I enjoyed being out of the kip-house, my days filled with domestic tasks, happy that I was now a married woman and my baby had a respectable mother and father and a nice home, on a busy back street in London. No one knew of my past. Except Tubular, of course.

My sores healed; I began to heal. And I knew that with time, I would lock the memories of the past few months in a box in my head, the key tossed away, buried in a recess that I would have to work hard to find.

I wondered what future Tubular and I would have. I thought about writing home, to tell them where I was, that I was now a married woman with a baby. But I was terrified of what had happened on the day I left, of what people knew or suspected. Brabazon had come looking for me that night in the kip-house, I was sure of it. If I wrote, telling of my whereabouts, then one day, a knock could come on the door, I would be found, and that would be that.

'Don't you want to write?' Tubular asked me occasionally, after I mentioned my mam or Michael or Patrick. I'd shake my head and say, no, I was never going home again. But it made me sad.

I concentrated on the sense of achievement I felt when I looked around me; at Oliver sitting in the little wooden chair, at the pots bubbling on the stove, at the floor that shone because I'd gotten down on my knees and scrubbed it.

I liked being in the house in the daytime, just me and Oliver. I pretended it was our own house, just the two of us, a little sanctuary from the cruel world I knew to be outside.

I'd made some changes to make the place more homely. Tubular had a mean streak and he didn't give me money for things I'd have liked for myself. I had to convince him that buying items were his idea, I had to hint and get him to make the suggestion that we buy a new blanket, or a vase or a toy for the baby.

When he brought something home, he'd be as proud as punch and I told him he was ever so lovely and sometimes I added that I was glad he brought me there.

I played the game. I had to.

In the evenings, I'd sometimes drop over to Mary's to avoid having to sit and talk to Tubular for an hour or two.

She was a lovely woman and she never asked any questions about where I was before this or why I brought a baby into my marriage. For all she knew, Tubular could have been the father anyway, and I was happy to let her think that. He would be his father growing up and I was starting to accept that now. That he would have an influence. I needed to learn to love him like a wife should. It was only fair on Oliver.

Mary and I drank tea, and the odd time she poured me a drop of port or wine or whatever bottle she had handy from the drinks cabinet. Mary's husband drank a lot and she said he never noticed what she took. I wished Tubular drank a bit more so that he might go off out to the pub and leave me in peace. But he wasn't a drinker - his favourite thing to do was to come to me and take me to bed - he couldn't get enough of my body, of my mouth, of my breasts.

I would sigh after I'd had a few mouthfuls of drink and think about buying my own bottle of alcohol for the house. I missed the whiskey tumblers I used to down at the kip-house. When I first came to Tubular's, I craved them something terrible, but after a while I got used to going without and as the days passed I noticed that my head was clearer and the dull headache I always had was gone.

Still, after those visits to Mary's, after I'd had a little sup, it always made things a bit easier and I slept better, forgetful, a bit stupored.

After the novelty of the first few weeks of marriage had worn off, when he'd gotten used to me being there every evening, with his dinner on the table, his laundry airing, and his kitchen scrubbed nice and clean, I noticed that his demeanour changed a bit, that it was almost like Oliver and I were getting in his way.

He would sigh if I stepped in front of him, or grumble when Oliver whined. One time he marched out of the kitchen and slammed the door because of *that child's incessant squalling.*

I wrapped my arms around Oliver and tried to get him to shush, but he was teething and his cheeks were on fire and

I'd run out of the teething syrup I normally pressed to his gums.

Tubular started passing comment and making remarks, lowly mutterings under his breath about me being a good for nothin' or useless and then one day, he said it, the word I'd been waiting for, the thing that he knew he could always hold against me.

'What did you say?' I said and I spun around to face him from where I was standing.

'You heard me,' he said and his face was in a grimace, ugly, snarled.

The word echoed through the air, the sound of it repeating over and over in my head.

Whore.

I walked up to him and went to slap his face but he grabbed my arm and with the back of his hand he struck me across the face.

My hands flew to the stinging, to the red mark he'd lain across my jaw.

'Get away from me,' he said.

We glared at each other and I felt tears threatening the back of my eyes. I willed them away with the anger I felt.

'Don't call me that,' I said and I realised how pathetic I sounded, that I should have been more forceful. He would call me whatever he wanted whether I liked it or not.

'Well, that's what you are,' he said and he sat down at the table and picked up his fork to start eating the fry-up I'd prepared.

I saw his eyes glance over at Oliver who was lying in his pram, his little chubby legs kicking.

'And he's the son of a whore,' he said, stabbing a sausage and putting it in his mouth.

I ran to Oliver and scooped him into my arms. I slammed the kitchen door and made my way to the bedroom where I dived under the covers with him and willed the tears to stay in my eyes.

I had nowhere to go and no one to come looking for me. I'd made the decision to marry Tubular and this is what came with it.

I wondered which was worse; being at the kip-house servicing many men or living in this house of tension, servicing just one? At least I had friends in the kip-house, Elizabeth, alcohol. Even Madame Camille, supplying things and marking them up on my slate.

I longed for my mother, for my family, for my country. I longed to be at home, in the fields, on top of Dowth mound surveying the landscape with nothing but my thoughts for company.

But there was no point wishing for that now. The most I could wish for was for Tubular to treat me with more kindness. I would have to find a way to convince him to do that. I'll go to the shops tomorrow, I thought. I'll get some groceries in and make him corned beef for his tea, his favourite.

That was my idea.

A treat for the husband who was turning against me, who was starting to make my life uncomfortable, making it miserable altogether some days.

I had no idea that there was worse to come.

That really, I didn't know misery at all.

And that was how I lost Oliver.

Chapter Twenty-Five

HENRY

He sold the lands on the edge of the estate. They fetched a meagre price, bought up by a consortium of other locals and some tenants keen to own their own land. He couldn't shake the vision, as he signed the paperwork granting ownership to these new land owners, of his father's face, angry and sore. He had done what his father had always managed to avoid; he'd lost land that had been in their family for generations.

But, he reasoned to himself; it was his father who had gotten him into this mess. Even if it was Henry who would go down in the Brabazon chronicles as having lost the estate. If it came to that.

He broke it to Arthur that summer that there would be no going back to Oxford. 'You can't be serious,' his brother replied, a tumbler in his hand.

It was late July and the birds were singing in the trees outside. Henry had the water turned off in the fountain. The garden was starting to look unkempt. He'd let all but one of the ground staff go.

'I know it's not what you want to hear, but it's the situation we're in. I can talk to the year head and see if they can delay for a year, maybe two.'

Henry turned away from the window now to look at his brother. He had told Arthur the news while looking out on to the gardens, thinking how they reflected the state they were in. A mess.

'And then if things are better you can go back, pick up where you left off.' Henry felt his shoulders shrug a little.

'My God, you are actually serious. You're *serious?*' His brother was furious, red spots burning on his cheeks as he lunged forward towards Henry.

'You get to go to Oxford for four bloody years and I'm whipped back home after mere months? No Henry. No, it's not happening. I'm not sacrificing my education to make you feel better.'

'Me ... feel better?' said Henry, his skin bristling at the confrontation with his brother. Their relationship had suffered lately. They argued regularly, Henry berating Arthur for spending money. He had made his way through their drinks cellar and started ordering malts and whiskeys in from all over the world. Henry told him they couldn't afford an alcoholic in the family. They'd already suffered a gambler.

'How does this make me feel better?' said Henry. 'Selling our land. Cutting back on every damn spend in the house. Telling you, now, that you can't afford to go back to Oxford?'

'There is money to send me to Oxford. You just want to hold on to it. To keep it for yourself, for here.'

'Arthur,' said Henry, feeling exasperated. 'If there's no here, there's no Oxford. Haven't you been listening to what I've been telling you? We are broke. Broke! Father left us penniless. We'll be lucky if we do hang on to the house.'

'You could have fixed this, Henry,' said Arthur and he threw his head back with the tumbler to his face.

'Oh really?' said Henry, annoyed that he was bringing Charity into this. 'It was up to me to change the whole path of my life to suit your lifestyle.'

'Well it looks like I've to change the whole path of mine to suit yours.'

He knew Arthur was biting out of frustration. His youthful charm got him everywhere, but with it came a stubbornness, a childishness, when he didn't get his own way.

Arthur turned and went back to the drinks cabinet. He removed the stopper from a decanter to pour more alcohol into the glass he was holding.

'Is that really going to help?' said Henry.

'No,' said Arthur. 'It won't. Nothing will help. But at least it dulls the pain. This,' he said pointing at the glass, 'makes me forget about this.' He waved his hand to take in the room and Henry.

'I know you miss Father,' said Henry, trying the direct approach. 'I do too. But we need to sacrifice now to build a future. To see that we hand Brabazon on, like it was handed to us. I know that delaying your studies is an awful thing to ask of you, but I wouldn't be asking it if it wasn't necessary. I don't want to see you torn away from doing something you want to do. But I'm serious, the fees, at this moment are not affordable. OK, we could probably push on for a few more months, but then what? Sell up completely?'

Arthur was quiet, unmoving, staring into the liquid in his glass. 'It's not fair,' he said, not looking up.

'I know,' said Henry. 'I know it's not fair. But I promise, if we can right ourselves, you can head back to Oxford as soon as it's feasible. I want you to have an education, Arthur, I want that.'

'I'm glad you want that,' said Arthur. 'And it's wonderful that you get to decide that.'

'Arthur,' said Henry, pleading now.

Arthur swallowed the drink in one gulp and walked from the room, slamming the door behind him. Henry wondered if he was going to the stables. They had reduced their horses in the stable yard and the hands there too. Henry had considered selling Arthur's stallion, a horse that would fetch a good price at stud. But he might try and hold on to him for a bit longer. Especially with the mood Arthur was in.

* * *

The fallout from the wedding that never happened had been costly to Henry, both financially and in terms of his reputation. When Lord Eustace watched his daughter break down in her white wedding dress, he vowed vengeance on Henry and had attacked him in a blazing row that afternoon at the house. They should have been sheltering in the marquee or seated, nibbling on hors d'oeuvre, waiting for the wedding banquet to be brought out. Instead, Henry was in the great room, his back to the fireplace, Lord Eustace reaching up to him, trying to contain himself.

'You, absolute bastard!' he shouted. 'How dare you? Who do you think you are? Embarrassing us like this. Doing this to my daughter. Don't you know who we are? Don't you know that this means?'

Henry let him rant and rave, accepting the spittle that landed on his cheeks.

'Your father would never have allowed this. This would not have happened under Seymour's watch. You absolute bollocks.'

Henry looked at him, trying to give him the respect he deserved, accepting the admonishments being rained upon him. Everything the man said was right. He did deserve to be roared at. To be spat at. To be told what a useless human being he was.

'I'm sorry,' he said quietly. 'I really am truly sorry.'

'Are you going to tell her that?' asked Lord Eustace. 'Are you going to tell her why? Why you've taken it upon yourself to go and ruin her future, her reputation. Her life!'

'I will tell her if you think that's what's best,' said Henry. 'Lord Eustace, you might not see it now, but I feel this is for the best. In the long run.'

His ex-future father-in-law was pacing the floor, treading marks all over the large Persian rug. He stopped at Henry's words and came over, right up to his face again.

'All I see is a broken-hearted girl and a thousand bloody

pounds wasted on an absolute blaggard like you. You will pay every penny of this back. Every penny. And I've a good mind to sue. For breach of contract.'

Henry let him express his anger. He stood, the fire burning the back of his legs, his hands clasped together behind him. This was part of it, listening to this man go on, shouting. But soon, Lord Eustace would have to leave and then it would be over. He would sell the land to pay the debt. The debt that the Lord and his daughter had insisted on. He would pay for painted eggs, hand-moulded chocolates, and paper decorations to place around the trees and stairwell. He would pay for the hire of the glassware and candles and coloured decorative sashes for the great room.

Henry would pay all of it back and then he could move on with the rest of his life. A life, at least, that would be free.

He could deal with being broke. He could deal with putting the lands up for sale to pay for an extravagant party that he never wanted in the first place.

It was a loveless marriage that he couldn't face. And when Lord Eustace left the great room, banging the door so hard that the windows rattled, Henry felt his shoulders relax and his neck soothe. What he had done today had been difficult, possibly the most difficult thing he had ever done in his life. But it was the right thing. And he felt so much better for it.

Chapter Twenty-Six

GLADYS

It felt good to finally have him in her arms. To know, that this was the one. That this was the one who would be staying, who she would be keeping, who would call her Mama.

He had surprised her, sitting there all by himself in the pram. Looking at her. Willing her to lift him up and take him away. She felt it in his face as he approached, that he knew perhaps. That he was looking into the face of his mother.

She had looked around her, making sure no one was watching. There was a woman on the other side of the street carrying a basket heading in the other direction.

Calmly, she picked him up, bringing his blanket with him and wrapping it around his legs and back. She walked as she did it, proud that she had lifted him so deftly, without being seen. She had learned from the last time. No dramatics. No people around watching.

He was a sturdy little thing, his chubby legs pushing against her. She couldn't wait to get him home and have a good look at him. She walked quickly to the end of the street, left then right again. A horse-drawn omnibus was pulling in at a stop just ahead. She ran, the baby's head bobbing as she leapt on to the step and sat down on her seat, breathing heavily. She had done it. She was leaving on a bus, her and her new son.

After a few streets, she changed buses. She didn't want

to take any chances that she could be seen, or questioned. Her heart was fluttering, an excitement rising in her chest, that today, she would finally bring their son home to Albert. What a shock he would get when he came in from work. How proud of her he would be.

As they neared the house, the baby started to grizzle, rubbing his head back and forth on her chest. She realised he was looking to be fed and she hurried, thinking ahead to all the things she would have to do this afternoon to get him and the nursery all ready for Albert when he came home.

She put the key in the door and struggled to open it while holding the baby and her shopping basket. This was her new life now. She would have to get used to a number of things, adjust to being a mother.

She boiled the kettle and added the formula milk to the glass bottle, savouring the task, having read the instructions hundreds of times. She scalded the yellow, rubber nipple and tested the temperature on her wrist. When it was ready, she laid the baby back and put the teat to his mouth. He turned his head away, twisting it back and forth. He didn't want to take it.

Tilting him forward, she tried again and then rubbed his back. The baby started to cry, loudly. After some minutes, she put the bottle down and lifted him against her shoulder. He calmed for a minute, then began to cry again, loud ear-piercing cries of hunger. She shook him, gently, hoping to calm him, but she felt a fluster rise run through her, sweating as she patted him on the back and told him to shush. She pushed the teat into his mouth again, but he refused each time, the gesture only making him more upset and angry.

She wondered if this had been a good idea after all, taking an older baby. Maybe she should have stuck with finding a newborn, one who would never know another mother, one who would take a bottle from her, who wouldn't make such a fuss.

Feeling like she was starting to lose control, Gladys decided to take the child upstairs. She carried him up to the nursery and laid him in the cot that had been made over and over for months. She had changed the sheets again only yesterday - perhaps sensing that her new baby was on its way.

She left the room and went into her bedroom, taking deep breaths to calm herself. She needed to do something to soothe him, to pacify him. She couldn't have Albert arriving home to a squalling infant. This wasn't how she planned it, how she had played out the scene in her head for months, years now. Pacing the floor, she thought of all the things that might satisfy the child. She wondered if she put him to her own breast, would he suckle and stop crying?

Then she thought of it. She only needed to quieten him for a little while. Until she could get the dinner made, the house ready, and herself made up for Albert coming home. She fetched the bottle from a small cupboard in her bedroom where she kept her perfumes and make-up - a good cough syrup she had bought at a pharmacy last year that had sent her to sleep within minutes. It had been so strong that she had not used it again for the light-headedness it had caused.

The baby was roaring, his cheeks and forehead red, his mouth opening and closing as he cried. What a state he'd worked himself into - she hoped she hadn't picked an unsettled baby. She took the lid off the bottle and stood over the child, carefully tipping the neck of it to his mouth. She poured a little on to his pink tongue and watched him gurgle a bit as it hit the back of his throat.

He shook his head again as though trying to clear his airways and then cried even louder, a sad and angry cry. She put her hand on his forehead to let him know she was there. After a few minutes, his loud cries became quieter and he put his fist to his mouth, sucking on it. She went downstairs to retrieve his bottle and again tried the large teat in his mouth, squeezing a bit so that the milk went on to his tongue. He took it, suckling on it carefully, before relaxing and getting the flow going on the glass bottle. After he had taken some, he grew tired, his lids drooping and his eyes heavy.

She took the bottle away and rubbed his forehead again, watching him fall into a twitchy sleep. She wrapped the red blanket around his torso and left the room, a smile on her face.

She changed into a dress with a nipped waist that she could wear now that she had removed all the padding. She powdered her face and added a light rouge, rubbing it into her cheeks and lips.

When Albert came in the door, he found his wife seated at the table, a plate of beef and potatoes steaming and a single candle burning bright in front of her.

'What's this?' he said, pointing at the candle and her dress.

'I have a surprise for you,' she said. 'But eat up first.'

They ate their meal together, Albert asking her to let him in on her secret and tell him what was going on. He asked her about Robert and whether she had been to see him that day. 'Not today,' she said, smirking, the delicious joy of what she was about to reveal almost too much to bear.

When he had finished his plate and she'd cleared it away she said she would take him upstairs and he was to follow her and not make a sound. Thinking his wife might be leading him to the bedroom, Albert slapped his wife playfully on her bottom and Gladys swiped him away and told him to be quiet.

On the landing, she made for the nursery door, opening it and stepping inside, up to the cot, where in the dark, the baby slept, deeply and peacefully.

She turned to see her husband silhouetted in the doorway.

'Albert,' she said, a smile on her face, her eyes shining in the gloom. 'Meet Robert. Your son. I got him home from the hospital today.'

Chapter Twenty-Seven

MOLLY

In the quiet of the mornings, after Tubular had gone to work, I would lie there and stare at a patch in the ceiling. When we had first married I had gotten up before him, set the fires, put on the water, stirred his porridge, boiled him an egg. I had been pleasant. Grateful for the bigger house I was in now. Happy that there was food on the table and for the coins he counted out for me to go to the grocers and the cobblers and wherever else I needed to go. He had given me a bit of freedom. And I appreciated that.

Now, I had no interest. I let him get up alone and make his breakfast like he'd done before I was here. The first few weeks or so he left me to it, but after he grew tired of that, he started to poke me in the shoulder and tell me I had to get up and get on with things. I ignored him, turning over on my side, not listening.

One morning, when I again refused to get up and see to him like a good wife, he came round my side of the bed and pulled me by the arms, forcing me from the bed. I let him drag me to the floor and then I got up and climbed right back in. He rained two blows down on my back, smack - smack, and I didn't flinch. I had no feelings left at all. All my pain was on the inside. My skin meant nothing. *Hit me again*, I thought. *Go on, do it.*

But he didn't. Instead he left, and I heard him banging pots around the stove and then the front door slam. He let me slip into my depression, where I said nothing, did nothing and stared. At Oliver's things. At his cot. At his pram.

I'd never felt so low.

When I did get up, usually around lunch time, I'd make weak tea and drink it to give me sustenance. Then I'd pull on my coat and I'd start my search. I always started at the shop where he was taken. I'd wait outside, watching everyone walking by, looking for his little fair head. If no one came I'd walk away and start where I had left off yesterday. I was combing the streets one by one. Knocking on every door, visiting every shop.

'My baby was stolen, I'm looking for him, fair hair, little boy. Have you seen him?' As the months passed I tried to imagine the changes in him. Would he be walking now? What words would he be babbling? Was he even alive?

The London Standard had covered the story twice. My hands shook as I read it, a small section at the bottom right hand corner page. *'Young Irish Mother Appeals for Missing Baby'.* It had my name. Molly Cotton. His name, Oliver Cotton. But I wanted to scratch out the words and put in what I felt were our proper names. It was Molly Thomas and Oliver Thomas. How would anyone recognise him with the wrong name?

And then it was a year. The 'Missing Baby' posters had fluttered off the lamp posts, the news articles where I was quoted, long gone from the papers.

On the bad days, I let it slip into my head that I would never see him again. That my search was futile, that I was wasting my time. But there was nothing else I could do. I could only walk the streets of London to find him. And that's what I did.

At first Tubular had helped me search, listened to me talk, met with the police with me, pinned posters all over the streets where we lived. But as the months turned over, he stopped wanting to talk about Oliver and instead said he wanted us to have a child of our own. But I didn't want another child.

I wanted Oliver.

I stopped letting him touch me at night. I refused his advances, turned away from him, hit back if he tried to hold me or force me. My depression was so great and my grief so bottomless, I lived through a fog of sorrow. He couldn't help, no one could help. And when I smelled smoke on him one night and scent, I saw it on his face, the shine, the post-coital glow, I knew that he had returned to the kip-house.

Eventually we formed a routine. An existence where we tolerated each other's presence. I returned to cooking some basic meals, fetching groceries, even cleaning. But we didn't talk and when he came in from work, I went to bed and when I heard him leave again for the pub or the kip-house or wherever he went these days, I would get back up and pour myself the whiskey I kept under the sink and drink it until I'd enough that would let me sleep for a few hours.

A thought was forming in my mind. It came mostly at night, in between the long stretches of fitful sleeping and uneasy dreams. I was going to write a letter home. I was going to tell them what happened.

It took me a full week to write the letter. I started it and stopped it, crumbling the paper and throwing it right into the fire. I had to get the words in the correct order. I had to say sorry for running away but not mention Mr McKenna at all. I wished I could get the letter to just my mother or my brothers, without his horrible hands ever touching it.

Dear Mam, Michael and Patrick, I wrote. I left out Mr McKenna, I didn't care at all. He could know that I was not writing to him, because I wasn't anyways.

I wanted to write to let you know that I am safe. I am sorry for not writing before. I hope you are all keeping well. I am in London.

I wrote carefully, forming the letters with a scratchy pen I'd found in Tubular's dresser. The ink turned brown as soon as it hit the paper. It reminded me of dried blood.

I am sure you are wondering why I went away and didn't write. I suppose I wanted an adventure. My news is that I am now married and my name is Molly Cotton. He is a good man.

My pen lingered on the paper, the ink marking the page in a range of little dots as I pressed it down, then took it back up again, leaning over it, thinking. Did I want to tell them about Oliver? I could say he was Tubular's, they would never know any different.

We had a baby and I named him Oliver.

I looked at the words for a minute, then kept writing.

Unfortunately, something terrible happened and someone took my baby. He is still missing. I search for him every day. They took him out of the pram one day on the street.

I read over those lines again, not believing the truth behind them. It was like something I read in a book. Or in my father's newspaper. It wasn't something that would ever happen to me. A tear slid right down my nose and plopped on to the page. It mixed with the brown ink and turned it a reddish colour. I blotted it quickly. It had taken me so long to get to this point in the letter. I didn't want to have to start again.

I am beside myself. I pray every day, but so far there has been no sight of him. The police have not been much help. I think they have all but given up hope.

I am very upset and I am lonely here in London. I miss you and I pray for you and I hope that you are in good health and Patrick is doing his studies. You have my address now, so I hope that you will write.

All my love,
Molly.

I folded the letter carefully, holding it to my lips while I contemplated sending it or not. This gave away my hiding place, it let them know where I was. It opened the door to Mr McKenna coming back into my life.

I put the letter on top of the mantlepiece in front of the

clock and I got back into bed and pulled the covers over my head. Writing the words down had done something to me. I realised that this terrible thing had really happened to me. It wasn't a dream. It wasn't something that was going to change if I slept long enough or starved myself or cried enough.

I'd been in denial, still in shock that my boy was gone.

I got back out of bed and took the letter and opened up the lid of the stove and popped it in, watching it melt and burn and disintegrate in the orange glow.

Then I took out my pen and paper and wrote a very short note saying that I was in London and I hoped everyone was well and I was sorry for running away. I tucked it into the manilla envelope and in the morning, after Tubular had left, I put my coat on and walked to the post office. When I pushed the letter through the red pillar box, I noticed something. I had not looked for Oliver on the whole walk there. The letter and thinking about my family had distracted me.

I wanted to go home.

Part Four

Chapter Twenty-Eight

MOLLY

Drogheda, Ireland, 1900

He had grown into a fine young man. I couldn't help but admire his strong jaw and kind mouth, the way he came out from behind the counter and stood close, listening to what the customer had to say. I'd listen from the back office, hearing how he held the conversation, placing the materials into the gentlemen's hands, never seeming like he was selling, but instead, helping.

I learned a lot from him, my brother Michael. Mr McKenna had shown him everything, he knew the shop inside out. I couldn't run the business without him. We'd customers come in from all parts, gentlemen pulling their fine carriages up outside. As our trade grew, our stock increased and we started importing materials and ready-made designs from London and Paris.

I smiled sometimes when I thought of it. Michael and I had turned the shop into something Mr McKenna had always wanted it to be. But he would never see it. The changes we'd made. The boost in profits. The gentlemen we attracted.

The idea had come to me not long after Mam had died. I peered at the pages the solicitor handed me, the bonds, the statements from the bank. Mr McKenna had saved it all and it had gone to Mam and now it had come to me. If we sold the shop we'd have enough money, my brothers and I, to buy a small cottage each. But I thought about it, as I pined for Mam, as I realised that all three of us were alone in the world now. The gentlemen in London - the fashion, the money they spent each season on their turnout. I'd seen it with my own eyes. If we invested in the shop, if we followed some of that style - we would attract in the money. And then we would have a solid income and could look to buy whatever we wanted, in the future, when we were older. Michael agreed, outright, he'd spent all his time in the shop anyway and was coming to the end of his apprenticeship. Patrick wanted to leave, to see the world, he said. So I gave him some of his share and he joined the merchant navy and we'd gotten two postcards from him since. I wondered if he'd ever return to us, to come back and see what we were building.

At the same time as we gutted the shop, tearing up the old, dusty floorboards and pulling off the peeling wallpaper, as we installed dark panelling along the wall and ordered new rails to hang the ready-made clothes we were buying in, we took the grey house apart, laying down a carpet runner on the stairs, pasting coloured wallpaper on the walls and adding new rugs to cover cold, bare floorboards. I placed ornate blue and white vases in the sitting room and made cushions and dried flower arrangements for every nook and cranny of the house. It was an homage to my mother, a reminder of what we had lost and what she could have had.

I ordered the men to demolish Mr McKenna's shed, to hit it with sledgehammers till it came crashing down in chunks and I watched them knock every bit of it, the dust flying at my eyes, arms folded, a hot feeling going through me. When they were finished, I went over to the rubble and pulled a splintered piece of wood from it and put it in my apron pocket as a reminder, a memento. The shed had been the start of Oliver and the end of the girl I'd been.

'A fine tweed, Mr Rankin.'

I can hear Michael admiring the man in his tweed, even though it's summer and we've had a week of sweltering heat. Mr Rankin mutters something back, something inaudible. The shop bell rings and I hold my text book, one of the journals I ordered in as part of my study, waiting to see if I'll be needed. Boyce, our tailor, is across town on an errand. He likes to get out once a day, marching like a soldier, coming back red-cheeked and refreshed. Sometimes the customers don't like to be served, or even greeted, by a woman, and they'll wait, tapping their foot until Michael or Boyce are free.

I listen to the greeting, seeing if I need to go out. Michael is talking with the new customer and I listen to the replies. Curt. Clipped. An upper-class gentleman.

The door is ajar and I lean back to peer out, past the rails, searching for Michael and the new customer. And there, standing in his top hat, in his leather gloves, in his riding gear, is Henry Brabazon. I feel the breath leave my body.

Without thinking, I pull the door wide and walk out, straight up to him, cool as I can.

'Miss Thomas?' he says, watching me approach. Still in his memory then, he hasn't forgotten my name. I never used the name Cotton in Ireland. I was Molly Thomas ever since the day I landed back.

'How nice to see you,' I say. And it was nice to see him. He seemed more handsome since the last time I had watched him, from behind a corner in one of the busiest kip-houses in London.

'Now I remember,' he says.

I can hear my heartbeat in my ears.

'You told me before, your step-father is the proprietor.' He waves his hand at the shop, a sweeping movement, his black leather glove fanning the air.

'He was,' I say. 'He's deceased. I am the proprietor now.'

'Oh,' he says. 'I'm sorry for your loss.'

There's no loss, I wanted to say.

'Thank you. What can I assist you with today?'

I could see Michael watching - realising who the customer is.

'I need a new hat.'

I bring him over to our hat display, an array of trilbys and top hats and some straw hats ready for the upcoming regatta.

'I've not seen you for some time,' he says.

'I went to London,' I say and I wait to see if he flinches. *Could* he have seen me that day and he's hiding what he knows about me? Is he here because he's heard I am back – is he here … to arrest me?

I realise that this is the moment I have waiting for. If he makes any sort of acknowledgment that he'd come to London to find me - if he indicates with a glance or a smirk or a hand on my arm that he alone knows I had the motive, the power and presence to do what was done to Flann Montgomery on that day, then my time is up.

'I was in London, too,' he says. He looks pleasant. Smiling even. 'Did you like it?'

'Yes,' I answer. 'I did. But I needed to come home. When my mother got sick.'

His demeanour has not changed.

I don't think he suspects me.

'Oh' he says. 'I'm sorry. Did she …'

And he leaves it hanging. I'm the proprietor of the shop.

'Yes,' I say. 'Three years ago.'

'I'm sorry,' he says again. The second time in only a minute.

All that time I'd run away, wondering if I could ever come home again. And when I had come home, nothing had been said and now I was here, with Henry Brabazon, the only man who had seen me in the area that day, that fateful murderous day and he is smiling at me.

'Do you see anything you like?' I say and point to the hat display.

'Straw,' he says. 'I'm attending the regatta. Haven't been in a few years. I had one, but Lord knows where it went. Probably tucked at the back of an auctioned wardrobe!'

The auction had taken place the year before. I had read the notice in the paper and read it out to Michael in a tone of smug happiness.

'Got what they deserved, those Brabazons,' he had answered.

But now that Henry Brabazon stood in front of me, with his genuine eyes, clasping at his riding gloves, I felt almost sorry for him.

'The auction must have been hard,' I say.

'These are the times we live in,' he smiles.

'Did Dowth sell?' I ask. I wasn't sure what had become of our homestead or the lands around it, or my beautiful, ancient mound. I'd barely been back to it since I'd come home to Ireland - I was too scared to head out in that direction, mostly in fear of meeting Henry. But now he was here in my shop. We had met anyway.

'That's still ours,' he said. 'I couldn't let it go.'

I realise that I'm in a very different position since the last time we spoke. Then, I had been only a girl, the daughter of a tenant, a farm hand turned shop girl who knew nothing of the ways of the world. Now, I could address him with confidence. I was a business woman. Standing in my very own shop.

I lift a hat from the display we had taken in for the regatta. Boyce had found a toy boat from somewhere and had set it up on a table, with the hats around it. Brabazon sits the hat on his head and looks in the free-standing mirror.

'A bit big,' he says and hands it back to me for another.

'Are you looking forward to the regatta?' I ask.

'Yes,' he says. 'As I said, I haven't been for a few years. There's been too much to attend to.'

'We're sponsoring a race,' I say. We had kept up Mr McKenna's tradition as a good showcase for the shop.

'I'm hoping to sponsor too,' he says. 'Maybe next year.'

'Aren't you taking part in the rowing?' I ask. I remember him in his white shirt, neck open, a tan across his face and tri-angled under his chin.

'Oh no, I haven't been training. There's been too much happening. Maybe next year too,' he says.

The third hat he tries, slides down on his head and sits in just the right place. He cocks his face at me and smiles.

'What do you think?' he says.

'A perfect fit,' I say. 'Is there anything else you need?'

He looks about the shop, his eyes darting among the jackets and waistcoats on display.

'Do you know, I think I could do with a new dicky bow?'

I take him to the counter where a display of cravats and dicky bows are facing up under a glass top. I take the boxes out and watch as he goes through them, taking his time, lingering.

He stops his finger on a purple bow, one with ridged satin.

'This one,' he says. 'I'll take this.'

'The colour of royalty,' I say.

'Yes,' he says. 'King of these parts.'

I go to laugh but when I look up, he's looking straight at me, no smile on his face at all.

'Miss Thomas, would you care to join me at the regatta? I'd be delighted if you would accompany me?'

I see Michael out of the corner of my eye, his head lifting and turning over his shoulder to look.

I look back down at the dicky bows, tracing the pretty material with my eyes.

'Yes,' I say, joining his gaze again, 'Yes, I would like that.'

He smiles, showing a set of white teeth and I notice that there is a crease on one side of his face under his beard.

'Marvellous,' he says. 'Write down your address and I'll send my carriage for you. We're having a soiree later that evening, it will be fun.'

I would be hobnobbing with gentry. I would be moving with people with fine tastes and fine accents and graces and ladies who had never worked a day in their whole lives.

Let them, I thought.

I have money now, too.

I hoped Daddy wouldn't mind.

Chapter Twenty-Nine

HENRY

Henry couldn't keep the smile from breaking across his lips. He felt a warmth move through his body. There was something about that girl. Something that made his mind sing.

It was a different feeling he noted, to the lust he had held for Amelia Aherne. With Miss Thomas, there was something more - a grounding, an understanding almost. It was tangible, he thought. He watched the trees go sailing by outside the window of his carriage. They looked fresh, in full bloom, growing fat with the leaves uncurling in the June sun. He hadn't noticed how summer had arrived all around him.

Rolling up the avenue to Brabazon House, Henry felt a stab of pride as he looked at the fountain, which was now clean, filled, and spraying a neat fan arc in the centre. The gardens had been groomed too, not back to their former glory, but they'd been shorn neatly and the gravel at the front of the house had been raked over.

He was getting back on top of things. Tonight was the first time they were having guests stay and be entertained since the massive land sale that had reduced their land stock to almost nothing. The decision to hold the auction to sell off possessions in the house - furniture and paintings handed down through the generations - had brought Mrs Johansson to tears, but Henry stayed firm.

'Less to clean,' he said cheerily as men in brown coats staggered under the weight of a walnut armoire.

Arthur had left for Dublin, unable to stay and watch his home disappear in parts before his eyes. Henry had been relieved, the tension between them now something less he had to worry about. He knew that his brother was gambling, sometimes winning and living like a king for weeks, at other times flitting from one town house to another, drinking, living off the family name and reputation.

'Brother!'

Arthur got up off the low sofa where he was seated, unfurling an arm from around a beautiful, young woman with brown ringlets piled high on her head.

'You're back,' said Henry and they embraced. 'I wasn't sure if we'd see you at all.'

'Oh, we should have been here yesterday,' said Arthur. 'But last night, golly, Henry, the card game, couldn't leave, haven't even been to bed.'

Henry noticed the red rims around Arthur's eyes now. He was bloated in the face, but still, the same cheeky Arthur.

'And this is ...' said Henry, gesturing to the woman still seated.

'Oh, Miss Chatham. Henrietta.'

'Henrietta,' said Henry, reaching for the woman's hand and kissing it. 'A very beautiful name indeed. I would call you Henri for short but it might get confusing.'

She giggled and looked demure. Henry wondered how long she'd been tagging along with Arthur.

'The house is looking well,' said Arthur. His voice was genuine, Henry could hear the apologetic note in it. It had been almost a year since they'd seen each other.

'Yes,' said Henry. 'I think we may have turned a corner.'

'Well then, let's celebrate,' said Arthur, striding over to the drinks cabinet which had been fully stocked ahead of tonight's soiree. He set about pouring shorts into three glasses and muttering about ice.

Henry looked at Miss Chatham and noticed the curve of her lips and gentle chin. She was very pretty, exactly Arthur's type. He thought of Miss Thomas, how she had a strong chin, a definite mouth. And how she would be here, in this very room, this evening.

Arthur brought the drinks on a tray and offered a glass to Miss Chatham and then Henry.

'To Brabazon,' toasted Arthur. 'To misfortunes allayed. To my brother. And to love.'

He pointed his glass at Miss Chatham, who giggled and took a long sip from hers.

'To love,' said Henry, feeling the liquid warm the back of his throat and sink past his windpipe to his stomach.

He was so looking forward to this evening. The first time in a long time that he could remember looking forward to anything at all.

* * *

Who is she?
A shop girl?
Doesn't he look pleased with himself?

He knew they were being watched. He felt the eyes bore into his back, caught the glances as the ladies huddled and whispered behind gloved hands.

They were standing in the tea tent, sheltering from the summer showers being thrown down on the river and its banks, muting the regatta crowd as they ran for cover. She was wearing a modern dress, one that reminded him of London. It was less extravagant than the other ladies' attire; a smaller bustle, her shape almost revealed instead of being hidden under a large circle of skirt.

'Don't you wish you were out there?' she asked. 'On the water?'

She was staying by his side, smiling, holding conversation. She had a confidence about her that was far removed from the coquettish smirks and laughter he was used to. She had something to say for herself. He was fascinated by her.

'In part,' he said. 'But then if I was out there, I wouldn't be here enjoying your company, would I?'

She laughed and told him he was funny.

He laughed too. People always said Arthur was funny.

He offered her a small glass of white wine and she took it firmly in her hand and sipped it.

He glanced across at the two ladies who were staring at them, their hands arched in whispered conversation. Let them talk. He wanted to show Miss Thomas off to the whole world. Miss Chatham, Arthur's guest, was standing beside the whispering women looking lost. Arthur had appeared in the arena for a short while, and then disappeared quietly. Henry suspected he could be found propped up a in snug in a pub across the river. He beckoned to Henrietta, calling her over and she caught his glance and smiled gratefully.

'Have you been abandoned?' asked Henry, when Miss Chatham joined them, the two whispering ladies following in hot pursuit.

'It seems so,' she said, her soft eyelashes fluttering.

'This is Miss Thomas,' he said, introducing Molly to the approaching ladies who reached out their hands in greeting.

'And you're a proprietor?' asked the younger woman, blond curls carefully placed around her face. She'd bustled forward to take a closer look.

'Yes,' she said. 'A shop I inherited. But soon I'll be opening a women's drapery. You must stop by and see our stock.'

'Oh yes,' said the woman. 'I will. I must say, I do admire the dress you're wearing. It's very... fresh.'

'Isn't she a wonder?' Henry said to the women, who nodded and laughed. 'A business woman, no less.'

'And a former tenant.'

The other woman who spoke was beautiful, her eyes flashing, dangerously.

'Yes, it's true,' said Henry swiftly. 'A former tenant. Isn't it surprising how life can turn?'

Henry watched a colour rise high in Molly's cheeks.

'Mr Brabazon, you always had a taste for the unusual,' said the blond woman, laughing loudly.

'I believe she could turn a profit to anything she turns her hand to,' he answered. 'She is indeed most unusual.'

'Perhaps that's why Mr Brabazon has his eye on you,' said the woman with the flashing eyes. 'He's hoping you'll turn the estate's fortunes around too.'

They all tinkled laughter again.

'I have the utmost faith in her,' said Henry.

He turned to Molly and looked at her.

'Are you happy to leave for Brabazon soon?'

'Yes,' she said, raising her emptied glass and looking him square in the eye. 'But I think I may need another one of these first.'

* * *

She seemed a bit reticent about coming inside. She stood for a moment on the steps looking up at the giant doorway, studying the lintel.

'Are you all right?' he asked, stepping back to her.

Other guests were arriving, queuing behind her, waiting to go in.

'Yes,' she said, before moving forward into the hall and looking up at the ceiling. The roof was painted bright red with white, ornate plasterwork criss-crossed in woven detail. It rose into a dome, sending white light cascading through the hall. Henry was used to people drawing their eyes up as soon as they stepped inside Brabazon's doors.

'It's beautiful, isn't it?' he said.

'Yes. I never noticed it before.'

It dawned on him that this was the first time she'd been in the house since the night she'd been evicted from her own home, all those Christmases ago.

'It must be stirring up some painful memories,' he said, gently.

'I just can't believe I'm here now, as a guest,' she said.

He led her into the great room and got her a drink, introducing her to some huddled guests. They eyed her with suspicion at first, but as she listened to their conversations and joined in here and there, they soon accepted her, and as the drink flowed, her nerves disappeared and she began to enjoy herself.

A small group of musicians were set up in the corner and started up some dancing music.

Henry took Molly by the hand and asked if he could have his first dance with her.

'I'm not used to such formal dancing,' she said as she walked to the space in the middle of the room, where the couches had been pushed back to reveal a polished dancing space.

He pulled her close as they turned, helping to lead her in the steps, complimenting her when she got the moves right and laughing when she trod on his toes.

'You're a natural,' he said.

'You're a liar, Mr Brabazon!'

When the music ended, he was sorry to have to let go of her, to lead her back to the group and take his turns with the other ladies present.

On a break from the music, he asked her to come outside with him and he held her by the arm and led her down the front steps, past the gathered carriages and out on to the lawn.

The evening sun had just set and tiny midges buzzed around the lanterns. The rain had lifted and the air smelled full of greenery, of cut grass and, wet soil.

They walked slowly towards the fountain, drawn by the trickle of water and the glow of the floating candles.

'Are you enjoying yourself?' he asked.

'Yes,' she said. 'I must admit, it's not the scene I'm used to, but I'm enjoying it. They're accepting of me.'

'And why would they not be accepting of you?' he asked.

'Henry,' she said and looked at him, solemnly.

'It means nothing,' he said. 'I can't tell you how bored I usually am in this company. How these gatherings pain me so.'

He stepped forward and placed his arms around her, his palms settling flat on her back.

She looked up at him and moved forward too, their lips meeting in a kiss.

She immediately pulled back, recoiling, putting her arms up to protect herself.

'What's wrong?' he asked, startled at her reaction.

'Nothing,' she said and she looked at him, into his eyes, her mouth moving as if she wanted to say something.

'It's nothing,' she said again, before apologising and turning and breaking into a run past the fountain to the house.

He stayed at the fountain, before walking slowly back into the house, scanning the room for her.

Perhaps she felt no lust for him at all, had no feelings towards him, like he had her. Perhaps he was being too forward, too quick, and he needed to give her a bit of space, to get to know him, to form feelings for him. Or perhaps she felt awkward, holding him responsible for what happened to her family, for the interference that had cost her so much ...

He spotted her, standing at the back of the room, clutching a glass of white wine. She looked shaken, as though his kiss had shocked her, awoken something terrible inside her.

'I'm sorry,' he said quietly, gently touching her on the arm. 'That was too forward of me, not very gentlemanly.'

She was quiet for a moment, before she whispered, 'That's where you're wrong, Mr Brabazon. It was too gentlemanly. Too gentlemanly for me. It's not something I'm used to at all.'

He scratched his head, trying to work out what she meant, and watched while her mouth broke into the slightest of smiles.

There were so many layers to this woman, so much depth and things to know.

'Am I forgiven?' he asked.

'Am I?' she said.

They both laughed.

'I doubt you have many sins,' he said, looking warmly at her.

She looked down at her wine, peering at it for a moment, the smile leaving her lips.

'That's where you're wrong again, Mr Brabazon,' she said looking back at him with a sigh.

Chapter Thirty

GLADYS

Sometimes, when they travelled into the city on the bus, strangers would tell her he looked like her. She would smile and nod her head and say, 'Do you think so?' The boy would look up at her, his slightly hooded eyes hidden behind wisps of fair hair. She had started lightening her own hair with ammonia and alum, in an attempt to look more like him. The mixture burned her scalp, but she enjoyed the stranger's comments, so she kept bleaching it, month in, month out.

It was another of the changes the child brought. She'd tried to keep to most of her ways, but it was difficult with him being so messy and playful and disturbing with the wilful way he had. He'd learned a bit now, but still she had to go hard on him, to show him how to be a good boy.

Before he came to them, Gladys didn't have much company. Now that he was growing up there were a few neighbours who were friendlier to her, who stopped her at the doorstep to ask after him.

A child was a great conversation starter. People would smile and engage her, or stop to chat and ask how she was getting on. She was getting on wonderful, she'd say. He would look up at her, pale faced and dark rings under his eyes and she'd smile. She didn't tell them about the hard days. About when she had to hold him down and put his dinner in his mouth because he wouldn't finish it and eat it all up, and grow to be strong boy.

About how she had to make him kneel in ashes at the back door to teach him to wipe his boots before he came in.

About how some days, when he was very naughty, she had to lock him in the cupboard and put the chair up against it and leave him there till he stopped crying, which could sometimes take hours and then he might soil himself and have to go back in again.

The truth was motherhood was so very different to how she imagined it. Some days she wondered if it had all been worth it after all.

On occasion she thought about his real mother. She thought about how she would have felt when she came back to find the pram, empty. But when she read about her in the paper that she was only a young girl, her heart had hardened and she didn't let herself feel pity for her. That girl would go on to have more babies. Gladys never would.

She knew the boy loved Albert more than he loved her. She wondered if knowing that sometimes led to her being extra hard on him. That she had done so much, gone through all that time before they got him home, with the pretence and the pressure and the planning she'd had to do. Why did he run to his father then and wrap his arms about him and smile so much around him and not around her?

She would be glad when he went to school. Then she would have her mornings back to herself. Then she could make her luncheon and eat it in peace, no little fingers spilling crumbs and wiping butter on the table. She could walk and count the trees and the cracks in the stonework and not have to keep her eyes ahead, watching him. September couldn't come quick enough. When she would finally get a bit of the old Gladys Eccles back. Yes, she looked forward to that.

Chapter Thirty-One

MOLLY

The telegram had arrived five days after I had posted my letter home. The boy rapped on the window, startling me over my cup of weak tea. I was just about to go and get my coat, to walk to the shop and wait and then to start up near the park where I think I'd missed a street.

I took the telegram and my hands shook as I opened it. I thought it was about baby Oliver.

Mr McKenna passed. Mam is very ill. Please come home.

I sat at the table, the shock working itself through my body and into my head. Mr McKenna was gone. My mother was ill. What kind of illness could it be? I had never known her to be sick her whole life. She was a strong woman, the kind who, even when she had a cold, could suppress it and get on with her work.

I thought of them at home in the grey house, Patrick and Michael, still so young and afraid. I put my head in my hands. I could leave and go home for a visit and come back and continue the search. But how could I leave my brothers, who would be orphans if something happened to Mam? It had never crossed my mind that anything could happen to them at home while I was away. I only thought of myself and what was happening to me.

My thoughts crashed inside my head, smacking off each

other, causing an ache in my skull. If I left here, I was leaving behind my baby. I was saying goodbye to the hope I held that I would find him. Walking away from London was like walking away from Oliver himself, who I knew would be toddling and learning to speak, right about now.

I rubbed at my face, mashing my cheeks and my lips in my hand, scratching my scalp, yanking my hair at the roots. I wanted to scream, to cry, to shout out loud in this kitchen that had not had Oliver's laugh in it, for longer now than I had held him myself.

'I just want him back,' I said and I rocked a bit, back and forth, something I'd fallen into the habit of.

But there was nothing, no answer, no sign or noise or anything to indicate that anyone was listening.

Slowly I pulled back the chair. I got up and looked around this kitchen that was too big for just one man and one woman. I pictured Tubular's face when he came home, as he went through the house, calling me, looking for me.

But I would be gone. I'd have taken my small bag, I'd have walked to the station and I'd have changed at Euston to take a train to Liverpool. I would stay in a small guest house that night, one with damp sheets that smelled of smoke and sailors and brought me right back to my days in Madame Camille's kip-house. And as I boarded the steamer at Liverpool for Drogheda, taking me home, back to my family, back to my land, I would be crying hot, wet tears for the baby, my son, I was leaving behind.

I felt as though I would never see him again.

* * *

It took some time for Mam to pass. She had an illness that the doctor couldn't diagnose. He thought it might be a lung disease, because of the incessant coughing and the blood that she drew up. She had shrivelled in just a few weeks, my brothers said. It started with a cold that she couldn't shift, and eventually, she had taken to the bed.

I walked into the grey house, not knowing how they would take my arrival back home, what reception I could expect.

It was Michael who saw me first and he rose slowly from the table where he was seated, came forward and gave me a silent hug. We stood there, just holding each other, not saying anything. I told him I was sorry that I hadn't been here and I hoped he'd forgive me.

Mam's face beamed when she saw me. Her skin had a yellow tinge, even the whites of her eyes stained, the same colour when you pour iodine out and wipe it away.

'Molly,' she said and she lifted her head off the pillow. 'You came back.'

'Yes, Mam,' I said and I sat on the bed. I couldn't remember the last time I had hugged my mother.

She came forward and I knew she wanted to be held so I put my arms around her and I leaned against her. I could feel the poke of her spine and the flat hard shape of her shoulder blades.

'You're married now,' she said.

So, they had read her my letter.

'Yes,' I said. Could I tell her I wasn't going to go back? Would she understand?

'Is he a good man?' she asked.

I looked up at her and an image of Oliver flashed in front of me.

'Oh, Mam,' I said.

I had cried in London, big sobs, helping me to get some of the pain and push it out into the air. But they were nothing like the tears and heaves that came pouring out of me there on my mother's sick bed, her arm across my back, as I lay on top of her and cried.

Mam rubbed and soothed and said, 'There, there,' over and over.

It was all I'd wanted to hear these past few months. My

mother's voice. Her sympathy. Mam knew what it was like to be a mother, to imagine having one of us taken from her.

But I couldn't tell her. I couldn't tell her that about the baby, that it was McKenna's, I couldn't tell her what had really happened.

When the boys came in, Patrick and Michael together, they thought it was for Mam that I was crying. They went away and came back again when I had gotten it all out of me and had withdrawn to a hard-backed chair pulled close to Mam's bed.

I was there sometime before I remembered to ask, about McKenna, about how he died.

'A disease of the liver,' said Michael.

'He had a shockin' time,' said Patrick and he withered under the look Michael gave him for speaking about such things in front of Mam.

I was glad to hear it. But I had come to know, from my work in London, that disease of the liver could mean many things. Especially for men like McKenna. I hoped he hadn't given anything to my mother. Or to me.

* * *

Mam stopped breathing on a cold July day. It was as though the heat and the sun had gone away for that day. I was upset laying Mam in the ground, watching her leave us for good like that. Losing Daddy was bad. But now we had no parents at all.

The one thing I had been able to do for Mam was to have her buried beside Daddy. She had told me she'd wanted that before she died, but I would have done my best to have made it happen, even if she had not said so anyway. The thought of her lying there, beside McKenna, his bristly moustache poking out among his rotting bones, would have been too much to bear. The priest had made a song and dance about it, but he stopped his hand-wringing when I pulled out the envelope, thick with notes.

I saw Nora at the funeral. She had two babies now. She embraced me and said her kind words and then she and he husband were on their way out of the graveyard and back to their farmer's cottage.

It was the first time I'd been out at Dowth since I'd come back home. It was lush and green and filled with all the summer sounds so familiar to my ears. I felt I could breathe there.

I wondered if I should look to move back, to buy a horse and trap and rent a cottage of my own. But when we decided to keep on the shop and the grey house, I pushed my cottage dream to the back of my mind.

I could see the shop needed work as soon as I stepped back into it. Mam and Michael had done their best with it after McKenna died, but they had lost customers and it was easy to see why. I didn't know much about men's tailoring, so I poached a tailor from Tully's, a skilled, chatty man, named Boyce. He was full up on ambition and I told him he would have control over the orders and the displays and a good pay rise.

All those walks with Daddy in the fields, all the chattering about orders and stock and sales had rubbed off on me. Business picked up. Boyce brought his own customers with him. We were profitable again.

I told everyone that Tubular was a soldier. That he had been called overseas. That was why he couldn't make the journey home to meet Mam before she passed. That was why he couldn't make the funeral. That was why my family would never meet him.

When the time was right I would organise to have word sent that he had passed. Missing in action and presumed dead. I had said he was fighting near Africa. It would take time for word to get back. Then that would be dealt with and I could continue with my life.

No one questioned me being back in Ireland, without

my husband.

I never expected to see Tubular again.

So, it was a very big shock when I did.

* * *

I hadn't given up my search for Oliver. I dreamed of finding him and bringing him back to Ireland, free from McKenna, free from Tubular. I could raise him with Michael, teach him everything I knew, bring him up with an Irish accent and our ways, pretend he was the son of a friend, an orphan. I would make up any story to get hold of him and rear him here, with me.

I scoured the local London papers weekly, which I had on special order for delivery to the shop. If anyone asked I told them it was to keep up with the latest business news in Britain's capital. But really, it was to see if there was ever a story: *'Boy Found'* or *'Young Child Abandoned - Search for Mother'.*

I had gotten the names of all the orphanages and care homes I could find and had written letters. I wrote that I was searching for a baby who may have been mistakenly placed in their care. I described Oliver, how I thought he might look like now, I gave my address and told them I'd moved from the address they had on file, where Tubular lived. Sometimes I got a letter to say a child had been found that matched Oliver's description. But when I wrote back to say that I would arrange to come over, to see if it was him, a reply would be sent back. The child's mother had been found. There had been a mix up. It wasn't him.

It was very easy not to tell Henry about my missing baby. I had wanted to. I thought it would be the honest thing to do. But I couldn't run the risk that by revealing the truth he would end our courtship. It was best that he knew nothing, that I continued the search myself, through the papers and the post and, if Oliver did turn up one day, if he was tracked down to a home where he didn't belong, well, then I could travel there quietly and I would tell Henry then. I would make him understand.

* * *

I threw myself into work, enhancing the men's drapery with daring new stock. I got posters printed up for the front windows to let everyone know who passed about items we were expecting in, new prices, the latest fashions imported from Paris and London.

I set about looking for new premises, a boutique where I could open a women's drapery. It didn't take me long to secure a shop just off West Street, with a low rent and a decent space to allow large fitting rooms, tailoring, and enough rails to hang ready-made stock in.

Within a few weeks I was preparing to open, and in the hustle of setting up the shop, a man arrived to paint the lettering on the front of the shop.

'Will you write out the name?' he said, handing me a piece of paper and pencil. 'Exactly as you would like it, to make sure there are no errors.'

I'd been thinking about the name for a long time, and it had come to me in the haze of a half-dream one night. My dreams were always about the same thing. I relived being in that street in London over and over again, the empty pram, the nauseous panic, the dread - they repeated in a looped nightmare, waking me sometimes in the middle of the night or disturbing my thoughts before I drifted off to sleep.

I wrote it out for the painter and he looked at it closely and shrugged. Then he disappeared outside, pressed a ladder to the front window and climbed it with a small tin of paint in his hand.

Inside I set up ladies' hats and scarves on half mannequins I'd rescued from a sale in Dublin. I added some handmade bags I'd bought from a market, and two fur shrugs.

I'd visited a number of boutiques in the capital to get a

sense of what they were stocking, but also how they were presenting the items. I wanted to be fashion forward, ahead of the times. I intended to earn a reputation as the finest women's boutique in these parts, just the way we'd built McKenna's business up too.

The little bell rang and I turned to find Henry, standing, gloves in hand and a smile on his face.

'Am I your first customer?' he asked.

'I don't think I've anything in your size,' I said and laughed.

He looked around and whistled.

'This is looking fabulous. You must be very pleased, Miss Thomas. Ever so well done.'

'Thank you.'

I loved getting praise from Henry. It felt like true praise - he didn't hand out compliments unless he meant them.

'So, you're all set then, ready for the grand opening?'

'I think so,' I said. 'Still a bit to do, but we're nearly there.'

The bell tinkled again and the painter walked in, cleaning his hands with a rag.

'Would you like to come and see, Miss Thomas, before I finish up?'

Henry and I walked outside and stood back on the street to take a look at the sign.

The painter had used a curly calligraphy, gold on cream, the shape of the letters forming into swirls. It looked exactly like I wanted it to look - elegant, sophisticated and fashionable.

'What do you think?' asked the painter.

'I love it,' I said. 'It's perfect.'

We stared at the sign and then to the window of the shop and Henry drew me close to him.

'*Bonny Oliver's*?' he said. 'After your father?'

'Yes,' I said, smiling, blinking back tears that were threatening the back of my eyes. 'Sort of'.

Henry thought the tears were for the hard work I'd put in - the joy at seeing my shop come to life. But he had no idea. He would never know of the real meaning behind the sign or what it actually meant to me.

* * *

As I got to know him on our walks around the estate, through Townley Hall Woods and across the back fields, I came to understand that under the accent and the Oxford education, Henry Brabazon was a kindly, learned soul. He and I shared an interest in many things, from the nature and wildlife we saw around us, to the news stories and court cases we read about in the paper, to the social movement where women were gathering together and campaigning to seek the vote.

By Christmas we were spending all of our free time together and when I wasn't free, spending my hours across the two shops or travelling to the city for stock and business errands, he would accompany me.

He became my confidante. My everything.

Michael and I received an invitation for Christmas lunch at Brabazon House and we spent a wonderful afternoon feasting, drinking, and being merry. Arthur had appeared with his beau and it felt like a true family occasion, the unlikeliest of pairings perhaps, yet it felt right - happy, normal.

Henry had already extended an invite to us for the Brabazon race meet too, on St Stephen's Day, but I hadn't accepted yet. The day was too fraught with memories, with bad feelings over our eviction and the death of our father.

'We should go,' Michael said, as we sat in the carriage on the way back to the grey house. Henry had offered us rooms at the house, but I wanted to get back to our own walls. I was afraid of committing too much, of giving all of myself to Henry.

'What do you think Daddy would say?' I said, wondering out loud.

'Daddy isn't here.'

'I know that, but what he would have thought matters to me.'

'Daddy would have thought that you should do what is right for you. He would have said, "Henry Brabazon is mad about you and you would be foolish to interfere in what is coming to you."'

'What do you mean?' I said.

But he didn't answer.

We rode the rest of the journey in silence, Michael's words playing over in my mind. Henry Brabazon. Mad about me? I didn't know what to think.

When we got back to the grey house, I took out my writing paper and penned a note of acceptance for the races and meet ball. It would be perfectly acceptable to attend with Michael and I would enjoy the occasion, seeing the house at its finest with the grandest of folks and their fashions.

I just couldn't shake the feeling that I was betraying Daddy. That I was treading in the steps of Flann Montgomery, becoming a part of what he was - a set that my Daddy never liked.

Still, I would never turn out like him - greedy, ruthless - a coward.

The one thing nobody could call me was a coward.

* * *

On the morning of the races, Henry invited me out to the house early.

'I can't stand the fuss,' he said. 'Come out and we'll go for a ride, it takes my mind off things.'

I was no horsewoman, but over the past few months Henry had been teaching me. I'd gone from being rather terrified atop of the great big horse he always set me on, even though she was a sure-footed, gentle creature, to enjoying feeling the movement of her barrel tummy under my thighs and the rocking motion as we trotted down the road.

We started going for faster country rides.

'Let's go in the direction of Dowth,' he said this morning. 'And if we like, we can take off over the fields then.'

I barely thought about where we were going until I spotted the lane leading down to my old home, the mound and tombs looming in the background. I was quiet as we rode past, not looking down the lane, not wishing to see what it looked like now or who lived there.

'It's never been lived in since,' said Henry, peering at me from under his riding hat.

'What do you mean?' I said.

'Montgomery's son moved out soon after his father's death and I never re-let it.'

'Why?' I said.

I knew Henry had struggled with finances on the estate - it didn't make sense not to gather the rent on our former property and the outhouses which still stood strong in the yard.

'I think I was saving it,' he said. 'For you.'

I didn't know whether to believe him. Was he saying it because he so obviously had a fondness for me?

'Would you like to see it?' he said.

'No,' I said, shaking my head. It would dredge up too many memories, remind me of my parents and the life I once had there.

We rode past the lane and just as our horses had clip-clopped past, I reined my mare in and stopped.

'Changed your mind?' he said.

'Yes,' I nodded.

We turned our horses and made our way down the lane, leaning back into our saddles as the horses rode the incline.

Brambles covered over the entrance gate, grass seeping into the muddy lane. Henry dismounted and cleared the gate to open and I rode in on my horse.

The familiarity of the place came flooding back, the sight of the house and the windows I'd looked out of every day, made me feel warm. And sad. It all seemed smaller somehow.

The place wasn't in too bad disrepair, nothing a few hours tidying and whitewashing couldn't solve.

I dismounted and walked round the yard, going up to the house to look in at the window, where my mother always stood, at the stove.

'So strange,' I said to Henry. 'I loved living here. In the country.'

'Why don't you move back?' Henry asked. 'I could give it to you, help you get it cleaned up. It would give you a bit of your own space.'

'You just want me nearer to you,' I teased.

'I guess I want to give back what is rightfully yours,' he said.

'It will always be yours,' I said. 'And the Trust's.'

'Things are changing,' he said. 'Lots of tenants own their own places now.'

'Do you still see me as a tenant?' I said.

'No,' he said, slightly indignant. 'I just want to put things right.'

I shook my head, tracing my finger along the dust on the window, cutting a sausage shape through it.

'It wouldn't make sense, living here, with the business in town.' I said. 'It's more convenient where I am. It's a nice idea, Henry, but it's not practical.'

'I have another nice idea,' he said. He stepped forward, wrapping his arms around my back, holding me as I stared in the window of my old home.

I turned around and reached up to kiss him, something we had been doing so often now, unable to keep our hands from each other whenever we were alone.

'Marry me,' he said. 'I don't have a ring. My mother's ring ... well, that got given away. But Molly, you are so dear to me, I can't bear to think of life without you.'

I let him embrace me. Could I spend the rest of my life with his man and his complications? Could I be Lady Brabazon, overseeing this land, this house that we had only a few years before, been forcibly removed from?

Yes.

I could.

I could be Lady Brabazon.

'Alright then,' I said, into his chest. 'The answer is yes.'

Chapter Thirty-Two

MOLLY

The bell tinkled and I look up from the ledger I was writing in. It's Nora, her face peering out from an old-fashioned bonnet.

'Nora,' I say. 'How lovely to see you.'

I come out from behind the counter, but we don't embrace.

She looks smaller somehow, worn - older than her years.

'Hello Molly,' she says. 'I thought I'd pop in for a look. I'm ever so pleased for you.' She looks around quickly. 'What a lovely shop.'

'Thank you,' I say. 'How are you keeping? How are the children - how many is it now, four?'

'Five. Twins last year.'

'Oh my!'

No wonder she looks tired. Her dress draws my eye. I notice how worn it is.

'Yes, a little surprise.'

A surprise she doesn't look happy about. I feel sorry for her.

'I heard you're engaged now,' she says.

'News travels fast.'

'Well, it is some news, Molly. Who would have thought it? All those years ago.'

'Yes. Sometimes I find it hard to believe myself.'

'You'll be a Lady.'

'I suppose I will.'

'You'll have to start acting like one, then.'

'Never,' I say and laugh.

It's so good to see her, to talk and chat, to joke with her.

She walks over to a rail and starts looking through the clothes. Her fingers linger on the material, touching it, feeling the texture.

'Such beautiful dresses,' she says.

'Would you like to try one on,' I ask her. 'It can be adjusted to your size. We have a lovely changing room here.' I point to the space where we've hung a curtain and mirror.

'Oh no,' she says. 'I couldn't afford it, Molly, I'm just looking.'

'We do a payback scheme,' I say. 'You can pay it weekly.'

'I can't,' she says and shakes her head.

I realise I am asking too much of her - that Nora probably hasn't had a new dress in years.

'Not to worry,' I say. 'But if you do want to try one, you're very welcome. And if you change your mind, whenever, I'll do you a very hefty discount. For my old friend.'

She smiles.

'When is the wedding?' she asks.

'Just a few weeks to go,' I say. 'It's creeping up on me.'

'It'll be a grand affair.'

'Yes,' I say. 'It will. Hardly my scene at all.'

We laugh again.

'Well best of luck, Molly. I hope it all goes very well for you.'

'Thank you,' I say, warmed by her sincerity.

She turns and walks to the door.

'It was nice to see you again, Molly.'

She puts her hand on the door and opens it.

'Bye,' I say and watch her leave, her shoulders hunched.

I watch her walk by the window and as she disappears

from view, an idea strikes me. I snatch a dress from the rail and package it quickly in brown paper. I open the door and look up the street - she's nowhere to be seen.

Running, I get to the top of the street and look left and then right. She's up ahead, almost at the church.

I run fast and get to her, reaching out to touch her back.

She turns around, startled, and I hand her the package.

'This is for you,' I say, panting. 'Say nothing, just take it, I want you to have it. I've to get back to the shop, but I hope I see you again soon.'

I turn and run, without waiting for her reaction.

But I know that a smile will have crept to her face, a grateful, happy smile but one tinged with embarrassment.

Nora is my oldest friend. But our lives are worlds apart. I see that now, how far I've come.

* * *

Working in drapery and having access to the finest materials had its advantages. I'd ordered in a rich cream taffeta and travelled to a dressmaker in Dublin. She made me a dress that suited me very well; little fuss, elegant, a smattering of pearls at the waist.

My wedding dress is in a large rectangular box, on the seat beside Ruth, a new maidservant Henry had taken on at Brabazon. Ruth was to be my new aide and she holds on to the dress box as if were a newborn baby about to be thrust from its sitting. Inside, the dress is wrapped in layers of paper, and I can't help but think about it and smile as our carriage trundles slowly home.

Ruth is chattering, agog after her first visit to Dublin.

'So busy, I've never seen so many people,' she says. 'And the shops. My, I would've loved to have stayed there all day, just to look, just to have a touch of the things. So pretty. Oh, your dress is so beautiful, Miss Thomas.'

She looks down longingly at the box.

I laugh a little.

'I'm parched,' I say. 'Let's stop at the Coachman's for tea.' Ruth looks relieved at the impending break. The tavern on the road to Slane is respectable enough for two ladies to enter and dine by themselves.

'You look very content, madam,' says Ruth, picking up on my good humour.

'And why wouldn't I be?' I say. 'It's not every day you pick up your wedding dress.'

I was glad we had hired Ruth. She was younger than me and I knew her sister from school. She was from a good family. I wanted a maidservant with a background like mine, someone I could relate to. I would need her confidences as I made my own way with Henry. He had fallen in love with me and he brushed aside my tenant girl past. Others wouldn't.

'I'm ever so excited for you,' she says.

I know that she is happy for me - that she does not begrudge the life I have made for myself, the opportunity I am marrying into. I think, after these recent years, of coming back to Ireland, of losing Mam and working on our shops, that I am the happiest I can remember being. I've enjoyed Henry's courtship - his constant attentions and persuasions to allow me to see a future life with him. It's hard to believe I'm in the position I'm in now.

Ruth holds the door open for me and I sweep into the tavern, waiting to be seated at a private table away from prying eyes. My grand clothes see that I am always afforded special attention now and I have grown used to being treated well, and kindly, with respect, from my regular travels with Henry.

We are seated at a table towards the back, beside a flickering fire and away from the men perched up on stools at the bar. We order sandwiches and tea and as I sit there and look at the flames, I wonder aloud what the weather will be like, in three days' time, my wedding day.

'I've the whole family praying for you,' says Ruth. 'A

nice fine day. No rain, wouldn't that be grand?'

'It would,' I tell her and I picture Ruth's parents and brothers and sisters, kneeling in front of the fire, saying prayers for me and the clouds. I wonder if they really are praying, or if it's just something she is saying to endear herself to me. I feel though that she is genuine, that she would not fib. A honest way is something I need in a maidservant and friend. She reminds me of Nora.

It's while I'm thinking of the weather and Ruth's family on their knees with their rosary beads, while I'm imagining rolling clouds and biting rain, that I see him.

It was the movement of the paper, a quick back and forth against his face.

Mr Tubular.

Tubular is here, in a tavern, a few miles from my home, in Ireland.

He has come to find me.

And he has managed to do that.

* * *

'Are you all right?' asks Ruth, examining me now in concern.

I barely hear her, there's no room for her voice in my head.

I look straight ahead, warning my brain to breathe. In and out. Ruth is speaking. In and out. Respond.

'Yes,' I say and I force my eyes back to her face and my mouth into a tight smile.

'You look like you've seen a ghost,' she says.

'Maybe I have,' I say and she laughs. I try to laugh too, but nothing comes out.

It takes me a while to make the connection. To match the face imprinted on my brain to the one shadowing behind the newspaper.

Tubular was here. It was him all right, I could make out the shape of his temples and his eyes. He was watching me.

Lowering the paper every minute or two to look across.

I turn my head away, my stomach folding into a knot. He had tracked me down. He had followed me to Ireland.

My current husband had arrived, just as I was about to marry my next one.

The sandwiches arrive on white plates. The teapot steams a little from the spout and drips on to the cheap linen tablecloth as Ruth pours.

I can't speak. I let Ruth talk on, nodding when I think I should, looking right past her, my eyes darting to where I know he is. How did he find me? Why was he here? Did he think he could take me back, to London?

I lift my sandwich and try to eat it but it sticks to the back of my throat like wet paper. I stop to take a drink. To think.

Unable to resist I look over again, this time letting my look linger. Tubular lowers his paper and waves his hand. Enough to get my attention but not to warrant attention from anyone else.

'Will you excuse me?' I say to Ruth and I get up and leave my seat, feeling the rush of my heartbeat in my ears.

He's aged a bit, more white flecks around his temples. His face looks lined, as if he's been staying up late, drinking.

'My dear,' he says as I approach and he stands up to take my hand. Every square of my skin pricks when he put his lips to my knuckles. The feel of his wet lips makes me want to retch.

I sit without being invited, my jaw set in lock.

'What are you doing here?' I hiss. I want to scream at him, to tell him to go away.

'I could ask you the same thing,' he says. 'Although I know the answer.'

'How did you find me?' I say.

'There I was, reading my paper over breakfast,' he says, his mouth set in the curve of a smile, his eyes glistening.

He's enjoying this.

'Egg in me hand, just going through the notices like I always do and I see that there's a Lord in Ireland marrying a woman by the name of Molly Thomas. Molly Thomas, says I - that name's familiar. That rings a bell. It couldn't be, could it? And do you know … it was!'

The notice in *The Times*. Henry had issued it before he told me. Said it was customary. He thought it would be a nice surprise when I opened the paper to read about our engagement. I'd seen such notices from Ireland in the London papers too. But it had never occurred, at least not in the forefront of my mind, that Tubular would pick up on it. He wasn't a paper man. But he had picked up on it and he'd travelled all the way to Ireland to find me. Three days before my wedding.

'What do you want?' I say. My voice is like something a snake might spit.

'I want my wife back,' he says.

I look around again, making sure there was no one listening. I could see Ruth looking over her shoulder wondering who I was speaking to.

'I can't speak here,' I say.

'Where would you like to speak then?' he says.

'I can meet you later. Somewhere else.'

I try to think of a landmark, somewhere he could find, somewhere that wouldn't raise suspicion.

'There's a mound at Dowth, a hill, you can't miss it.' I told him. 'I'll meet you there.'

It was a place out of town tourists sometimes visited. If anyone asked I could say he was a relation, someone who happened to be passing through the area. Interested in history.

'Is this about money?' I say, wondering how high his price might be. He had bought me before, maybe now he wanted his investment back.

'This is about you,' he says. 'And your plan to commit bigamy.'

He had me over a barrel. And he would spill about Oliver too.

Chapter Thirty-Three

HENRY

'I'm very happy for you Henry.'

Arthur was standing in the great room, his arms clasped behind his back.

'Thank you,' Henry replied. He was seated on the low sofa, a book in his lap. He was trying to relax after a busy few days organising last minute wedding details.

'I think you will be very happy together.'

'I do too,' he said. 'Well that's the plan anyway. No point going into it if you're not planning to be happy.'

'No,' said Arthur. 'You learnt the hard way about that, didn't you?'

'Yes,' said Henry, frowning. 'But let's not bring all that up. It's something I'd rather forget about. Hardly my finest hour.'

'She'll be very disappointed to hear you are getting married again.'

'I'm sure she will, but what's done is done. Besides, she's married herself now.'

Henry still felt sorry for Charity. After the humiliation she suffered with his last minute decision to cancel their wedding, she had taken back to Carlow and spent a year mourning the loss of her relationship and the future life she'd planned with a man she'd been in love with all her life. After the year, her father told her the only way to deal with her heartbreak was to marry again, and he presented an array of suitors to choose from, all keen to marry into the family and wealth. She went with a mild-mannered man from the same county, who came from a monied background. Henry expected she didn't love him, but she probably couldn't bear the thought of a spinster life. She had vowed to never travel to the north-east again because of the memories it dredged up.

'Well, I am pleased for you - I think she's a lovely lady, Molly. I think I'd like to find what you have.'

'You mean Henrietta doesn't satisfy you?' asked Henry, raising an eyebrow in mockery at Arthur.

'Henrietta is a doll. And great fun. But it's hardly true love.'

'No, I suppose not,' said Henry. 'Just as well I'm the heir, isn't it. Brabazon would never survive if it was waiting on you to get married and produce a set of legacy children.'

Arthur looked down at the floor.

'I'm only joking, old boy,' said Henry, when he saw his remarks had hurt.

'I know,' he said. 'But you are lucky to find Molly. Remember that.'

Arthur turned, walked to the drinks cabinet, poured himself a tumbler of whiskey and left the great room, looking mournful. Henry felt a pang of pity for his brother. He wished he could find happiness. Or at least whatever it was he was searching for in the bottom of every glass.

* * *

The wedding was to be held at Brabazon, but Henry had learned from his previous nuptial experience. There would be no marquees or champagne fountains or chocolate rabbits or expensive niceties - it was to be a small, simple affair, with a short guest list and little fuss. This suited Molly, who was shy in large crowds. She was finding it difficult to adapt to the number of soirees, balls, and parties they were being invited to, but she was learning to smile, to stand, and listen, to put on a brave face in front of the numerous questions and comments she was subjected to. He found that people were drawn to her, fascinated by her fashion sense, by her business sense and by the fact that she had captured Henry's heart and would soon be Lady Brabazon.

His mood had improved immeasurably since his courtship began with Molly. All the problems he'd faced over the past few years seemed to have faded into the background. He had overcome the bulk of the financial strain from Seymour's death and the cancelled wedding. He had established himself as a capable landlord of the house and what was left of the land.

Molly and he had decided to keep on both drapery shops after she got married. They were turning good profits and Molly had worked too hard to let go of them.

Their future was bright. They were going to be very happy. That, he was sure of.

Chapter Thirty-Four

MOLLY

Ruth knew there was something wrong, that the man I had met had upset me. I told her he was a relative who didn't have good relations with my family. She sighed and reached across the table in the tavern and patted my hand. We waited until he left before we made our way out to our carriage and she left me mostly in silence on the way home, my wedding dress in its box making a mockery of who I was. Who I am. A bigamist. A prostitute. A mother who lost her own child.

'Weddings will always bring out the worst in family,' she said sensibly, as I watched the road rush by. I felt the tilt as the horse leaned into the steep descent coming into Slane. We cross the river, over the stone bridge, before slowing as he strained, dragging us up the almost vertical slope.

Tubular fills my mind and it races ahead to our meeting tonight. How had I not thought that this day would come? That he would find me? That he would track me down, to here, to my home? I should never have told him where I lived all those years ago. I knew it was a mistake, saying the words out loud in that pit of a place.

What could he want from me? And how could I make him leave? I didn't think he had it in him. The gumption to leave London and follow me, here. I didn't think he'd care enough. I never thought he was one for revenge, that he'd come to haunt me, to hurt me.

If he talked, it was the end of Henry and me. It would be the end of all that I knew here. I would be disgraced - I wouldn't even be able to return to the shop. Who would buy from there, knowing of what I'd done in London, of my reputation, that I'd been a whore? And that I had a son out there somewhere, who I'd just left behind?

I listen to Ruth's gentle voice, lilting as she talks. She's excited about the wedding, about the dress in the box, about the finery she would see in three days' time. She talks of how lovely I will look and how she is going to be part of that, making me beautiful.

Beautiful on the outside. Soiled and dirty on the inside.

I was a disgrace.

* * *

Tubular was there before me. Early. A smirk on his face. There was a time when I thought he was a good man. That he did care for me and wanted the best for me. But his love for me had disappeared the day I had. And now, he wanted revenge.

I dismount my horse and feel his eyes on me. I look nothing like the girl in London. I'd filled out, my hair styled, my dress a fine material and cut to my shape.

'Ireland suits you,' he says as I stand to face him.

'Yes,' I said. 'It's my home.'

'No,' he said, shaking his head. 'It's not.'

I'd forgotten how small he was, how ill statured and weaselly he looked. He was nothing on Henry. Henry was a finer, truer man than he would ever be.

'What do you want?' I say. 'What do you *really* want?'

'I told you,' he said. 'You are my wife. And I want you.'

I shake my head. He couldn't be serious. How could we have a future now? After all that had happened and all that had passed?

'No,' I say. 'I am no longer yours. You bought me. But I am no longer yours.'

'You are my wife,' he says. 'And you are mine. You *do* belong to me.'

I watch him pat his breast pocket and open the flap of his jacket. His fingers flitter and take out a white piece of paper. He opens it up to show me our marriage certificate, the calligraphed letters curving round into a decoration. He holds it in front of me and reads in a mocking voice.

'Molly Thomas,' he says, tapping at the paper in his hands. 'Married. Cotton. That's me. I own you, whether you like it or not.'

'You don't own me,' I say, my voice quiet.

'Oh, you think I don't,' he says. 'But the truth is very different.'

'How much?' I ask.

'What do you mean?' he says.

'How much to see you gone?'

'This is not about money,' he says and he laughs. 'I don't need money. What I need is my wife. Back in my kitchen. Back in my bed.'

'Hah,' I say, scoffing at the thoughts of me ever joining him in that way again.

'Oh, you laugh,' he says. 'But it didn't stop you climbing into bed with hundreds, *thousands* of others.'

His words sting. It has been so long since I'd been confronted with my past, since I had to face what happened to me and what I had done. I was quiet for a moment. Thinking. I had been prepared to give him money. To take what I was pouring into Brabazon and reroute it to him.

'Stopped searching for your boy, have you?' he says. 'Your precious Oliver?' He follows it with a throaty laugh, one that reaches into my very core and makes me take my strength and come at him, flailing, my hands making contact with his face.

'Oi,' he says grabbing my wrists and holding me in place. He was small, but he was strong and he stops me in my tracks. 'All right, calm down, calm down. I actually came to give you some news.'

I stop moving, and watch his face for a smirk.

'News?' I say.

'About your boy. I know where he is.'

'Where?' I say, surrendering to his hands, to his grip, which he loosens when I stop fighting him. His words swirl through my head. I wasn't even sure if I was hearing correctly.

'The police were in touch. They found a boy in Newcastle. They think it's him.'

'Newcastle?' I say. 'But how did he get there? Newcastle?'

'Yes, well, I didn't want to go to see without you. And then I read the notice in the paper. And here I am now.'

He was lying. It couldn't be true. But Newcastle? It did make sense. It would explain why I never found him in London, after all the streets I'd walked. He never turned up, because he was never there in the first place.

'You need to come back with me,' he says. 'We can go to see him together. And if it's him - well - we can start up where we left off.'

'And if it's not?' I say.

'I will file a petition for divorce,' he says.

I couldn't read his face. I didn't know him to be a liar. He was wily, yes. A peruser of prostitutes. But not someone who had proven themselves so dishonest that I expected nothing but lies from his mouth.

He steps towards me and reaches out.

'Molly,' he says gently. 'I've missed you. We had a life together. I know you were upset ... devastated at what happened. But we could have had our own children. We would have gotten him back if you gave it time.'

I bowed my head. News of Oliver. It was all I had dreamed of; all my waking thoughts had imagined. And now this news, three days ahead of my marriage. To a good man, who loved me and I him.

I had to go back.

I had to see if it was him. This was the first positive news I'd had in years. And if they had contacted Tubular, notified us at that address, well then it had to be Oliver.

'I'll go back with you,' I say, quietly. 'But if it's not him, I wish for the divorce. You must petition like you say.'

'Of course,' he says.

'I will have to tell my fiancé. We'll need to delay the wedding.'

'Yes.'

We were standing at the bottom of the mound, our horses pulled in from the road.

We are silent but I'm thinking about how I can tell Henry. Should I tell him the truth? Or make up a lie and a reason to suddenly depart to England?

'What is this?' says Tubular, pointing at the hill behind us which rises from the earth like a beehive.

'It's a tomb,' I say.

'Let's climb to the top,' he says.

'No,' I say. This was not the time for sightseeing. But Tubular had turned. He was climbing the mound, clasping at the clumps of grass like I used to when I was child. I watch him get to the top and stand surveying the view, watching the houses all around, small lights in the windows.

'Come up,' he says. I didn't want to. My head was whirring. But I found myself walking towards the mound, climbing, smelling the earth in my hands, remembering what it was like to scale this height.

I view the land around me, my eyes drawn, as always, to where my family home had been.

I feel Tubular standing close, feel his breath on the back of my neck. His hands wrap round my waist and I get his hands and fling them from my body. But he persists and steps in closer, again.

'Molly,' he says gently. 'I know this is hard for you. I know it's a shock. But I'm still your husband. It's still me.'

I remember the smell of him, now that it was here in

my nostrils, on my skin. I remember his bony fingers, pressing my flesh.

I feel him kissing my neck.

I was going to have to go to England with him. I was going to have to get through these next few weeks to get back to my son.

'You know what you are?' he says. 'You know, even under that fine dress and that lady's hair style, you're nothing but a whore?'

He was right. But I hadn't heard that word in so long. I was back in London. The same feelings. I was nothing. Nobody. My body was not my own.

'I tried to help you, Molly,' I hear him say. 'I gave you everything. And look what happened. You threw it all away.'

He was lifting my dress.

Whore.

Kissing my neck.

Whore.

Fingers inside.

Whore.

I hear his breathing getting heavier and he sniffs, deeply, pulling me closer to him. I could feel it against me, poking, like all those men had felt against me before.

'You'd believe anything, wouldn't you?' he says.

Then I hear him laugh and feel his hands paw at my exposed skin.

I bend down as though offering myself to him and I feel his lust jump, a grunt out of his mouth as he grips at me.

There it is in front of me, lying in the dark, one of the stones like my daddy lifted to build our farm, covered in lichen, burnt with rain. It was a stone brought and carved by people we could never know, by our ancestors who knew more about the sun and the moon than we did.

I curl my fingers around it, pull it up into my palm, turn and smash it into his head, right into his temple, coming from the side, with the most force I could. He crumples in front of me, bent at the knees and falls, his trousers half open, the smirk leaving his face.

I stare at him and then tentatively I kick his body, at the shoulder.

He does not move. I bend down and turn his face over, black blood trickling from the wound on the side of his head.

Panicking, I pull his body to the edge of the mound. He's short but he's heavy and I feel my shoulders almost snap from their sockets as I strain to move him. I lie on the ground and put both boots against his side, pushing him and watching as his body slowly disappears down the side of the mound, falling and landing with a horrible thud.

I scan the road from my vantage point and feel breathless as I realise what I have done.

Have I really killed another man?

This time, there was no power, no force through my head and my hands.

This time it was all me.

I climb down the mound quickly and run to untie his horse, leading it over to where he has fallen. Gathering all the strength I can muster, I manage to get one of his feet into the stirrups, and I pull the horse, to drag Tubular, his head lolling on the ground, down to the swollen river.

I roll him off the bank, hearing his body hit the water and watching it submerge, before it floats to the top again and is taken by the fast-moving water. I don't wait to see where it ends up - whether it gets caught in a tree or by a low hanging bush or whether it sinks again.

I take off the horse's saddle and toss that in the river too. And then I slap the horse and send him racing over a ditch and out of the field.

I leave, cantering my horse out of the field and down the road, back to Brabazon, where Henry is busy with the final arrangements for the wedding we'll be having in three days' time.

He said he would do anything to please me. Henry Brabazon, the most loving man I had come to know. And he had no idea that he was marrying a woman capable of murder - twice.

* * *

There were so many faces I was overwhelmed by it all. Henry had said it would be a small gathering, but for me, there were still too many. Sophisticated, refined ladies. Gentlemen with top hats so shiny, if they bent down I could have seen my reflection in the flat surface of their heads.

My wedding face, painted and rouged. Beautiful, they told me. I looked beautiful.

Henry held a smile as wide as the moon. He did look happy. Marriage, it seemed, would suit him very well.

Better than it would suit me.

'Lady Brabazon.'

It was the daughter of a landlord who owned an estate near Navan. I had seen her before, but she looked different now. It was so hard to tell who was who in the mass of faces, all congratulating us, all gripping my hand and kissing the air beside my cheek; the smell of their oils and perfumes going up my nose.

The fires burned hot in the grates. I could feel sweat glistening at the base of my back where the dress sat, tight. It was hard to breathe.

I wondered if he might have been found by now. Where he was, if he had washed up, out to sea? How long did it take to float from our river, out past the wide tide, where the banks met the park and the bridges and through the marshy land? What if he got stuck? What if the steamer was passing over him now?

I thought of the mullet, speckled and brown, their great mouths sucking and lumping the pieces from his cold, wet flesh. Then I thought of the children who might catch the mullet and take it home to be cooked for tea, how a family could be sitting around the dinner table, munching on that fish and the flesh of Tubular right now.

'What a wonderful ceremony. And you look exquisite. A very fine dress, so delicate. I've never seen the likes of it before?'

The woman was looking me up and down, her eyes resting on my stomach, where the dress maker had stitched a set of pearls.

'Yes,' I said. 'A new design. I ordered the material from London.'

I'd said those words a hundred times today. Perhaps it had been a bad idea to go with something so different, so modern. A talking point.

Henry appears by my side. He grips my arm and I am grateful for his presence.

'Would you like a drink, my darling?' he asks.

I nod. My throat is burning. Acid is leaking from my stomach, cutting me raw on the inside. It is the worry. I feel almost dizzy. It is so hot in here, so many people, the press of damp clothes and perfumes.

'Henry,' I say as he goes to walk from me and I pull at his arm. 'I ... I need some air ...'

Concern crosses his face, he takes in my white cheeks and my wide eyes.

And then I see him rush towards me as I fall, forward, spiralling, a shutter of black closing in around my eyes, slowly blocking out the faces and the swirl of the crowd pushed into our great room. Celebrating our wedding. Celebrating the union of Henry and me.

I fainted. On my wedding day. In front of all our distinguished guests.

* * *

A fan flaps at my face. The cool air waves in sheaths over my cheeks and nose. It's nice, I like it.   But when I open my eyes

I feel like I can't breathe again.

My dress, I need to loosen my dress.

Henry is there, looking concerned. Poor sweet Henry.

They've pushed sugary tea into my hand, but it's quivering. They hold it to my lips - the liquid surprises me, burns me. But I take some into my mouth and let it go down.

'Darling, are you alright?'

No.

Don't cross me Henry. I hurt any man who crosses me.

Where is he now, out to sea? Floating? Or under?

They bring me upstairs and Ruth loosens all the cord at the back of my dress. I lie down on the bed and want to take the whole thing off.

She sits with me and I let myself fall into a rough slumber, one where the room is spinning around me, where I think, *get up, Molly, it's your wedding day, you can't sleep through it, you fool.*

But this is my second wedding day. My first was in a small register office in Whitechapel, London.

And look how that one ended.

That husband, cold and wet and floating down the river out to sea.

Chapter Thirty-Five

MOLLY

It was foolish of me to think that I could get away with what I'd done. That it wouldn't catch up with me - that it wouldn't take its toll. I'd spent all my life being brash and getting on with things, facing up to what needed to be done, pushing through my problems and my circumstances, never really stopping to reflect on who I was, what I had done, what I had become.

When I should have been floating through the first weeks of marriage, I was instead falling down, further and further into a well of despair. Henry watched his bride turn sullen and silent, refusing to get out of bed in the mornings and staying up late at night, raiding the drinks cabinet, knocking back crystal tumblers of whatever alcohol I could find until the feelings went away. Of unrest. Of fear. Of blood on my hands.

I watched the newspaper, listened to the gossip from the servants. Had he been found yet? Where was he? Was there any way it could lead back to me - had I been careful enough?

The horse had turned up on a neighbouring farm, a stray, and they had kept it after asking around the locality. No one laid claim to it and it was a fine beast. The stables where Tubular had hired it from would have been looking for it and they'd have his name. I worried about it constantly - so much so that I thought about going to the farm in the middle of the night and perhaps slaughtering it, seeing it brought off to the knacker's yard. It seemed death was always my way out.

Wondering about Tubular brought up the fears I had around Flann Montgomery and being caught. I couldn't walk down the road to Dowth without reliving the night I left Ireland, the night I'd drawn my knife, the night I'd taken his life.

It was something I had chosen to do - to avenge the death of my father. But was it the right thing to do? Could there have been a different way - could I have found a way to punish him without extinguishing him completely?

I was surprised how the sadness reignited feelings I had buried around losing Oliver and even my father and mother. All of my fears jumbled into a great black sadness that closed in around me.

Henry took me to the doctor. I was prescribed opiates and laudanum and I took them all, washing them down with alcohol. The medication helped and I fell in to a routine of having good days with bad, but functioning all the same. I hired help in the shop, but I still made it weekly and I found when I did get in there and attended to some of the business, it took my mind off things, helped me heal a little.

We had planned to expand, to open up shops in neighbouring towns - Navan perhaps or Dundalk, but with the way I'd gone since we'd gotten married, with my moods low and the headaches, and sickness I suffered from the drink and the medication and the sadness, we put things on hold. Managing two shops was enough for the moment.

Then I found out I was pregnant.

* * *

Henry was overjoyed at the news. He swept me up and kissed me and subjected me to a barrage of questions about how I was feeling.

'This is the news I've been waiting for,' he said. 'I'm so

happy, my love, fantastic, you're going to be a mummy. I'm going to be a father. I can't believe it.'

I wanted to tell him that I was already a mother. That somewhere out there, my little boy had turned into a long-legged child, with feelings and wants and a personality that I knew nothing about.

Having suffered such a blackness over the past few months I worried that the pregnancy would send me over the edge, but it had the opposite effect. I had something to look forward to.

The months where I waited for the baby to grow and tickle in my belly were more enjoyable than I'd expected. Once the flush of the first weeks had passed and the nausea that took hold of my stomach all day and all night disappeared, I felt a joy that I had been unable to feel with Oliver.

This time, there was nothing to hide. When my stomach swelled and Henry put his hands there, to feel the baby growing inside, he looked at me with such pride that I couldn't help feeling proud myself. I'd made him happy. And what joy to be with child so soon after our wedding?

Mrs Johansson fussed and Ruth asked after me every minute of the day.

'Are you quite well, ma'am, is there anything you would like me to fetch for you?'

But I carried the pregnancy well. I started to bloom with it, to grow rosy cheeked and healthy, the hormones and swelling suiting me more than I could ever have imagined.

When it came time to birth, I worried about the pains that were to come, but with the support of an attending doctor who offered me a rag with a substance on it to ease the baby's entry into the world, I got through it quickly, the baby arriving with a slip on to the bed sooner than I expected, giving me a shock to see her - blue, breathing and wet.

Henry cried when he met her, coming into the room immediately after the birth, taking her into his arms, going quiet, staring, the tears sliding down his cheeks in a torrent.

'My beautiful ... beautiful girl,' he said.

I was glad it was a girl. That it was different. A boy would have been too much, I think.

She was a bonny baby, light haired with dark eyes. I held her close to me, smelling the strands that had formed on her scalp, plastered there with an intoxicating scent.

We called her Sarah.

A few days after the birth, as I struggled with painful breasts and the baby squalled incessantly, the tears came back. They came from a well deep inside me. They poured through the night and when I awoke from a scratched, wretched sleep, they were there again, waiting in the morning.

With the crying, came an utter despair. My feelings disappeared, only to be replaced with a nothingness, a blackness, a space where my emotions had been before. I could control nothing. I wanted for nothing.

I realised I was searching for something, longing for something to cover up an aching chasm that had opened like a crater inside.

I was looking for Oliver.

My first born was the only thing that could have pulled me from the pit I had fallen into. And even if he was found, even if Henry himself walked through the door, hand in hand with a tall boy now, I had already missed so much. His first steps. His laugh. His discovery of the world of trees and building bricks and the books he loved to read and the songs he liked to sing.

How could I not have found him, through the police, through the children's services, through my own ability as a mother to track down her child?

I didn't deserve to have another baby. One, as bonny as this.

I didn't deserve happiness, or to be married to a man like Henry in a house like this.

I didn't deserve anything. I was nothing. Nobody.

And that was what fuelled the tears. Until they too dried up.

Until I had nothing left to give at all.

Chapter Thirty-Six

MOLLY

It was worse when I saw it.

Between his legs.

That he was a boy.

It was worse than Sarah.

A different kind of pain. One that went more inside, a darkness, a blackness inside my mind, that I would never lift myself out of.

I could see it now. The rest of my days. Without him. Without Oliver.

This was my punishment. I would pay for my sins.

And it was as though everything stopped that day.

The search.

The hope.

The thoughts that I would ever see my first boy again.

I had my new family now, a girl and a boy.

I would live for them.

At least I would try.

I would try through the blackness.

To be the mother I should have been.

Chapter Thirty-Seven

HENRY

Brabazon House, Co Meath, Ireland, Christmas 1915

Henry smells the pine needles as soon as he steps into the hall. The tree is fresh, taken from the woods that morning. He pictures his father and Arthur and Mrs Johansson standing in the hall, holding out glass baubles, Mrs Johansson having done most of the work, their mood good, the memory as clear as though they were all standing there in front of him.

He thought about Mrs Johansson, how she was the only constant in the house. She was getting old now and he knew that soon, she would retire. How he would miss her presence about the house, her words of comfort, her bad humour when she was tired and irritable. She was the closest thing he'd had to a mother.

He looked forward to seeing Arthur later - he so rarely came back to Brabazon these days. He wondered how he would be, how he would look, how he would act. You never knew with Arthur these days. He was so volatile. He hoped he'd be in a good mood and that they would have a nice time together, no dramas, from anyone.

Henry worried for Arthur the same way he worried for Molly. There was a blackness among them, a heavy cloud that sheltered them, that shadowed their faces. It hung in the air around them as though it were tangible and he could reach out and tip their melancholy.

Molly had been carrying her cloud for years. It seemed to have appeared on the day they married, when she fainted in front of everyone. It was as if she awoke a different person, a worried, sorrowful soul.

When Sarah was two weeks old, he had found Molly in the nursery, crouching over the baby, her arms wrapped around the newborn's body, rocking back and forth. She was trying to suppress her sobs, but it was the screeching sounds that escaped that drew him.

'My love,' he said, putting his hand on her shoulder, prying away her arm to check that the baby was OK, that she was breathing. 'What is it?' he asked, desperately searching the child for signs of life. Had something happened? Had she died?

But the child moved, wrinkling up her forehead and stretching out her miniature body. He watched as Molly pulled back and the child arched, the stretch reaching to her small toes.

Molly stopped her sobs but didn't look up at him. He shook her gently, bending down to try to look at her face. She turned her head away and stared at the nursery wall.

'You wouldn't understand,' she said quietly.

And she was right. How could he understand? She must have been traumatised. Perhaps it was the emotions coming out after the birth in a way that they never would from him. Women cried.

He was enthralled by Sarah. He found it hard to understand why Molly was not as attached to the baby as he was. He would come to the nursery each evening and sit with her for a time, feeling the weight of her in his arms, running his finger over her soft dark eyebrows. He was fascinated by the curve of her mouth, the dip above her lips, the scent of her as he held her against his neck and patted her back.

On the days when he worked at home in his study, he

would visit the nursery and tell the nanny to take a break. He found himself longing to hold her when he was away from her. Molly though, was different.

She avoided the nursery. In the evenings when the nanny would carry Sarah down to them in the great room, Molly would take her stiffly, her back straight, her arms reaching, almost reluctantly. Most evenings, after a moment of staring into the child's face, the tears would come again, streaming down her face, often dripping, wetting the baby's chemise.

'Are you quite well?' he had asked her on many occasions. But she was angry and would scowl and would make him feel as though he were stupid to think that anything was wrong.

He had waited for the doctor's check-up visit, and took him aside down the corridor when he came out of Molly's room.

'I'm worried about her,' he said. 'She's been crying. Uncontrollably sometimes. I know there can be emotions ...' His voice trailed off. 'I know it can be a difficult time. But I don't think this ... she ... is normal.'

Henry felt guilty as he spoke. As though he were telling tales on his wife.

'She is distant,' said the doctor. 'And tired. I have prescribed some medication that shouldn't interfere with the baby. I'd suggest some fresh air and good, wholesome meals. I can arrange a test to check her iron level.'

'I think there's more,' said Henry. 'I'm not sure if she's ... well. In her mind?'

The words leathered his tongue. He felt he was betraying Molly.

'This can happen,' said the doctor reassuringly. 'The blood loss can leave a woman quite depressed. But in a few weeks, she will back to her normal self. If you have any more concerns, come and see me. It'll probably pass.'

* * *

Henry did feel reassured by the doctor. And for a while it did seem as though things were settling. Molly got used to the baby and her care, the tears subsided and she started to cope better. She returned to some of her old self, even going back to the shops some days, to take stock and check accounts and meet customers.

But with the birth of James, just a year later, the blackness returned. The worry Henry had that it would was realised the day Molly went missing, leaving James crying in the nursery and Sarah toddling, all the way down to the basement kitchen.

When he pulled up that evening, stepping out of the trap, he was met by a panic-stricken Mrs Johansson.

'Molly's missing,' she said, her face white as a sheet. 'There's a search out, they're walking the fields.'

Henry had raced to the fields where the house staff were out with walking sticks calling Molly's name. They found her sitting at the top of Dowth mound, her hands hugging her knees, freezing, no tears, just staring out over where her family used to live.

It was after this that Henry had her put on complete bed rest and given a mixture of tonics and painkillers, mainly laudanum, each day. The doctor said she could be one of the unfortunate women who suffered hysteria.

The words made Henry's skin crawl.

As the years passed, Molly would have dark times and good. Sometimes it would be clear when an episode was about to strike, other times, it crept up on them, from nowhere, a black mood that would see Molly take to the bed, crying for hours, other times, sleeping, it seemed, for days.

This Christmas, Henry hoped she would cope well. It was a difficult time for her, stirring up memories of her father and her mother and her childhood.

'We both lost our fathers at Christmas,' Henry reminded her.

'Yes, but yours died at home, in this beautiful house,' she would say. 'Mine died on the side of the road.'

It was something that never went away, even though they had long joined their histories and had fallen deeply in love.

Deep down, she still blamed him.

He had long stopped trying to argue his case for fear it would trigger another depressive period. He never stopped worrying for her. Even as he watched her, sitting by the fire, her hair pulled up and put back, her face beautifully made up, it was as though something was missing. As if a piece of her had been lost.

And maybe it had. Maybe every woman who gave birth felt as though a piece of her had been removed. That she had lost some of herself, that pre-mother self.

He worried for Molly and for their children, now old enough to understand. His own mother had suffered with her nerves and he knew, even though it had never been spoken of, that this was the reason she died when he was six. He feared Molly would go the same way. She had that same look in her eye. That distant glint. A look, that scared him, more than anything else in this world.

***

James is looking at him with the same expression that Molly uses. It's a type of pleading and angry look. His eyebrows have narrowed and there's a furrow that cuts all the way above the bridge of his nose, deep into his skin.

'But Father, this is my right. I have a right to go if I wish.'

'A right to be slaughtered?' said Henry.

'Don't you feel for our country. For our men? They need people like me, people who will stand up for what is right.'

'I have feelings for my family,' said Henry. 'For my son. For his mother who will sit and stare out that window and not leave it until the day you come back. *If* you come back. And what if you don't? What then? She's bad enough now.'

'So, this is about Mummy,' said James, his expression now turning into a scowl. 'It's always about her. Always about what she wants, never about me.'

'Your mother loves you,' said Henry. 'That is why I am not going to watch as you sign up and throw your life away in a hole of a trench in France. You have everything going for you. More than I had when I was your age. When I was your age, my father was in the middle of squandering everything we had. Don't you know how hard we've worked to get that back? Your mother and I? Is this the way you wish to repay us? Signing up to a bloody war that you have no act or hand or part in. The answer is no, James. I understand the lure - the excitement of it. But believe me, this is not something you want to volunteer for.'

'I would have thought you of all people would understand,' said James.

'I owe nothing to England,' said Henry. 'And you don't either. What you owe is the peace you can bring your mother. Going to war will bring none of that. I won't allow it, James. This is the end of it. You will finish school and then start your studies at university, just like has been arranged.'

James left Henry's study, flinging the door behind him into a slam.

Henry realised he had been the same with his own father. Battling to find his place. Pushing forward his opinions. Walking out of the study in a temper and slamming the door shut.

The war was a millstone around all their necks. Already thousands of Irish had left for the continent, enticed by a sense of duty to join those who had gone before them and by the rallying cries on their own shore. And now there was civil unrest too, with the Irish Volunteers swirling to bring about Home Rule again. Henry cared none for politics these days. He only cared how it might affect him and his family's livelihood. And Molly.

Christmas 1915 had been one of the happiest of recent years. Her mood had been pleasant. She'd presented him with a small book of black leather-bound stories with a message inside:

To my darling Henry, for all that you do. You are, my love, Molly.

He had warmed on Christmas morning when he read it. Sometimes it was difficult to tell if she did love him. If she had the same feelings he had for her. If their love that had formed so many years ago, was still alive, underneath all that suffering, under that depression that lingered through their lives.

It was in the days after Christmas that James had started his campaign - his persuasion battle to go to war. Henry warned him to say nothing to his mother. 'If I hear that she even has a breath of this, I'm cutting your allowance ... off!'

James had an uneasy soul. He carried some of his mother's melancholy with him and had been a quiet and inward child. He flitted from interest to interest, going hunting in phases, then stopping and moping about the estate. He had learned to fish and then threw the rods in the long sheds at the back of the farm and never reached for them again. He asked for a hive to keep bees and after a few weeks, was badly stung and left it to the gardener to harvest the honey and see to the swarm.

Henry knew that his son's desire to go to war on the continent was another phase. He was always looking for something new, some excitement. He had no idea what war meant. The boy was too soft, he would never last in an army environment. But James's new found interest was keeping Henry awake at night. He had a troubling ache in his stomach. He feared they would get up one morning and James would be gone.

It was Sarah who brought Henry most peace. She had taken on the role of confidante; becoming a caretaker for the family. Even as a child they had enjoyed long walks together, chatting. He'd relished teaching her as she grew, watching her interest in nature flourish, taking to books, talking about countries she read about and wished to visit.

She was quick to laugh and he missed her vibrancy terribly when it was time, each term, for her to return to school in south Dublin. The house felt empty without her.

Most of all she could read Molly like he never could. She could predict her moods, let him know when another episode was coming on, reading her mother's warning signs in an innate way.

There were times when he walked past Molly's room and found Sarah sitting in a chair reading to her, Molly lying back with a relaxed expression and her eyes closed. She seemed to bring her some solace, a comfort that he was unable to.

He thought about Sarah's marriage often, how he wished her to make her own choice, someone who could secure her future, someone, he thought, who was a bit like him.

For some reason, he couldn't imagine handing Brabazon over to James. He was so flippant, so quick to change and easy to temper. What sort of future would it face under his hands?

He wondered if he should confide in Sarah about her brother's desire to go to war. Ask her to have a word with him. He often spoke with her when he felt the situation was getting out of hand, that a sister's word in James's ear would be more powerful than his.

But this was different, this felt like something he should be able to handle. Something that James had to understand. War was no place for a boy. And James Brabazon, was after all, only a boy.

Chapter Thirty-Eight

Dowth, Co. Meath, Ireland, 27 April 1916, Easter Week

It was 5.30 a.m. when James Brabazon walked quietly from Brabazon House, out the back door used by the servants, past the orchard and through the gate that led to the woods. He carried a small white canvas bag with some bread, water, and an apple. In his brown leather bandolier, he'd packed spare socks and a little notebook and pen. He thought he might scribble a few notes if there was time, or if they were lying in wait and there wasn't much to do.

He walked with his black bicycle all the way to the entrance gates, the gates that gave access to the back of Brabazon House. It was twenty minutes before two other volunteers arrived to meet him, their green caps black in the dark. They smiled and hollered when they saw him and he felt his pulse rise. Already, he knew this was the start of the biggest adventure of his life.

They cycled through the dark, their dynamo lights whirring against the wheels. They made good time on the windy road to Slane leaning into the bike right then left, as they manoeuvred the bends. They felt the bogland beneath them as they pedalled over the road that led to the main highway between Slane and Ashbourne. Up and down. Up and down.

James thought about the motor vehicle his father had

been talking about getting. If he'd had a motor car, James would have taken it, picked up these volunteers and made their way quickly to Garristown where they were meeting the rest of the garrison. It would have saved time, and a vehicle would have earned him the respect of the troops.

In Slane they met three more volunteers and the group of five cycled as the morning became light, down the hill and up again. They were quiet and watchful. They could be stopped at any time. James was pleased when they met the garrison leader who was waiting at the bottom of a small country road as they cycled into Garristown. They had made it to the battalion. They had gotten this far.

He felt proud to be dressed in his Irish Volunteer uniform. He had packed it into a small, brown suitcase and hidden it in his room after he received it, locking his bedroom door and warning the housekeeper to stay away. She did as she was asked, used to James and his strange habits, aware that they were living in secretive times. No one could be too sure of anyone nowadays.

The rest of the volunteers had not long since arrived and they were setting up camp, fetching water, laying fires, handing out rations and getting the farmhouse they would be sleeping in that night ready. They had marched from Dublin that morning and some were sitting, tired. James saw a volunteer polish up a long, black-brown rifle and his heart fluttered in his chest. Soon he would have a firearm, a weapon he could call his own.

He thought about his father and his refusal to give him permission to go to war at Christmas last year. He thought him still a boy, the baby of the family, incapable of making a decision or doing something for himself, on his own terms. Now war had come to their own land. A cause that James believed in, something true to his heart. His father could do nothing to stop him now.

The volunteers welcomed James with open arms; here was the son of a landlord, an heir to an establishment they were rallying against, who would fight for them. He felt accepted and needed, useful for a change.

Before lunchtime the man leading the battalion called the group to attention. They gathered round, standing with their arms folded and chins tilted to the grey white sky.

'There is no bravado here,' the leader said. 'This is not somewhere you should be if you are here for the wrong reasons. If you aren't fully committed, if you're not sure in your heart that this is something you could leave your family for, you could die for, then now is the time. No judgment will be made. We are not forcing anyone. Please, think, and if you know yourself that you shouldn't be here, then walk away. The same for the sick. I see some of you limping. You will not be coming with us.'

James thought about the man's words. Some men were nodding, some looking thoughtful. They were separating the men from the boys, putting together the strongest force they could. He worried, with his youth, that they might tell him to go home too. But he would tell them, show them. He was a true patriot.

After the speech, James could feel energy coursing through his veins. He was ready to fight. He was ready to bring Home Rule back to Ireland, to stand up for his country, *their* country.

He watched as some men stepped forward to speak to the colonel, shaking their heads, he shaking their hands. They gathered up their white knapsacks and left their brown bandoliers behind, taking off their volunteer hats and jackets, ready for someone else to wear. They were leaving the farmhouse, going back to their families, exhausted from their previous days' fighting in Dublin.

James thought how he was now an asset, fresh blood, new energy, ready to take on the attack they had planned for the small town of Ashbourne, only a few miles from here.

In the afternoon, he was given a rifle and shown how to use it. It felt heavy and smooth in his hands, the smell of gun powder touching his nostrils. He told them he already knew how to use a gun, having often shot using his father's, taking part in shooting parties when they had visited other estates. They were impressed at his knowledge and he beamed as he was ordered to help others, to teach them how to hold the gun, how to load it and how to shoot it, on target and without injuring or dislocating their shoulders.

As evening fell, a large pot of stew was prepared on an open fire with small, fatty bits of meat floating among the carrot and onions. It was watery, but James lapped it from his metal tin, hunkered round the farmhouse with men, older and wiser, full of tales and patriotism. He felt like a man. He thought of the hundreds of fine dinners he'd eaten at polished dining tables. This was really living.

They were ordered to sleep early, to conserve energy and prepare for the battle the next day - when they would rise in the dark hours and make their way to Ashbourne.

Before the lights were put out, James listened to some of the men singing ballads, and, laid out on a sack and tucked in a light sleeping bag, he thought his heart might burst out of his chest with pride.

When he awoke the next day, it only took a moment to realise where he was and he jumped up quickly to wash his hands and face and eat a breakfast of bread and dripping being passed around.

Today was the day. Today was the day he would go to war.

* * *

James was quiet, watching the men around him, some saying a decade of the rosary, others using a rag and spit to shine their buttons and boots. The battalion assembled, a group of fifty or so, and as the sun tried to shine through a cloud, they were split into their columns. James liked the look of his, a group with energy; they'd been given most of the rationed ammunition they had.

They set off on their bicycles, two spotters cycling ahead. It was a clear April day. Small, white butterflies flitted on the hedgerows which were just taking on their summer bloom. James thought about his parents, who would have discovered him missing by now. He half-expected his father to come across them, to appear from nowhere and shout 'stop!' He was so interfering, his father, always trying to make him into something he didn't want to be.

They took a back road into Ashbourne, the columns then splitting and going to the points they had marked out and studied on the map. James's column was to oversee the barracks, a small cement block building in the centre of the town. They'd been told to attack, if it hadn't been disarmed already.

When they reached the deserted streets of the small town, they threw their bikes in a ditch and walked, crouching low on approach. Up ahead they could see two RIC officers outside the barracks, rushing to barricade it. Two of their column went back and got their bikes. They cycled at speed towards the officers, pointing their rifles and telling them to surrender to the Irish Republic.

James followed the orders and crawled along the roadside ditch, and lay down pointing his rifle to cover the two volunteers who had stormed the barracks. The officers disappeared inside and the cyclists shot at the windows, before abandoning their bicycles and diving over the ditch. Within a minute the gunfire was returned and those who had weapons were ordered to fire at the barracks in unison.

James shot his gun and felt the pull back. It was the first time he had ever aimed it at anything that wasn't a pheasant or a rabbit or a rusty tin can. There were people inside the barracks, officers. He was shooting at real live people. His father's face flashed before him. He would be so disappointed in him. Pushing the image from his head, James reloaded and fired again. This was not about his father - it was no time to be thinking of him. This was about the future, about Ireland's future.

More shots were fired and more returned. James lay there, waiting to be told what to do. They had limited ammunition. Did they want to use it on these bricked up barracks?

The second column had positioned themselves behind the building. James could see them moving in, crouching down like they were, the tips of their guns flashing in the April light. They waited, listening to the gunfire coming from within. They would raid the barracks when it was surrendered, take whatever was left and reinforce their own troops.

James watched as one of the men from the second column crawled across the field opposite and up the side of the barracks, as near as he could get to the door. The man drew his knees up into a hunker, quickly stood up and tossed a stick that looked like a mallet with a lit fuse attached. It landed right in front of the barracks under the iron bar windows. Blinking, James wondered what it was, until a loud explosion rocked his ears, the blast knocking out his eyesight for a second. A home-made grenade. It blew a small crater in the gravel road.

The explosion frightened James. He hadn't been expecting it. It was much louder than the gunshots going off, and it had shaken everything around him. He looked down at his hands and saw that they were blackened. He wiped his face and felt the dirt smear against his fingers. He was shaking. This wasn't what he had expected. What if the barracks tossed a grenade at them? They were only a few feet from the door. It could lodge in the ditch before they had time to run.

To their right he heard more commotion. He strained his neck to see a fleet of cars arriving, police cars, filled with RIC officers. He heard more gunfire and thought it was coming from one of their own columns who were stationed near to where the cars had pulled up. He felt trapped, with the barracks up front and a tranche of new manpower arriving to his right.

He listened to the sound of more tyres arriving. Reinforcements from Slane, far more than they had in their own columns. They were on bicycles and on foot - how could they compete with trained troops and automobiles?

Not knowing what to do, he lay and listened, hearing the shouts, boots running on the stone road, the loud crack of gunfire. Perhaps if he got a better look, if he could see beyond the men and pinpoint where the split column was, he could make a run for it, or crawl back and cross the road to where they were. He stood up, straining his neck, his arms outstretched, his rifle pointing towards the barracks.

A shot rang out, fired from a gun poked through the barrack's bars, barely visible through the clearing smoke of the explosion.

The bullet passed through the air, whistling, its tail swirling like a firework pinwheel. It ricocheted off James's head, taking half his forehead and most of the right side of his brain with it. His face registered the shock as he fell backwards into the green grass, his hand still wrapped around his rifle, his skull exposed, its fragments falling around him.

From the barracks, the shooter watched the young man fall, and felt a pang in his own heart. He had been in Ireland only three weeks, drafted in, as Britain battled on in the continent. He had expected to join the ranks in France, to go where all the men he'd known before him had gone. He hadn't heard of anyone being posted to Ireland.

But his mother has said it was a sign from God when she heard, and she'd curled up her nose in distaste.

She wasn't able to say why.

The shooter's name was Robert Eccles.

Chapter Thirty-Nine

GLADYS

She didn't expect that he would up like that. Leave. She didn't think he had it in him. He'd surprised her, had Robert. Maybe she'd taught him a thing or two after all.

She was proud the day he left. His bag over his shoulder. His new uniform gleaming on him. He filled it well.

She was proud that he finally had the gumption to get up and do something with himself. To go and represent their country, like she'd be telling him it was his duty to. She thought of all the other soldiers heading off, their mothers sniffling after them. She wouldn't be sniffling. She was glad to see him go. She'd get the house back to herself. And if anyone asked, she could tell them her son had been called up and he was gone, just like the other lads on the street.

Robert had been annoyed about the Ireland posting. He hadn't expected it, thinking he'd be on a boat to France, where his class mates had gone. He felt he wasn't really going to war, that he wasn't good enough to go where all the others had gone, that his was a phony posting, something else he'd gotten wrong before he'd even started.

But Gladys found it all rather amusing. Back to his home country. Back to his mother's land.

He'd never really been hers. Maybe he'd find himself over there, with his own people.

When he was gone, having kissed her on the cheek as she stood leaning against the doorway, watching him walk away, she had an urge to tell him, to pull him back by the arm and blurt it out. To lead him by the hand up to her wardrobe, where at the very back was a small wooden box and in a hidden shelf tucked at the bottom of its velvet floor, three yellowing newspaper cuttings. The year he was born.

'YOUNG IRISH MOTHER APPEALS FOR MISSING BABY'
'BABY TAKEN FROM PRAM – POLICE APPEAL FOR WITNESSES'
'SECOND APPEAL FOR BABY TAKEN FROM PRAM'

She wouldn't have to say anything. Just show him. She wanted to let him know that he wasn't really hers and that she'd never cared for him the way Albert did.

Albert doted on that boy. She remembered him now - arms out for an embrace every time he came through the door. Taking bits of toys out of his pocket that he'd made on his lunch breaks, carving little stumps with his penknife. There were soldiers and hollowed out boats and dice. And the face on the child when he took out some liquorice, or apple drops or oranges.

What did he bring home to her after she'd brought the boy home for him?

He knew with her sulks that she hadn't been happy after Robert had arrived into their lives. But he said he couldn't help himself. 'He's my boy. Look at his little face.'

She'd looked at his face day in, day out. She was tired looking at his face, his sandy hair, and his rounded cheeks, looking nothing like her or Albert. It had gotten worse as he'd grown, seeing how he didn't resemble them. Knowing that he wasn't theirs. Knowing that he didn't belong in the family, that he was an imposter.

The feelings, the longings she'd had for him were well gone, replaced with some other feeling that took over her stomach and her head. All the preparation she'd done to get him here as a baby. Getting him ready for the world, toughening him up so that he could stand on his own two feet. Albert was too soft on him, undoing all her hard work. And that was why she was always trying to teach him. To show him that life was disappointing, that you didn't always get what you wanted in the end.

She did miss Albert. Nothing had been the same since he'd died, keeled over in the maintenance yard of the council, pulling a large cart laden with brushes.

But now, at least, she could get back to her routine, get the house the way she wanted and not have the disturbance of Robert coming in at all hours, getting in her way and treading footprints on her scoured steps and floors.

When he came back from the war he could find his own place. He could get a woman and settle down. She'd had enough of him. It was time, at her age that she had a bit of peace and quiet.

It was time that she'd hoped she and Albert would spend together.

But he was gone now. And being on her own was the next best thing.

Chapter Forty

HENRY

Brabazon House, Co Meath, Ireland, 19 December 1916

Henry watches Sarah's face and notices the whites of her eyes. They're showing, startled. Frightened.

'Mama's missing,' she says.

Henry is in his study, a glass of whiskey on the papers he's been reading. He's taken to sipping whiskey in the evenings now, from a bottle exactly where his father used to keep his supply in his desk. Funny, how son becomes father, eventually.

'Since when?'

'I don't know,' said Sarah. 'This afternoon.'

'Is her horse here?'

'Yes.'

This wasn't the first time Molly had disappeared this year. The blackness that returned after James's death was similar to the days after James's birth. Only this time there was no light, no hope for the future to heal.

Henry got up from behind his desk and walked with Sarah from the study.

'And you've checked with all the staff?'

'No one saw her leave,' said Sarah.

She stopped him as he walked and put her hand on his

arm.

'Daddy, I'm frightened.'

'Don't worry,' he reassured her. 'We'll find her.'

But the panic was setting in for him too. On most of Molly's disappearances she had turned up a few hours later, muddy and tired having walked for miles. The last time she'd gone missing, one of the footmen had found her in a barn on the farm yard, loitering dangerously near the edge of the hay ledge, a rope in her hands.

It was the first place Henry checked now, pulling on his coat as he went out of the back door, telling Sarah to gather together the house staff for a search party.

'It's too dark for her to be out by herself,' he said.

There was nobody in the barn, only the snuffle of mice among the hay. He found a lantern and lit it and checked all the other buildings that were open, holding his lantern up to check the rafters. What a thing to be checking, he thought.

The staff were gathered at the back door and Henry returned to give instructions. He sent three of the staff up to the back of the estate, through the woods and out near the church.

'Circle,' he said. 'And make sure you call her name, good and loud.'

He would take Sarah with him down to the river and out across the fields to Dowth.

As they rode down the sheltered drive, Henry's anguish rose through his stomach, knotting it into lumps. They had been through so much this year. He found it hard to believe when he woke each morning that his son was no longer in this world. That he would never take another breath. He thought how he would give anything to hear him slam the door of his study one more time or to find his broody presence in his bedroom, reading, moping. Reminders of his hobbies and projects were strewn about the house and yard, but their soft boy, with his dark hair and childish smile, was gone.

The loss had impacted Molly in such a way that Henry had been forced to quell his own grief, to hide it, to be strong, to act as though James's loss was something that could be gotten over and all they needed was time.

He could not have imagined the impact of their son's death on Molly.

Her grief was a mountain, visible for all to see. She was broken, not even a shell of her former self.

'You wouldn't understand,' she mouthed through tears, when he sometimes found her, crying on the floor.

And he wanted to tell her that of course he understood - that James had been his son too.

* * *

There was no sign of her in the woods or in the fields. They had checked any spots where they thought she might have gone but it was so dark, their lanterns barely made an impact on the blackness. They called her name over and over again, but they were met only with the sound of their footsteps on the frozen grass, or the horses' hooves, as they stomped where they stood.

Henry rode with Sarah down to Dowth, cantering the horse in the dark, the fright of falling off superseded by the need to get to Molly, to rescue her from the mania that she must be in.

Sarah was quiet in her worry. This was the longest their mother had ever been gone and it was freezing. She hadn't taken her cloak with her - Sarah had lifted it and thrown it across her horse, so that when they did find her, they could put it on her. Where could she be?

They reined in their horses, tying them up quickly and running to the mound.

'Molly!' roared Henry. But there was no response.

They both climbed, tackling the mound like a stepladder. Henry helped Sarah to the top as they scanned the mound for her.

She wasn't there.

'I really thought she'd be here,' said Sarah, tears threatening her eyes.

Henry pulled his daughter into an embrace.

'We'll find her,' he said into her hair.

They stood for a moment, panting from the exertion of the climb, trying to calm the panic in their chests.

'We'll check the old farmhouse,' said Henry. 'She could have gone back there. Actually, maybe she went to the graveyard, to the graves? Let's split up, I'll check the house, you go to the church.'

The church and graveyard were located in the shadow of the mound. A new church had been built on the grounds of an ancient dwelling and gravestones were scattered around the ruins. Molly's parents had been buried at a simple grave to the back to the church, a flat flagstone in the ground to mark the spot. James had been buried close by, a new gravestone recently added, fresh and light coloured amongst the weather-worn stones.

'Are you all right going on your own?' asked Henry, as they left Dowth and rode quickly away.

'Yes,' said Sarah.

Henry thought how brave she was, how resilient she was in the face of the frightening situation they found themselves in.

He raced down the lane, swiping at a briar that hit him across the jaw.

He dismounted to open the gate and lead the horse in, calling Molly's name over and over.

There was no response.

He let the horse loose, running to the outhouses to check if she might have gone in there. His worst fear was that she would have returned and gotten in and done the unthinkable.

In two days' time it was her birthday, and in less than a week it was the anniversary of the eviction and her father's death. Christmas always sent her into a spin - it wouldn't have surprised him to find her here in her sorrow.

Large padlocks secured the great wooden doors to the barns and were untouched. He walked quickly round to the small windows on the sides of the buildings, shining his lantern in, cupping his hand to try and see inside.

There was no light, no movement. He didn't think she was here.

He ran to the house to check it too, calling her name over and over.

Still, there was no response.

He mounted his horse again, his heart pounding in his chest. He feared if they didn't find her soon, it would be too late.

Cantering up the lane, leaving the gate to the farmhouse wide open, Henry rounded his horse on to the road and towards the small lane to the graveyard. He could see the swish of Sarah's lantern up ahead, moving in the darkness.

He rode the horse towards it and as he got to the door of the church, she appeared, her face shadowed under the light she carried.

'She's not here,' she said.

'She's not at the farmhouse, either,' he replied.

'Where else could she have gone, Daddy? She hardly went towards town?'

'I don't know,' he said. 'Let's go back to the house. Maybe she might have turned up.'

But they both knew it was wishful thinking. Wherever Molly was, she needed to be rescued from there. She was too far gone to make her own way back.

Chapter Forty-One

MOLLY

I think those feelings are the same. The ones I'm experiencing now. I'm not quite sure, I can't be really sure, what I felt then, what I feel now. There have been so many medications over the years. Opiates. Laudanum. Wine. Port. I take them all. I hope that one and all will cure these feelings. But nothing does. I can numb it. Black out. And then wake up more wretched than before.

There's this feeling of dread that won't go away. It's the feeling I had on that evening Oliver was taken. It's the feeling I had as I rode my horse to meet Mr Tubular at Dowth. It's the feeling I have now.

I rub the stone, the one I've picked, the one I went all the way up to Dowth to collect, to pull from the grass and wipe the soil from it. I carried it all the way down to the river in a cloth bag. I wonder if it is the same one I murdered Tubular with - if it's caked in his blood, the dark liquid rusted deep in the pores of the stone.

And now I sit here and I cradle it, thinking of all the times these stones have crossed my life's path.

Underneath me as we rolled down the mound, my brothers and I bumbling, falling, laughing.

Over my head, in the lintel of our doorway, of our farmhouse, laid there by my forefathers.

In the outhouses, stone on top of stone, pushed into the render by my daddy.

Crushed against Tubular's head. Stone on bone. His blood on my hands.

And now here, in my hands, a rough scratchy rope tied around it, the end fastened around my neck and tangled down my arm.

I have been thinking about this for a long time.

I thought about it in the dark days after the children were born, when my moods had sunken low and the thoughts of Oliver had rushed back, more present than ever in the little writhing bodies of my newborn children.

I longed to tell my secret - to have just one person know where my anguish came from.

But I could not. Ruth would not understand. Henry never would. Sarah would never know, that somewhere, out there, she had a brother, living.

I thought about it every day since James had died.

It was wrong to go on living when so much had been taken. I couldn't face another Christmas without them. I couldn't face another winter solstice without Daddy, without Oliver and now without James.

I've been sitting for a long time, my breath like steam in the air.

I still have those broken feelings that I did then. Empty. I see Sarah's face and Henry's. Sweet, sweet Henry. But I have caused him so much pain. I am a penance. A stone around his neck.

And that was how I thought of it. A stone. A rope.

When they told us that James had died, a soldier, for a cause, I knew then. I could not take any more pain. I would not.

It was best to go this way. At my favourite place. At the river, with the rock around my neck, pulling me down to meet my father and my mother and my James. And in time, Oliver would join me too. Wherever he was now.

Henry would forgive me. I was releasing him from his worry for me, from the constant suffering I brought.

I love this river. I love this place.

I see them now. My mother walking with her arms folded across her, on her way to mass. Daddy sailing by in the trap, old Ned pulling him along. And James, playing by the water, like he did when he was a child, skimming stones, laughing, scanning the water for jumping fish.

And in those moments, as the cold hit my face and the brown water rushed round my ears and I felt myself move down, pulled by the stone, deep into the blackness before the water rushed into my mouth and lungs and caused me to choke and not breathe, before then, for a few moments, I felt it.

I was free. Happy. Back in the days where my brothers and I were rolling down the hill at Dowth. Back where my mother made her omelettes and dusted her apron and scolded us for walking grass into the house. Back with Daddy on our walks, through the fields, the dipping sun on our backs, our chit chat murmuring among the bedtime twittering of the birds.

Where Oliver was in my arms, gurgling and laughing. Where my children, Sarah and James, and my husband, my beautiful Henry, were beside me smiling and loving and setting me free.

I was free.

I was finally free.

Chapter Forty-Two

HENRY

As they rode in the dark, the horse's hooves sparking on the ground, the road silent up ahead, Henry thought about everything he had been through with Molly.

They had overcome so much to be together - he'd always known breaking the engagement to Charity had been the right thing to do and when he met Molly, it became clear why.

She had not found it easy in the early years - marrying into a lifestyle she wasn't used to, becoming a lady and all the social servitude it brought. She had overcome the melancholy she suffered after the birth of their children - at least in part, but she had never returned to the woman she had been when they met - the spark of joy rarely glimpsed, the way it had shown itself so often in their courtship.

But they had gotten through her dark days and had grown into a more settled existence. Keeping busy was the key. Having projects helped occupy her mind and he could tell after James's death, when she withdrew from work at the shops and started to spend all her time in bed, or going for long rambling walks by herself, that the sadness would return and it did - with a vengeance.

They came to the end of the road and were about to cross over to take the long driveway back to Brabazon House when they heard a noise, some commotion.

They stopped and listened - it was coming from the river.

'Come on,' said Henry and they turned their horses right, thundering down towards the noise along the river bank.

As they approached, Henry thought about where they were headed to - it was the stretch of river he'd often sat at - where he had met Molly all those years ago, before she left for London. Why had he not thought of checking here earlier?

Up ahead they could hear raised voices, panic in the air.

'What's going on, do you have her?' roared Henry as he pulled his horse up to where his stable hand and footman were standing.

Molly lay, white faced on the ground, a rope pulled from her neck. Her hair lay spread around her, matted and black with water. Her eyes were closed.

Henry and Sarah rushed to her, crouching down. Henry cupped her face with his hands.

'Is she breathing?' he roared.

'We're not sure, sir,' said the footman. We were checking along the riverbank and we heard something go in. We went straight in after her, but it took us some time to get her out. She was under for a while, sir.'

Henry tilted Molly on to her side, remembering how he'd watched his classmates revive a man who had fallen into the Isis while rowing. He pulled her head back, arching her mouth and opening her airway.

'Mama,' said Sarah. 'Please, Mama.'

The footman and stable hand looked on in silence. Sarah began to cry, her fearful sobs carrying over the rush of the water swollen with winter rain.

Henry put his head down to Molly's, laying his forehead on the side of her face.

She was wet to touch, cold and clammy.

'Please, my love,' he said. 'Please, darling.'

He shook her vigorously, as though trying to shift the

water from her lungs.

Still, she did not respond.

Leaning back Henry looked at her, shaking his head. Then he stooped and shook her again, rattling her shoulders, willing her awake. They stood waiting, for a breath, for a sigh, for a response. But there was nothing, only the sound of the rushing water filling the black, dark night.

Sarah began to wail.

'Mama!' she roared. 'Mama!'

Henry got up and walked to Sarah's horse, taking down the cloak she had thrown across its back before they left. He went to Molly and laid it on top of her, lifting her gently to wrap the rest of it round her, like a shroud. As he lifted her, cradling her in his arms like a child, tears flowed down his face. He walked away from the river, from the overhanging trees, into the dark, across the road and up the driveway to Brabazon House.

Behind him Sarah walked, pulling Henry's horse and hers, her sobs piercing the forest that guided them back up the winding lane.

The footman and stable hand hung back to give the family some privacy, before following them too, leading their own horses behind the husband and daughter cortège, carrying the lifeless body of the woman they loved most in the world.

Chapter Forty-Three

MOLLY

I saw him, you know. When I was down there. He came to me. But he wasn't a boy. He was a man. And he said he was sorry. Over and over again, sorry mama, I didn't mean it, I'm sorry.

I told him I was sorry too. I mouthed it under the weight of all that water. As it poured into my lungs. As I got past the spluttering and the choking and it filled me up like a jug.

I tried to reach out to him. I stretched my hand in the water, through the murk, through the dark depths of the swollen river.

I watched him reach for me too, his baby face grown up, his limbs long, muscular.

His fingertips reached, his hand was near mine. And just as we were about to touch, I felt it, the clutch of the stone, on my neck, yanking me and dragging me back, down.

The pain ripped through my skin, the weight pulling me further and further into the depths.

And that was when I went. After I had seen him and the water had gone too far and I had to sleep, for just a moment.

And I knew he was out there, somewhere. Oliver was alive and well and I felt a comfort. A comfort I hadn't felt since before he was taken, all those years ago.

Chapter Forty-Four

Drogheda Argus, Christmas Edition, 1916

The funeral has taken place of Lady Molly Brabazon (nee Thomas) who died suddenly at Curley Hole, Oldbridge, on Tuesday, 19 December 1916. Lady Brabazon is fondly remembered by her husband, Lord Henry Brabazon and her only surviving daughter, Sarah Brabazon; her brothers, Michael and Patrick Thomas and her brother-in-law, Arthur Brabazon.

Lady Brabazon was laid to rest on Thursday, 21 December at Dowth cemetery, a special four o'clock burial the day of her birthday, noted as the sun set on the Winter Solstice, for which Newgrange, Knowth and Dowth passage tombs have world renown.

May she rest in peace.

Chapter Forty-Five

Brabazon House, Co. Meath, Ireland, April 1921

He watched her as she edged closer to the front. Shoulder. Neck. Snout. She was leading by a nose. He roared, the sounds tumbling from his throat, jumping up and down, his boots splatting in the light mud.

Around him came the cries of the crowd who had gathered to watch the race, the highest prize, the biggest turn-out for the day. Twenty-five horses started. And Sarah was leading them all.

She had come from behind. Sitting back strong. Moving up and overtaking each horse, one by one. At the turn at the fence, she belted the horse with her crop and crouched lower to its neck.

Henry strained to see her, placing his hand on a man in a cap who was blocking his view. And then he saw them approach, the racing pack, his daughter at the front, her face dark with concentration.

The cries got louder as the finish line came closer. Henry felt as though his head might wrench from his neck with the strain as the horses thundered past, a mass of galloping hooves and flashing coloured shirts.

And in seconds, they had passed the post, Sarah in front by a length, the crowd hopping up and down, caps thrown in the air. He wondered how many had wagered on her, how many had taken the chance on a girl?

Arthur threw his arms around Henry, his usual flamboyance out of control in the moment. But Henry didn't pull back, instead, he smiled and laughed out loud at the wonder that was his daughter.

They made their way to the top of the track, weaving under the fence to join in with the horsemen, who were grabbing at the racehorses by their bridles and rushing to congratulate Sarah, who was still atop of her mount.

She stood up in the short stirrups when they approached and shot her hand in the air.

'I did it!' she said, as Henry came up to the horse and held her hand to help her dismount, with a leap on to the ground.

'You did it,' he said and they embraced.

'Your grandfather would be so proud,' he murmured into her hair.

Sarah pulled back and looked at her father's joyous face.

'So would Mummy,' she said. 'I could feel her with me. Like a power.'

* * *

It was Sarah who got him through those silent days. The ones afterwards, when the emptiness of the house rattled him. He wondered, in his melancholy, if this is what it had felt like for Molly, the sadness inside, a pit of despair, nothing easing the physical pain he felt in his bones or the crushing thoughts in his mind.

Sarah had cried too, sometimes breaking down when she found something belonging to her mother. A note scribbled in a book, a handkerchief dotted with her perfume. But she had a strength that restored itself and, in time, she used it to help him. To take him out for long peaceful walks, to let the silence sit between then, gently.

He took comfort in what Molly had left behind. A

daughter, with piercing eyes and a quick laugh, a spirit and a strength, a desire to move forward and make the best of the circumstances they had been given.

It was her idea to keep going with the races. To maintain the track, to mend the fences, to entice the sponsors to keep the prize money up and the great horses returning to compete at the Brabazon meet.

He watched her now as well-wishers came up to shake her hand, her riding crop hanging low by the racing britches she was wearing.

She was a woman of her time, a woman who could only be admired. She reminded him so of Molly and sometimes, his own mother too.

He looked at the house in the background, the grey facade glinting under the light summer sun.

* * *

They barely heard the doorbell among the din. A record belted from a gramophone in the corner, warming up the crowd before the band would lift their instruments and fill the atmosphere with their music.

Sarah had washed and changed into a simple dress. Its dropped waist suited her boyish figure and she loved her new short bob, which took little time to dry and which Ruth now delighted in styling after she got over the shock of seeing her mistress's tresses disappeared.

Sarah knew that some of the guests did not approve of her racing and were very much aggrieved that she had won the cup today. Because of this, she ensured that she greeted and made conversation with every one of the disapprovers. It delighted her to see them squirm. She was speaking to a man with white sideburns covering the entirety of his jaws, his expression barely containing his disdain for 'lady riders', when Ruth tapped Sarah on the shoulder and asked to speak with her.

'Your father wishes to see you in his study,' she said.

Sarah noted the worry in her assistant's eyes and wondered if her father was unwell. What on earth was he doing in his study just as the ball was about to start?

She followed Ruth out into the hall and when she opened the study door, she was surprised to see a man, seated in front of her father.

Her father looked pale, an expression on his face that she couldn't quite read.

Henry asked her to sit and she sat herself down on a chair opposite the sandy haired man.

'Sarah,' said her father, 'If what this young man is telling us is true, then I need you to prepare yourself for a shock.'

Sarah darted her eyes to the man and took in his face, trying to gauge what sort of news he was bringing to their house, on this happy occasion. She followed his hands which were nestled in his nap, clutching a worn looking envelope. She turned her eyes back to her father.

'What is it, Daddy, what's wrong?'

Henry gestured to the man, indicating to the man to give Sarah the envelope.

The man leaned over and held out his hand, the paper quivering in his shaking hand. There was something so familiar about him. As if she'd seen him before.

'What is this?' she said, looking to her father.

'Open it,' he said, quietly, his voice strained.

She opened the envelope and took the contents out - three yellowed cuttings from a newspaper and a white page, handwritten and marked St Anthony's Mothers and Baby's Home, London. Behind it was another piece of paper, folded.

'What is this?' she said, looking to her father,

Sarah scanned the headline on the article – 'YOUNG IRISH MOTHER APPEALS FOR MISSING BABY' - before turning her eyes back to the man's face.

'It's about your mum,' he said. He had an English accent. He was dressed simply in a shirt and jacket, his clothes pressed, his face clean shaven.

She unfolded the piece of paper. It was creased and crinkled as though it had been read a thousand times. [L4]

Her eyes glanced over the page - *I lost my baby - my baby was taken - his name is Oliver - did anyone hand in a boy of this age?* It was addressed to the same home marked on the white piece of paper and it was signed Molly Thomas with a bracketed line saying - (*may go by the name of Cotton.*)

'I don't understand,' said Sarah, looking at her father and back to the man. 'Who are you?'

'I'm Oliver,' he said pointing at himself. 'Robert, my new name is Robert. Your mother had me before she married your father. But I was raised by someone else. It's taken me till now to find you, to track your mum down. I'm devastated that she's gone.'

Tears glistened in his eyes.

Sarah stood.

'This can't be true,' she said, to her father.

Henry shook his head.

'Sarah, look at the writing.'

She looked at the letter, close up, squinting at the letters and the signature. There was no mistaking Molly's distinctive scrawl, the curl of the letters on her name. The colour drained from her cheeks. Sarah looked at Robert and then back to her father.

'I don't know what to say,' she said, shaking her head slowly.

'We could start with hello,' said Robert, holding out his hand to shake hers. 'I'm ever so pleased to meet you.'

Epilogue

Ireland 3,200 BC

And when it was time, when the day had come and the sun had moved high enough to reach the temple, they gathered in the morning, in the darkness, in silence.

They felt the sun's rays fill the chamber, crushing the dark, touching their skin and sending light into their very souls.

And now it was that the spirits were alive.

There was much dancing that day, around the fires and the smoke, with the eating of the flesh and the drinking of the liquid that warmed their blood and throats.

When evening came, dropping in like a cloak, surrounding the hills and the valley and the river babbling black, they gathered again, at Dowth, to enter the chamber to see the Gods send their sun once more before it set.

When it entered the tomb and they fell again and felt the dead arise and go, having been alive and with them that day, they felt a sadness, at another winter solstice over, at their sacrifice complete.

The young were told that this was a special place, that this was where the dead lived and came alive, each year in the temples where the sun shone.

That babies born on this day were the most special of all, that they carried a spirit with them, a power, from the depths of the temple, from the body of the stones.

It was lucky to be born on the solstice, for great strength did it bring.

A spirit and a power and a strength sent by the Gods themselves.

THE END

Acknowledgements

Vanessa Fox O'Loughlin was one of the first people I contacted when I decided to take writing seriously. An assessment I undertook with her while writing this book ultimately shook the novel out of me. She is a positive force within the creative and publishing world. Seek her out.

One of the best things I've discovered in trampling my path in the world of publishing is the fantastic supportive network of writers, bloggers and publishing professionals. The following writers have conversed, chatted, tweeted or private messaged all along the way and it's been a pleasure getting to know everyone and learning about their own writing careers. Thank you in particular to Carmel Harrington, Margaret Scott, Andrea Mara, Cat Hogan, Catherine Ryan Howard, Hazel Gaynor, Elizabeth Murray, Orla McAlinden, Sharon Thompson, Elizabeth Reapy, Sharyn Hayden, Lorna Sixsmith, Susan Lanigan, Tric Kearney, Sadhbh Devlin, Shane Dunphy, Pam O'Shea, Alana Kirk, Sheena Lambert, Pauline Clooney, Margaret Rowe and Caroline Busher.

As a blogger myself, I am all too aware of the hard work and passion that goes into writing and maintaining a working blog. Writers in recent years have come to rely on book bloggers as not only a wheel in the publicity machine but a generous, supportive network, who work tirelessly to support writers and share news, updates and a general love of books. I am slowly getting to know book bloggers, both in Ireland and the UK, but in particular I would like to single out Lisa Redmond of *Lisa Reads Books* for her very kind beta reading early on and Linda Green at *Books Of All Kinds*, who also read some early work and offered valuable critiques.

One of the closest friendships I have developed in recent years is with Margaret Madden, book blogger at *Bleach House Library*. We have enjoyed many a book chat and journey home from a Dublin based launch and I'm delighted to have her launch December Girl in our shared home town of Drogheda. .

To my best friend Caroline English who introduced me to reading as a seven year old (I refused to move to books without pictures until she MADE me) and was a beta reader. To Ramona Ward, who also volunteered her time to read a very early draft, all the way from the US.

To Gareth Yore, who wrote the original essay December Girl is based on and who kindly took me to the sites explored in the book. Walking the land where my imagined characters walked was invaluable in the writing process.

To Tracy Brennan of Trace Literary Agency who works tirelessly to place her authors with the right publisher. I am lucky to be represented by her and I look forward to our future endeavours together, wherever they take us.

To my family, for the babysitting services, to my brother Alan for his historical expertise, to my husband Ronan, who never wavered in his belief that I would achieve the dream and who allowed me the space and time needed to write and edit. We are still negotiating on installing a library in the house – but I know I'll win out as always.

To Sam McGrane, who was possibly more excited when the news of a publishing contract came through than I was and who will drop anything to help our family, which she has adopted as her own.

To my beautiful children, August and Bonnie who simply by

being born, helped inspire me towards writing and finishing this book. I wanted to leave something behind for them and I found writing was an incredible place of expression among the difficult early days of parenting.

To all the team at Bombshell Books – who first signed this book, particularly to Betsy Reavely, Emma Mitchell and Sarah Hardy.

Finally, I would like to thank my English teacher Margaret McCartan, who shone a light on my writing skills in my teen-age years and helped form the idea that one day I would write a book. I wonder how many other writers found themselves feeling warm and fuzzy whenever they received praise for their writing in school? It is for this reason that I have dedi-cated the book to English teachers all over the world – who in-stil a love of literature, encourage good writing skills and help hone the belief in budding authors what they write can have an impact on someone, somewhere.

I hope that this book in some way, somewhere, will do that.

———————————